FACT The Unbroken SECRET

Behind the Story

In 1912, the collector Wilfred Voynich discovered a selection of ancient books hidden in a chest in Mondragone Castle, Italy. Among the texts was a manuscript written entirely in code. It became known as the Voynich Manuscript.

For a century, academics tried to break the code. But not a single word or phrase in the 245 pages of the Voynich Manuscript has been read.

In 1944 a group of code-breakers working for the US government formed a Study Group to try and decipher the text. They failed. Between 1962 and 1963 a second Study Group was formed. Eventually Americans joined with British code-breakers based at Bletchley Park Mansion. They failed.

In 1969 the manuscript was donated to Yale University and registered simply as 'MS 408'. It is kept hidden from general view in the Beinecke Rare Book and Manuscript Library. Since that day, the secret code has remained unbroken.

What the fans are saying about
SECRET BREAKERS . . .

'I like that the settings are real places like Cambridge where I live – I have seen the mathematical bridge so now I know everything in Secret Breakers is real! Helen is a brilliant storyteller . . . I like going on adventures with the Secret Breakers.' Aaron, 8

'You just keep on guessing about what's going to happen . . . the whole book is like a code to be broken!' Alice, 10

'It's the kind of book that makes you want to hide under the bed cover and keep reading late into the night.' George, 10

'This thrilling kids' code-breaking adventure will blow your mind!' Bailey, 11

'It's so exciting that they're solving real mysteries and codes. I was desperate to read on!' Zac, 10

'I enjoy trying to work out the puzzles before Brodie, Tusia and Hunter.' Indiana, 11

'Couldn't put it down . . . Can't wait for the next one!' Nina, 14

'Exciting! Funny! Definitely want to read more!' Jacob, 10

'The best book this year!' Phoenix, 11

SECRET BREAKERS

THE POWER OF THREE

H. L. Dennis

Illustrations by Meggie Dennis

Hodder
Children's
Books

HODDER CHILDREN'S BOOKS

First published in Great Britain in 2012 by Hodder Children's Books
This edition published in 2016 by Hodder and Stoughton

12

Text copyright © H. L. Dennis, 2012
Logbook illustrations copyright © H. L. Dennis and Meggie Dennis, 2012

The moral rights of the author and illustrator have been asserted.

A CIP catalogue record for this book
is available from the British Library.

ISBN 978 0 340 99961 5

Typeset in AGaramond Book by Avon DataSet Ltd,
Bidford-on-Avon, Warwickshire

Printed and bound in Great Britain
by Clays Ltd, St Ives plc

The paper and board used in this book
are made from wood from responsible sources

Hodder Children's Books
An imprint of
Hachette Children's Group
Part of Hodder and Stoughton
Carmelite House
50 Victoria Embankment
London EC4Y 0DZ

An Hachette UK Company
www.hachette.co.uk

www.hachettechildrens.co.uk

For Meggie,
for Steve
and for Mum and Dad.
Thank you for believing!

Then Arthur looked at the sword, and liked it very much.

'Which do you like better,' said Merlin, 'the sword or the scabbard?'

'I like the sword better,' said Arthur.

'You are most unwise,' said Merlin, 'for the scabbard is worth ten of the sword.'

Adapted from *Le Morte D'Arthur* by
Sir Thomas Malory,
Book 1 Chapter 25

Following the Call of the Code

Brodie Bray held the writing towards the light.

It was then she saw them.

Holes.

Amazing really, she hadn't seen them before. It was only the angle of the sun, streaming through the window, which made them visible now. Tiny pinpricks pushed through the surface of the birthday card.

Eleven.

The holes weren't random. They'd been precisely placed.

She grabbed a piece of paper and pen and wrote out each letter marked with a pinprick. Then she read the message aloud.

Tuesday 10am

HAVE A TREMENDOUS TIME

AND ENJOY SO MUCH THE

DELIGHT OF

A GREAT DAY

Wishing you a very

Happy Birthday

HAPPY 10TH

BIRTHDAY

BRODIE MAY

Now she was scared.

Someone was trying to send her a message. And she had no idea who.

Everything about today's delivery from the postman was confusing. An unsigned card when it was nowhere near her birthday; her name written incorrectly inside; even her age was wrong. And the bright orange socks she now wore, which had come with the card, were far too big.

She put the card down on the floor and her hand knocked against the glass of water by the bed. She jumped up too late to stop it falling. Water splashed on her feet.

It was only when she knelt to sponge up the mess, she saw the orange stains across the back of the card. Ink. From the socks.

And there, marked clearly now, was a map.

And three words.

Light is knowledge

4

Mr Smithies was a member of a secret organisation. It was such a secret organisation even Mr Smithies' wife didn't know anything about it. As far as Mrs Smithies was concerned, her husband worked at the tax office. She packed his sandwiches every day and watched him leave for work every morning, waving him off from the kitchen window wearing her bright yellow Marigold gloves. Every evening she set Mr Smithies' dinner on the table at six o'clock sharp and when they'd eaten they went into the lounge and watched Mrs Smithies' favourite television programmes. They never talked about his work. Which was just as well as Mr Smithies wasn't allowed to.

The organisation Mr Smithies worked for had an unusual name: the 'Black Chamber'. Black Chambers had existed in one form or another for centuries. They'd always been secret organisations created to find out secrets. The very best brains in the country (Mr Smithies was very proud of this part) were specially selected and trained by the British Black Chamber simply to do this job. The problem was there really wasn't much that was 'simple' about it.

Clearly, the best way to keep a secret is not to tell anybody.

But sometimes information has to be shared. Just

not with everyone. That's when codes are used. Writing messages in code means only certain people can understand what's said. This is an excellent system for controlling who knows what. Those who understand the code have power.

Black Chambers make codes. And break codes. Codes that contain secrets. Sometimes the secrets are exciting; sometimes they are dangerous; and sometimes they change the course of history. So, however hard the codes are to crack, it's important the workers in the Black Chamber never give up. Mr Smithies believed this. He really did. And Mr Smithies loved his job. At least, he *had* loved it. Recently things hadn't been going so well. Things were changing and Mr Smithies was not a man who dealt well with change.

However, today Mr Smithies had other things on his mind. He had a meeting to attend and he was feeling very awkward about the whole thing.

Mr Smithies had agreed to meet Robbie Friedman in a small café at the edge of Russell Square. He spent a few moments checking he hadn't been followed, then opened the café door. Friedman was already there; a tall man, with fair skin, and hair wild around his face like a thick blond halo, a golden necklace glinting at the base of his throat.

'Good of you to agree to see me again, Smithies,' he said.

Smithies felt this was a bit of an understatement. If anyone from the Black Chamber knew he was meeting Friedman there'd be trouble. Friedman and trouble seemed to go together, like eggs and bacon or bangers and mash. Smithies ordered the full English breakfast, pulled out a chair and sat down.

Friedman hadn't always been trouble. There was a time when he had been one of the most important code-crackers in the country. That was all before the rather unfortunate mistake he'd made. Now Friedman was in exile and Smithies was taking a huge risk in meeting him. But Smithies wasn't afraid of risk.

'It's done,' Smithies said. 'Operation Veritas has been reactivated. I've sent out the invitations.'

Excitement flashed in Friedman's eyes. 'You're sure we can do this?'

'No. But you and I both know we've got to try. It's what we always agreed. If we ever discovered any new information about the manuscript, then we'd relaunch the Study Group section of the Black Chamber.'

'So who've you asked? The best minds in the country? New graduates just out of university? How many from Oxford and Cambridge?'

Smithies' hand froze in midair. A globule of egg

slipped from his fork and slopped into a puddle of baked beans. 'None,' he said.

Friedman's lip twitched.

'Look, it's complicated, Robbie,' Smithies whispered. 'Modern code-cracking's all about computers and targets and internet security. No one's interested in a five-hundred-year-old manuscript nobody can read. People don't remember the work of the Study Groups any more. Veritas disbanded forty years ago.'

He lifted the chipped spotty mug to his lips. When he put the mug down, he wore a milky white moustache.

'And anyway, MS 408's a banned document. It's got a "D notice" on it. No one can go anywhere near it legally.'

'So who've you asked, then?'

The end of the milky moustache dripped a little. 'Children,' he said.

Friedman took a moment before he answered. 'Are you totally insane, Smithies?'

'Possibly. But that's hardly the point. And with all due respect I don't think you're exactly in a position to be making comments like that.'

Friedman shuffled in his chair.

'The fact is, Robbie, I had a spark of inspiration. Like a fire. We were just children ourselves when we were first involved and so to me it made perfect sense.'

Friedman now wore a face which made it look like he'd swallowed some particularly vile-tasting medicine.

'Using children's the answer. I know it. Children have nothing to lose. They don't know what's OK to see and what isn't. They haven't got the weight of expectation on their shoulders.'

Friedman still looked a little green.

'Most importantly, children haven't been put off code-cracking and replaced by computers in their work. There's still a chance they'll have a love of the code. Don't you remember how it used to be? When we were young and unafraid? When there was the thrill of the chase?'

Friedman's eyes lightened a little but when he spoke his voice shook. 'Children, Smithies. Is that safe? You know . . . after everything?'

It was Smithies' turn to look uncomfortable. 'There's no other way.'

'But the risks involved. We'd be putting them in danger.'

Smithies ran his finger along the rim of the mug. 'It's children. Or it's over.'

Friedman took a while before he looked up. 'Go on,' he said.

'I've chosen carefully. Grandchildren and great-grandchildren of code-breakers who worked in the war. And obviously descendants of the 1960s Study Group Veritas. They'll be less likely to ask awkward questions. They've secrecy running through their veins! And the children are most likely to be naturally good at accepting a challenge.' He paused. 'We'll just have to be careful.'

Friedman jabbed at the yolk of his egg with his fork. 'How will it work?'

'Ahh, now this is the part I'm particularly proud of.' Smithies beamed. 'We're going to run the whole thing like a home-school learning project. There's some loopholes in the law I'm making use of. We'll set up a sort of Code and Cipher School using some of the old-style code-crackers as teachers.'

'Teachers?'

'Yep. I've put the word out, secretly of course. Tried to draw in some retired code-breakers who can pass on what they know. Old-style stuff. That doesn't rely on computers. You know the sort of thing, Robbie. Teaching an eye for subtlety, a nose for connections, an ear for a link.' He leant forward in his chair. 'I've got interviews set up for this afternoon. We should end up with an excellent team of children and a top-class team of code teachers.' He pushed his empty plate across the table. 'This time we're going to be lucky, Robbie. I know it. The time to make sense of MS 408 has finally come.'

* * *

Tandi Tandari, Mr Smithies' secretary, winced a little and lowered her head. A flurry of tight black curls tumbled over her shoulder. 'I'm sorry, sir. He was the only one to turn up.'

Smithies peered through the frosted screen door at a man wearing a pair of pyjama trousers tied up with a garish yellow necktie.

'And you didn't feel the need to get rid of him?' Smithies hissed.

Tandi clutched a pile of Manila folders tightly to her and shook her head defiantly. 'No, sir. I didn't feel it polite to "get rid of him". He was, after all, the only one to come.'

'But where are the others I invited?'

'Dead, sir.' She paused. 'Or in prison. And these two here,' she flicked to the uppermost files, 'are in institutions apparently. This one hasn't spoken a word for nearly ten years.'

Smithies grimaced. 'Oh well, Oscar "Sicknote" Ingham will certainly make up for that then.'

'Sir?'

'Never mind.' Smithies pushed open the door and made his way into the board room. 'Oscar,' he said with a fair degree of effort. 'How've you been?'

'Oh, you know, Jon. Never without pain.'

11

Smithies counted to ten silently in his head.

All things considered the interview went quite badly. Oscar Ingham was enjoying his retirement, hated the thought of working with children and was appalled at the idea of being on the staff of a Code and Cipher School.

'So why *exactly* did you answer the call?' said Smithies, biting back the urge to also ask why a fully grown man had decided to arrive at a meeting he so obviously didn't want to be at, and hadn't even bothered to change out of his pyjamas.

Ingham reached into his pocket and took out a small container of tablets, emptied two into his hand and swallowed them before speaking. 'MS 408,' he said with an urgency that made Smithies' heart quicken. 'You said there's a new lead.'

Smithies reached into his briefcase and very carefully, as if afraid it may turn to dust in his hand, he drew out a small yellowed envelope. Across the back of the envelope was a seal pressed into thick red wax. It showed a bird in flight. A phoenix with wings spread wide. The mark of the Firebird. The seal was broken. The envelope open. And with hands that shook a little, Smithies drew out a folded sheet of paper and laid it on the table.

2

Search for the Light

Brodie Bray stood on the footbridge that spanned the river and waited for her granddad. She knew he'd arrive on his scooter. Not the sort of scooter that looks like a golf buggy and that old ladies with blue curly hair ride at top speed down the middle of the pavement. A proper scooter. A silver one with two wheels and a footboard; that you scoot on.

She didn't mind that her granddad rode a scooter. She was just glad he'd grown out of his rollerblade phase.

She rolled up the left sleeve of her jumper and looked at her watch. He was late. She rolled up her other sleeve. Her second watch was set to show the time in New York, America. It was behind English time. But whichever calculations she made to allow for the time difference, Granddad was still late. She kicked a loose pebble with her foot. It rolled across the pavement and then dropped into the river. It made barely a ripple. 'Too small,' thought Brodie to herself. 'Just too small to make a difference.'

She peered down into the water. It looked thick and black like oil, her reflection rising and falling so her freckled nose seemed to grow and shrink. She kicked another pebble. This time a bigger one. The image in the water swirled beneath the weight of the pebble. She waited for the image to settle. But it still didn't look like her. Not the person she saw in the mirror with wild straw-coloured hair that never hung smooth, and a crooked grin where her teeth stuck out a little because she'd sucked her thumb as a baby. This shimmery water version of her looked strangely scary. She kicked one more stone. The largest she could find. The reflection in the water shattered into a thousand pieces.

'So you found it all right?' Her granddad's voice behind her made her jump. 'Been waiting long?' He was loosening the strap on his helmet and unfixing the cycle clips from around the hem of his trousers.

Brodie gave him a quick hug. 'Just arrived,' she lied.

At first her granddad had been dismissive. The map on the card was probably a joke. A clever trick played by someone in her class. It wasn't. Brodie was sure. So he'd said he'd go with her; that she wasn't to be there on the bridge alone. And she was suddenly very glad he was here.

Brodie looked down at her Greenwich Mean Time watch. It was nearly ten. The streetlamp flickered above them. In precisely three minutes she and her granddad would find the mystery solved.

Tandi Tandari was waiting. She had her arms folded, her eyes narrowed so thin lines wrinkled the skin of her black brow, and she was tapping her left foot impatiently. 'You're transferring to Bletchley Park Museum?' she said, any attempt to disguise the annoyance in her voice failing miserably.

'Ah, yes, about that. I was going to mention—'

Tandi didn't let Smithies complete his sentence. 'Five years I've worked as your secretary and you didn't think to let me know you'd be moving on.' She snorted, making a sound very much like a muffled sneeze. 'As if taking a post at Bletchley is *moving on*.' Her voice was getting higher and a little shriller.

Smithies steered her rather abruptly through a nearby doorway. It led to a cleaning cupboard and amid the mops and buckets he tried to calm her down.

'Tandi, please.' A tin of furniture wax to his left clattered to the floor.

'Why on earth would one of the Chamber's best code-crackers want to work at a museum? I thought that role was just for those who wanted to build up their pension before they retired. Why on earth would you want to transfer there?'

Smithies picked up the tin of furniture wax and cradled it in his hands. 'It's not what it seems,' he said.

'Well, that's good because it seems to me you're giving up code-cracking and had forgotten to mention it.'

Smithies put the tin of furniture wax down on the shelf. 'Would you let me explain?'

There was something about the way his secretary swept her hair dramatically behind her shoulders that suggested he should!

'It's true I'm making a move to Bletchley Park but I won't only be working at the museum there.'

He held his hand up to stop her interrupting.

'Bletchley Park Mansion was a hugely important code-cracking centre in the Second World War and the museum does a great job of telling people what went on. But I plan to do something else with my time there.'

'Like what?'

'I intend to set up a secret Code and Cipher School for modern-day code-crackers. I want to choose a team of successful candidates to work with me, covertly, in a secret section of the Black Chamber, on a particularly tricky manuscript.'

Tandi drew her hands up to her face and pressed them tight against her mouth. 'You're going to work on MS 408 again?' she spluttered.

'I didn't say that.'

'You are! It makes total sense. All the people you hoped to interview yesterday used to be connected to MS 408.'

Smithies could feel the panic rising in his chest. It was usually a source of pride to him that his secretary was thorough in her work and meticulous in her quest for details. Now, it was particularly awkward.

'Tandi, please. Maybe we're going to be looking at MS 408.' She made a yelping noise then which he couldn't be entirely sure signalled distress or pleasure. 'But no one must know. It's *entirely confidential*. It'll be like a secret in a secret. I've waited years to look again at MS 408 but since the ban on the manuscript, what I'm doing is highly risky.' He hesitated a little. 'That's why I didn't tell you.'

'But a Code and Cipher School. You want to use *children*?' It was clear she was finding it hard to breathe. 'What about the rules? What about the risks?'

'No one'll know. I'll be careful.' Smithies wished he

was as confident as he sounded.

Her forehead wrinkled again. 'Let me come with you.'

He stepped back against the shelf and the tin of furniture wax toppled to the floor again. 'Don't be ridiculous.'

'I want to come. If you're looking at MS 408 then I want to be part of it. What greater challenge is there than trying to read an unread book?'

Smithies tried to argue but no sound came out.

'I was a teacher. In Jamaica. Before all this.' She waved her hands around and the tins on the shelving wobbled. 'Teaching's what I did. And I loved it.' She drew herself up tall to her full height. 'Let me come and teach.'

Finding any words at all was now impossible.

'Smithies, if you're packing up and going to work as part of a secret Code and Cipher School then I want you to count me in. I can't believe for a minute you thought I'd stay behind and work here without you.'

He lifted the tin of wax once more and this time she took it from him and placed it on the shelf. 'You sure?' he said. The idea was brilliant. It might just work.

Her smile told him that when he left for Bletchley Park, Miss Tandari would not be far behind.

'Well, whoever it is, isn't coming,' Brodie's granddad said quietly, leaning his weight on the lamppost.

Brodie pretended not to hear. What was the point in arranging to meet someone and going to all the trouble of sending them a map if you weren't going to turn up? It wasn't worth looking at either of her watches. She knew how long they'd stood there. She'd counted the minutes in her head.

'Shall we give them till eleven?'

That just made her feel worse. Granddad being all understanding and patient. It'd been much better when he'd suggested the note was from someone at school and perhaps she should ignore it.

'No one,' she said at last. 'We've seen absolutely no one. A whole hour and not a single person's walked by. No one ever uses this bridge – that's the problem. Don't know why they bother having a light here,' she snapped, kicking out with her foot at the base of the lamppost. 'No one needs it.'

Her granddad chuckled. 'Well it's good to kick out at when you're angry. Good to lean on when you're tired. I think it's great it's here,' he said.

The light flickered in the bulb.

'Doesn't even turn off,' she said. 'It shouldn't be on in the day. It's wasting money. And we're wasting time.' She linked her arm through her granddad's and pulled the scooter from where it was leaning against the railings and began to roll it forward. 'Come on,' she said. 'Let's go home.'

Her granddad didn't answer. He just walked along beside her, his helmet hanging from the handlebars and the bicycle clips linked like bracelets around his wrist. 'Light is knowledge,' she sniffed. 'What a joke.'

They'd just reached the door of the Pig and Whistle pub when it suddenly dawned on her.

'Granddad, I need your scooter!'

'What?'

She could tell her granddad had half a mind on a pint of shandy and a packet of pork scratchings.

'Your scooter. I need to borrow your scooter.'

It took less than three minutes, but every one of them felt endless. She couldn't believe she could have been so stupid. If no one used the footbridge then she wasn't supposed to look for a *person* at the bridge. She was supposed to look for a *thing*. And there was only one thing on the bridge. That was the lamp. A streetlamp that'd flickered on just before ten o'clock and now blazed brightly in the middle of the day.

She skidded to a halt and threw the scooter down. Her heart was racing. She circled, looking up at the flickering bulb. 'Come on,' she hissed. 'Come on.'

Light is knowledge, the note said. She circled again, running her hands along the post. She knelt on the tarmac and scrabbled at the floor. Then, when she could think of nothing else, she slid down to the ground and sat with her back against the post, and looked up at the sky.

There was a click.

Pressure in the small of her back.

She twisted round and behind her, in the base section of the post, a tiny door latched open.

Once on her knees it was easier to see. The door opened to reveal what looked like a tiny cupboard. Inside was a sheaf of paper tacked together in a thick Manila folder tied with red ribbon. On the front of the folder was a picture of an elephant holding a key in his trunk. The word VERITAS was written at the top and along one side the name 'Brodie Elizebeth Bray'.

By the time Brodie reached out to take the folder, her granddad was beside her. He was panting and beads of sweat were across his brow. He nodded as she looked up at him. Then she closed her fingers around the folder and took it out of its hiding place.

There was a gentle hiss, a soft click and the light from the lamp went out.

* * *

Smithies lifted the paper from the table and stood up slowly. A list of names. The chosen ones. All the children he'd invited.

He was anxious about their safety. He'd be careful. He'd have to be.

He made his way across the room towards the shredder then pushed the sheets carefully between the cutting blades. It no longer mattered who'd been asked. It only mattered who accepted the challenge to come.

'I'm not going.'

Brodie Bray had spent the last hour discussing the contents of the document from the lamppost with her granddad, and as far as she was concerned, it was the most ridiculous idea she'd ever heard.

'There's no way I'm going to go and live in a museum.'

'It's a mansion. Bletchley Park Mansion, otherwise known as Station X actually.' Her granddad was rummaging around in the bottom cupboard of the dresser, searching for something he'd obviously decided was absolutely vital to find while in the middle of rowing with his granddaughter.

'That document said it's a museum,' she snapped to the back of his head. 'How come you know different?'

'Because I used to live there.'

Brodie slumped down to her knees beside him. 'You what?'

'Used to live there.'

'And you never thought to mention it?'

'Not until now. There were strict rules until the Veritas section of the Black Chamber was recalled.' He added the second part of the sentence almost apologetically. 'But I did believe this day would come, you know. If we just waited long enough. I bet others have given up. But me . . . I believed it would happen.' He seemed at last to have found what he was searching for. 'Here,' he said, 'there's something I want to show you.' In his hand he held a metal biscuit tin. He put it down on the table and tapped the lid almost ceremoniously, opened it and took out a small discoloured photograph.

'Veritas,' he said deliberately. 'It's Latin for "truth" and that's what we were after. The truth, you see.'

'Who's we? What truth?'

He waved the yellowed photograph in his hand. 'Look. Here's me, looking pretty dandy if I do say so myself. And there's your grandmother. Splendid woman. Truly splendid. And there's your mother. Must've been about your age then. Next to her friends, Jon and Robbie. Not officially part of the team, what with them being only kids, but that didn't stop them trying to help.' He let the memory wash over him. 'Fantastic times. All of us together from all parts of the world working to find the truth.'

Brodie was getting exasperated now. 'Yes. You keep saying. What are you talking about? What truth?'

Her granddad peered at her over the edge of the photograph. 'You know we believed then it was the only truth worth knowing. The truth of MS 408. Of course it wasn't called that then. We knew it simply as the Voynich Manuscript. It was named after the man who found it one hundred years ago. A book with pictures of places we couldn't understand and words we couldn't read. But a book that drew you in, like a fly being pulled into a spider's web. There was no escaping the pull once you'd seen the pages of the book for yourself.' He ran his fingers through his thinning grey hair. 'You know, Brodie, I've dreamt of this day. Longed for it to come. The day when Veritas was recalled. Your mother would've been so proud to know you'd been chosen. So very, very proud.'

'My mum?'

'MS 408 wrapped her tightly in its web, I can tell you. She spent much of her life trying to break the secrets of that book. And on her very last trip to Belgium, when she was so cruelly taken from us, she thought she was on to something new about the

24

document, you know. She really did.'

'Veritas and this weird book were important to my mum?' Brodie asked softly.

Her granddad looked uncomfortable.

Brodie picked up the yellowed photograph. 'And she'd want me to go to this Code and Cipher School then?'

Her granddad looked more uncomfortable still. There was something he wasn't telling her. She could sense it.

'You'll need to be brave,' he said.

'To look at a book?' she laughed.

'It's complicated.'

'Bet it is, if it's all in code.'

'No. I mean *things* are complicated.'

'But I should go?'

Her granddad thought for a moment. 'You should. If Smithies is involved.'

'Smithies,' she said. 'You know him?'

Her granddad pointed to a small boy in the photograph who had a wide and cheeky grin. 'Oh yes. And so did your mother. Jon Stephen Smithies was one of her very closest friends.'

It was perhaps putting it a little too strongly to suggest that Ms Kerrith Vernan hated Mr Smithies. But it really wasn't so very far from the truth. Smithies, in her opinion, stood for everything that was wrong with the state of the Black Chamber. He was old-fashioned, stuck in his ways and a terribly bad dresser.

Kerrith Vernan prided herself on three things. The first was her fast, and some would say exceptional, acceleration through the ranks amongst the staff at the Black Chamber. The second was her acceptance and love of the new order, the improved way of doing things, the future. And the third was her very carefully managed appearance. You didn't get to be as good-looking or as well presented as she was today without expending a lot of energy at the gym, or spending a lot of money on your stylist, two words she knew without doubt didn't even exist in Smithies' vocabulary.

Smithies was the thorn in Kerrith's side. And also the man in the next-door office, and simply sharing the same floor level as him, and therefore occasionally the same elevator, made her unhappy.

But Kerrith had heard a rumour, a rumbling among the staff at the office, and she longed with all her heart for the rumour to be true.

It was Thursday. In forty minutes Kerrith had an appointment with her box-a-thon trainer followed by two hours with her beauty therapist. She shuffled the papers on the desk into a neat pile and slid them into a

Manila folder labelled '*CLASSIFIED*' before opening the top drawer of her filing cabinet and slipping the folder inside. When she looked up, her secretary was standing in the doorway.

'It's true,' the secretary said purposefully.

Kerrith's fingers clutched tighter to the key in her hand. Her heart began to skip a little. 'You're absolutely sure?'

'Confirmed just now. He's off to work at Bletchley Park Museum. Some sort of early retirement package.'

Kerrith stood up, flexing her neck a little like an animal in the wild focusing on its prey before preparing to pounce.

'Perfect,' she said, her tongue lingering over each syllable. 'Now at last this department can move out of the shadow of the past.' She smiled a rather uneven smile. (The work with the orthodontist hadn't been entirely satisfactory and she was awaiting a follow-up appointment to complete the corrections.) 'Absolutely perfect. We need to keep an eye on what he does there though. He may be out of sight but after what he did, he'll never be out of mind.' There was a sense of venom laced through her words that caused the secretary to leave the room rather quickly.

Mr Bray snapped on the light. His heart was pressing

27

hard against his ribs. He looked at the bedside clock. Four fifty-two. Less than eight hours left.

He could change his mind. Tell her he'd thought things through. That he *needed* her to stay.

If he said that, she'd never leave.

He rubbed his chest.

It was important then, that he said nothing. Despite all the rules and all the risks, surely he had to let Brodie go.

The Chosen Ones

It was a week since Brodie Bray had found the document in the lamppost and there was about an hour to go before the car arrived to take her to Bletchley.

Her granddad sat down on the edge of the bed and sniffed a little.

'Here,' he said, after wiping his nose on a rather garishly patterned handkerchief. 'I want you to have this.' Brodie thought for a moment he was talking about the handkerchief (a prospect she found a little worrying) but then he reached into his jacket pocket and pulled out a small package wrapped in yellowed tissue paper. Brodie held out her hand. 'It was your mother's. It was with her things when she died. She was a mighty fine code-breaker, you know. One of the best. I think she'd want you to have it.'

Brodie unwrapped the tissue paper carefully to reveal a silver locket. Pressed into the centre was a large oval stone that appeared at first to be white and blue. Brodie moved the locket in the light and the stone flashed pink. It hung on a thick twisted chain. She held it up and it swung freely in her hand, catching the light like a bevelled glass. 'It's beautiful, Granddad,' she said. 'I'll wear it every day.'

'Here,' he said, slowing the swing of the locket with his hands. 'Open it. My fingers can't manage the catch any more.'

Brodie rested the locket in the flat of her palm and pressed her fingernail against the seam. The locket sprang open. Inside was a small sketched drawing of what looked like a castle. Brodie peered up at her granddad for an explanation.

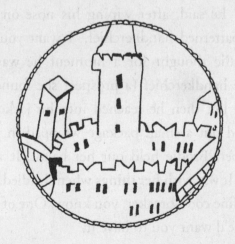

He blew his nose loudly. 'It's a picture copied from MS 408,' he said. 'The picture fascinated your mother. Your grandmother too. It was as if all the mysterious words and diagrams from the Voynich Manuscript would eventually lead to this place. This hidden place.'

Brodie traced her finger across the towers of the castle, the ridges of its walls.

'It was always our hope one day to find the castle,' whispered Granddad.

Brodie pressed the locket closed and held it tight for a moment.

Then she hugged him and together they put the chain around her neck and fixed the clasp. The locket was warm against her skin.

Brodie tried to think of something sensible to say, something important about how she'd carry on the quest and that she'd try her best. But in the end no words came.

Several hours later, Brodie stopped crying. Her stomach was knotted. She wasn't sure if this was due to travel sickness, the fact she'd eaten half a bag of toffees or because she missed her granddad.

'So, what d'you reckon?' the driver asked as the car climbed up a hill towards a large gateway. Brodie was too busy trying to take everything in to answer.

At the end of the drive was a sprawling, red-brick mansion. There was a mixture of designs; some window frames painted white, others black and edged with stone. There were sections of pitched roofs, some turrets and green-topped domes. In places there were thick black beams criss-crossed along the plaster, but some walls were covered in a creamy pebbledash. There were high chimneys and jagged archways, wooden doors and glazed ones, and in front of the main entrance a gravelled forecourt with a circular lawn. It looked to Brodie as if no one builder had ever quite taken control. It looked unfinished, as if things here still needed completing.

The car slowed to a halt.

Brodie stared at the front door of the mansion. In the story she told herself in her head, it looked like an opening to a new world. She was scared. Unsure again, if she wanted to go inside. Two stone statues stood like guards either side of the door and above their heads hung a single lantern. A candle burned inside, the light of the flame bouncing against something small and shiny.

Brodie bit her lip as the driver of the car unloaded her cases from the boot. She thanked him, checked the time on both her watches and the car pulled slowly back down the drive.

Then she turned and ploughed straight into the path of a boy riding a unicycle.

The crash wasn't pretty. Her case burst open, spilling an embarrassing load of clothing and books on to the ground. Brodie landed in a heap next to the boy, who'd fallen with an ominous crunch on top of the unicycle. As Brodie fought to catch her breath, chocolate toffees rained down on the pair of them.

'Where the deep-fried Mars bar did *you* come from?' His voice tailed away as he rose from the ground and rested the unicycle in his place. The wheel looked more than a little bent.

'I don't believe it,' Brodie groaned through teeth clamped tight together.

'Well, you better toasted sandwich believe it. Unless it's raining sweets and knickers and you've decided to take a quick kip on the pavement, then we've really just crashed. It's my nineteenth circuit and the path's been totally clear every time.'

Brodie flicked a toffee from her shoulder and pulled herself up to sitting. 'Well, it wasn't clear *this* time!'

'No. I see that *now*. Sorry! *Really* sorry.' The boy towered over her, his face ringed by the sun as it broke through a cloud. He looked tall, although it was hard to tell from so far below him. He was perhaps her age, probably a year or two older, and his hair was fairly long, a fringe flopping in front of his eyes and a freckled nose blushed red with embarrassment. He swept his hair back from his face then offered his hand out towards her.

She wanted to yell at him for not looking where he was going; scream at him for making all her books burst out of the case. But he looked so incredibly awkward and his hand shook so much as he offered it, all she could bring herself to mutter was, 'Thanks.'

The boy knelt down and scrambled to repack her case. His hands hesitated over a nightdress with a rather large rabbit printed on the front, and she thought for a moment he was going to comment, but then as if thinking better of it, he scooped up the books and pressed the case lid shut. 'There,' he said purposefully. 'Like I said. Very sorry.'

Looking down at where he knelt beside her case, Brodie could see a toffee was still wedged in the collar of his jacket. She bent down to remove it then looked across at the unicycle. It was clear now the wheel was completely buckled. 'Oh, your bike,' she said, 'unicycle, thing. It's all wonky.'

He lifted the unicycle from the ground. The wheel squeaked as it spun. 'Doesn't look very well, does it? Oh, well. I can always use my stilts to get around.'

Brodie wasn't sure if he was joking.

'My name's Hunter,' he said. 'Hunter Jenkins. And yes, it's my real name. Why would anyone make up a name like Hunter?'

Brodie considered the question for a moment.

'It's a family name. My parents say I'll grow into it, which makes it sound like a winter coat or something.' He waited. 'At least you can take a coat off. I'm stuck with Hunter.'

'It's unusual.' Brodie chose her word carefully.

'You?' he asked.

'Brodie. Brodie Bray.'

'BB,' he said. 'Like it. Got a good ring to it. I arrived earlier. My stuff's round the back. And I was just riding around the front here to suss things out, really. Being nosey.'

'But you've been inside the house, told them you're here?'

'No,' he said.

'Oh.'

'Door's locked, see. No sign of anyone. I was beginning to wonder if this is all a joke. You know. A sort of set-up.'

'Perhaps we're just early,' she said hopefully, looking down again at her Greenwich Mean Time watch, and then frowning. 'But they should be expecting us. You've rung the bell?' she added, turning a statement into a question.

'Can't find one.' He looked back despondently into the gloomy porch where the light from the candle lantern pooled against the door.

Brodie sat down on the front step. She unwrapped a toffee and popped it into her mouth.

Hunter stared rather longingly.

'Here.' She passed him the sweet she'd retrieved from his collar.

'Thanks, I'm starved.' He sat down and began to chew.

Brodie twisted her toffee paper into a bow. 'I suppose we just wait,' she said eventually.

'Yeah. Well, I can't ride my unicycle any more. So that little bit of fun's been taken from me.'

Brodie felt a twinge of guilt. 'Perhaps we should look back at the document we were given.'

'Done that,' Hunter said, reaching into his open backpack. He pulled out his rather crumpled version of the document Brodie had retrieved from the lamppost. 'What?' He obviously noticed Brodie's look of displeasure. 'My dog sat on it. She's a big dog.' He shook the pages out in an attempt to straighten them. 'I can still read it.'

'But you didn't think of ironing it flat again?'

'Oh yeah. I often go round ironing papers.' He

looked thoughtful. 'The other thing we could do, rather than just sit here, is open that box.'

'Box? What box?'

'That one,' he said, pointing. There was a small cardboard box tucked inside the porch. The lid was closed. 'I wasn't sure,' Hunter added. 'Seemed a bit rude. But after nineteen circuits of the lawn, I'm running out of ideas.'

Brodie wasn't sure it would help. Neither was she sure it was allowed. But a struggle had begun inside her. A wrestling to know what was inside the box even if they weren't supposed to look. Surely it was better than just doing nothing? 'I say we go for it,' she said. 'Agree?'

Hunter winked and prised open the lid.

It was instantly clear to see what was inside. Stopwatches. 'Nice,' mumbled Hunter. 'Welcome gifts, you reckon? Not sure you'll really be needing one as you seem to have the whole time issue covered.'

Brodie pulled her cuffs down quickly.

'But there's loads here so I guess we can take one each.' He passed her out a stopwatch and hanging from it was a piece of paper. 'They've all got notes attached,' he said. 'Looks like they're all the same. What's it say?'

Brodie read the message aloud.

Welcome to Station X. We see you have an eye for seeking out answers and this is impressive. However, before we get down to formalities and welcome you inside the mansion, I think a little puzzle is in order. A game. You must use all your powers of problem solving to retrieve the key in order to open the door before you. The clues you solve will lead you to that key. But keep in mind the very good advice that was given to you before your arrival. Nothing you needed in the past can be forgotten. All the best puzzles rely on what we have already learnt but think we have forgotten. Good luck on your quest.

JS Smithies.

<u>*Clue number one*</u>*: report to the guards.*

Brodie turned the note over. There was more to read.

Oh, and by the way, to add to the excitement, there's a catch. Fail to find the key before the alarm sounds on the stopwatch and the game is over . . . your adventure finished before it's even begun. Good Luck!

'They're timing us,' Brodie spluttered. She stared at the stopwatch display and the figures counting down. 'We've got thirty minutes.' Panic bubbled in her throat.

'Half an hour to get inside, or we're going home.'

Hunter's face had drained of colour. 'OK. We shouldn't panic. Let's take things steady.'

'Twenty-nine minutes, Hunter,' Brodie groaned. 'We don't need to be calm. We need to be quick!'

'OK. OK.' He slipped the cord of his stopwatch around his neck. 'Guards then. We need to find the guards.'

Brodie knew she should remember something important. A piece of a story perhaps, but she couldn't work out what it was. 'Can't see any guards,' she said. 'That's the problem. I can't see anyone at all!'

'To be fair, *you* couldn't see a unicycle careering towards you, so we can't entirely trust your vision, can we?'

Brodie peered in desperation at the entrance.

There was no bell or knocker, just a door between two pillars. At the base of each was a stone animal. Both had the body of a lion but wings like an eagle and Brodie was pretty sure they were griffins, although one of them was looking a little worse for wear, its beak and forehead chipped and weathered. 'There are no guards,' Brodie said again. 'Griffins are supposed to keep watch for treasure seekers but they didn't stop us getting the watches, did they?'

'Guards,' Hunter blurted suddenly.

'Excuse me?'

'Guards.'

'Where?'

'There, you doughnut. The griffins. That's what you've just said. *They're* the guards. I reckon we have to report to these griffins.'

It seemed too obvious to point out the griffins weren't real, although now she remembered she *had* thought the statues looked like guards when she first arrived. Fact was though, they were really just lumps of stone, but Hunter seemed undeterred and began to inspect the statues like a doctor urgently checking over the body of an accident victim.

'Here,' he said, 'there's something under its feet.'

Brodie knelt down beside him. 'Is it the key? Have we done it already?'

Hunter shook his head. Wedged between the talons of the most damaged griffin was a roll of paper. He eased it out and began to read the message aloud.

Well done. I see you've made yourself acquainted with the guards. You're doing well . . . although I hope you remember the clock is ticking.

Brodie looked at her stopwatch. 'Twenty-one minutes,' she said. 'What else does it say?'

Hunter turned the paper over.

Clue number two: You must demonstrate true northerly direction when riding the winged horse in the shadow of six o'clock.

'So?' Hunter re-rolled the message and tapped his knees with the paper. 'What d'you think?'

'I think we've got twenty minutes,' she said.

Hunter began to read the clue again. 'Repetition,' he said in explanation. 'Helps the details sink in. It's to do with numbers.'

'Numbers?' Brodie was totally confused.

'Numbers,' he said again. 'They're my thing. Like books are obviously yours,' he said pointing back to her case. 'Based on the fact you had twenty-four of the things packed in there. And as numbers are my thing we need to hone in on the use of the number six.'

'Brilliant.'

'Yes. Maybe *brilliance* is actually my thing.' He read the clue again.

It was on the third reading aloud that Brodie sank down dejectedly to the ground.

'What's the problem, BB? Beaten already? We haven't even tried to solve it.'

'It's no good,' Brodie mumbled. 'We're late.'

41

'Pardon?'

'Late. We're late.'

'But we've got eighteen minutes,' Hunter said, clutching at his stopwatch.

'That's not important.' Brodie rolled up the sleeves on both her arms to reveal each of her two watches. 'Whichever time zone we use, we've missed six o'clock.'

'Oh.'

She kicked a pebble with her foot. She couldn't believe she'd failed already. Her granddad would be so disappointed. How could she tell him it had all gone wrong so soon?

'So that's it then?' asked Hunter. 'All over. Just like that?'

'Looks like it.'

'So what? We just wait here for them to come and ship us home? My parents aren't going to be happy about me bowling back a failure already, I can tell you.' His voice was quite high, as if he was scared.

'What can we do? We didn't get the key in time.' Hunter looked so sickened by the thought of defeat Brodie scrabbled to find something which could make things sound better. 'We could go round and get your stuff and then we can try and tell this Smithies guy about the accident. We can tell him the story of what happened and maybe he'll feel sorry for us? Let us try again?'

'I don't think we can make it sound like a multi-vehicle pile-up, B. But they might feel bad for us. We can give it a go.'

They rounded the corner at the back of the mansion and stopped.

Brodie could hear the sound of heavy breathing coming from above her.

'What the cream cake's that?' gasped Hunter.

Brodie tried to shield her eyes from the sun and peered up at the roof. A girl about her age seemed to be clinging to the metal base of a wrought-iron weather vane swinging slightly in the breeze. And she definitely didn't look comfortable. In fact, Brodie was sure now she was hanging on for dear life.

Hunter grabbed a heavy wooden ladder propped against the wall behind him. 'It's OK! I'll save you,' he called.

An indignant voice called down from the turret. 'I don't need saving, thank you very much.'

'Doesn't look like that to me!'

'You think just because you're a boy you can rescue me!'

'No. I think just because I've got a *ladder* I can rescue you.'

Brodie tried her best to calm things down. '*Why* are you up there?' she shouted, glaring first at Hunter in a way she hoped showed him she didn't want him to speak.

'Pegasus,' the girl yelled, waving one arm towards the weather vane, causing a loose tile to skitter across the roof and come crashing down. 'I got here at six and saw the winged horse and climbed up. That was a while ago.'

'She's trying to *ride* the winged horse,' Brodie hissed.

'Well, she's not doing a very good job of it, is she?' Hunter hissed back. 'And I'm not being funny, but do you really think the note meant anyone should actually ride the thing?'

'Got that right!' came the voice from the tower.

Hunter craned his neck upwards.

'You're not being funny, I mean.'

'Surely she knows it's after six and the game must be over,' said Brodie, a weird tightening growing in her stomach. Was there a chance they'd misunderstood the clue? A possibility that the game wasn't over at all? That they still had time? 'Six o'clock,' she blurted. 'Maybe it doesn't matter where we were at six o'clock but where the *winged horse* was.'

'Well, I'm here to tell you,' called a voice from the roof which was becoming more than a little strained, 'that the weather vane was here at six, firmly attached to this roof – that is why,' she appeared to be spitting now, the words sharp and furious, 'I'm up here!'

Brodie was trying to organise her thinking but ideas and words were crashing together in her mind. 'Read the clue again, Hunter.'

'*You must demonstrate true northerly direction when riding the winged horse in the shadow of six o'clock.*'

'It's talking about the *shadow* made by the vane!' Brodie scrabbled for her stopwatch.

'How long have we got?' said Hunter.

'Thirteen minutes.'

'OK. It's not over. So let's focus. What else is in the clue?'

'*Northerly*,' said Brodie. 'That's got to be important.' She peered up at the vane and the arrows below the horse pointing in each direction of the compass. 'We need to think about where the shadow from that northern arrow was when it *was* six.' Brodie glanced over in the direction of a low-roofed building to the left, where a shadow from the clock tower and the weather vane above it was stretching across the brickwork.

'Perfect,' said Hunter, following her gaze. 'The shadows are on the wall. But they must have been a bit further back along the wall when it was six, don't you think?'

'Erm. Hello. Still up here.'

'Thought she didn't want rescuing,' sniffed Hunter. 'I say we leave her there.'

'I simply meant you shouldn't *presume* I couldn't get down without you,' the girl snapped.

'Oh, this is ridiculous,' said Brodie, dragging the ladder along the wall herself and propping it in reach of the girl's feet. 'You two haven't even properly met. How can you be so mean to each other already?'

It was a question neither of the others seemed prepared to answer.

The girl worked her way down the ladder and reluctantly Hunter held out his hand to her as she neared the bottom rung. She seemed to take great delight in rejecting his offer of help and jumped the last few steps instead. Brodie sighed. 'Look, you two, we have a clue to solve. And twelve minutes to do it in.' She looked at the girl from the roof. 'Are you with us or not?'

The girl appeared to be thinking.

'It's not a difficult question,' snapped Hunter. 'Are you in or out? Eleven minutes. Have to hurry you!'

'OK. We'll work together. I'm Tusia.' She made a noise which sounded remarkably like a sneeze. 'It's Russian. Well, I'm Russian. Fourth generation. It's said "*Too shka*".'

46

Hunter struggled for a while trying to make his mouth form the word as Tusia wanted. He gave up. 'We've got ten minutes. I'll call you Toots,' he said. 'She's BB.'

'Brodie actually. And he's Hunter. And it's best not to ask about that now. We haven't got time.'

'Nine and a half minutes,' pressed Hunter. 'Let's get solving. The shadows are changing all the time. They're moving along the wall of that building. If we leave it too long we'll have no idea where the shadow was falling at six o'clock.'

The arrows on the base of the weather vane worked like a sundial, and the shadow of the northern arrow was like a line against the bricks.

'Well? We've got nine minutes, people!'

Brodie ran her hands along the brickwork, moving in the opposite direction from which the shadow was travelling fraction by fraction as the moments passed. 'We have to go backwards and work out where the shadow was at six o'clock.'

Hunter scrabbled to his knees beside her. 'What the cheese cracker are we looking for, exactly?' he asked. 'On a brick wall, I mean. Even if we do work out where the shadow was, it's just a line of bricks, surely?'

Brodie's mind was whirring. 'Where are the arrows

on the weather vane?' she snapped.

'Erm. Under the winged horse,' suggested Hunter tentatively.

'So. We've got to find where the shadow of the vane arrow was at six. And look *under it*,' said Brodie. She wished she was as confident as she sounded.

Tusia was waving her hands around, pacing up and down.

'Erm, Toots. Not helping.'

'Actually, I'm *calculating*. About a third of a brick per minute, I reckon, and so . . .' She moved Brodie's hand along the wall. 'There. Six o'clock the shadow would have been about there.' She looked at Brodie. 'Anything?'

Brodie's fingers locked on a loose brick wobbly in the grouting. With a tug she pulled the brick free. Underneath was a small rolled-up note.

'Perfect!'

'What's it say?' urged Hunter.

Well done, my careful code-crackers. It seems you are not to be deflected in your quest for the truth. So now for the final task, in order to gain entry to the Station that seeks to welcome you.

<u>*Clue number three:*</u> *At the end you must return to the beginning.*

48

Tusia repeated the clue then placed the note back beneath the brick. 'Everything back in its place,' she said by way of explanation.

'Return to the beginning,' mumbled Brodie, a sense of panic rising again in her stomach. 'What's that mean?'

'Back to the box of stopwatches?' offered Hunter. 'We searched that. There was nothing else.'

'Maybe it just means the front door?' offered Brodie hopefully. 'That's where we started. It was the beginning.'

Tusia was shaking her head. 'I've banged on the door. There's no bell. The door's locked. There's no way of getting in without a key.'

'We have to look again,' urged Hunter. 'We've got six minutes.'

They ran to the front of the mansion. Brodie noticed the candle in the lantern had shrunk in size. It was as if it mocked them, burning relentlessly lower as they searched for answers. For the second time since she'd arrived, the idea she should remember something nagged at her mind.

Hunter steadied himself against the griffin.

'I read a story once about a griffin,' Brodie said, trying to move the game back on to ground she understood.

'Really?' Hunter didn't seem surprised. 'Stories are her thing,' he said to Tusia, 'like clambering all over things is obviously yours.'

'Shape and space is *my thing*, thank you very much,' Tusia snapped. 'I have a highly developed sense of organisation of locations,' she said.

'Nice,' mocked Hunter. 'Must be so useful. We've got five minutes. How's your shape and space thing working for you now?'

'Actually—'

Brodie cut them off. 'This story,' she said. 'The griffin in it was a guardian of light.'

'Could he stretch time, this guardian of light?' asked Hunter. 'Four minutes now. We're into our last four minutes!'

'Shh,' Brodie hissed in exasperation. Something about her memory of the story had sparked an idea and she was sure if she didn't grasp hold of it, the thought would drift away like smoke.

'You all right, B?' Hunter said, lifting his head to look at her.

Brodie sheltered her eyes against the glare of the sun. 'BB?'

'At the end we must return to the beginning,' Brodie said again.

The stopwatch said three minutes.

'How d'you get your invite to this place?' Brodie asked.

'Birthday card,' mused Hunter. 'A hundred and seventeen days late.'

Tusia's eyes widened. 'I got a card too,' she said. 'And holes had been spaced under the letters to let light through the message.'

Brodie clapped her hands. 'Exactly. *That* was the beginning. And then?'

'Message in a lamppost.' Hunter grinned, finally cottoning on.

'So at the end we must return to the beginning,' confirmed Brodie. 'And at the beginning of all this was the *light*.' Her pulse was racing. They had two minutes.

She looked up at the candle lantern.

Glinting in the glow of the single flame was something metal. Brodie peered into the light to see. It was a key!

'I guess it's time to use that ladder again!' yelled Hunter.

Dust lifted from his feet as he ran and the end of the ladder carved a snaking line in the gravel on the forecourt.

'One minute, Toots,' he shouted as Tusia climbed the ladder. 'Fifty-nine seconds. Come on!'

Brodie steadied the base of the ladder. She tried to steady her nerve. A bead of sweat trickled down Tusia's neck and dripped on to the floor of the porch.

'Twenty seconds. We have twenty seconds, Toots!'

The lantern cage swung open. The flame of the candle guttered in the breeze. The key tumbled into Brodie's hand.

She slotted the key in the lock and turned.

An alarm on the stopwatches pierced the air.

But the door of Bletchley Park Mansion swung open wide. They were inside the Black Chamber.

'There's only three of them?' Oscar Ingham spat the words out before moving back from the window of the ballroom. 'All this preparation and there's only three of them?'

Smithies tried hard not to panic.

'How many did you ask?' Ingham's voice was sharp like a blade.

'I asked those I thought would come.'

'And all we have is three?' Ingham spluttered into his hand and then, taking an asthma inhaler from his pocket, he pressed firmly on the trigger and inhaled deeply.

'I don't think we should panic,' offered Tandi. 'I mean there's still a chance some have been delayed, isn't there, Smithies?'

'Not really.'

'Oh.'

'So this is it then?' Ingham stood up from the chair, his pyjamas held up today by a vivid red necktie which almost matched the patchy skin of his hands and arms. 'Just three children.' He coughed into his balled fist.

'True. True,' replied Smithies, in a voice he hoped sounded self-assured and confident. 'I agree I'd hoped for more. I can't pretend not to be disappointed. But it's the calibre of the children we've got that'll matter. The strength of their aptitude for the code and their love of a challenge that'll make all the difference. After all, it's our job to teach them while they're here.'

'They nearly failed against the clock to get inside.'

'But they didn't.'

'So what about these children makes them worthy candidates?' Tandi asked in an obvious attempt to be encouraging.

'Well, let's see. The boy on the unicycle, he has a way with numbers and his parents both lecture at Oxford so I'm sure we're on to a winner there.'

'He was reluctant to open the box, though. Till the girl arrived.'

'So, he's not a natural leader,' said Smithies, 'but we've time to work on that.'

'And the girl on the roof? We've time to instil some

53

sense of safety in her, do we?' mumbled Ingham, sipping at a mug of now very cold tea which he seemed reluctant to put down on the table.

'She was a local chess master at ten,' said Smithies, trying to sound impressive.

'And the other one? She was quick to think she was beaten.'

'Alex's girl,' said Smithies gently.

No one spoke for a while.

'You think that's wise, Smithies? After all that happened?' Ingham was speaking but his voice was softer now.

Smithies refused to answer but walked instead towards the door.

Ingham coughed into his hand again before he spoke. 'You still haven't told us, Smithies, how this set-up will work with just three candidates. Do we tell them, what they're up against? What they're really involved in?'

Smithies looked at the ground. How could they with only three children? Explain everything and they could lose them all.

'We tell them only what they need to know,' Smithies called over his shoulder. 'It'll work.' He added the last part in a voice that could barely be heard. 'It'll have to.'

4

Drawings in the Ice

'Welcome. Welcome. So glad you enjoyed our little game.'

Brodie wasn't sure 'enjoyed' was the best word to describe the panic of the last thirty minutes, but she said nothing.

The man before them wore a smart three-piece suit and a small pair of glasses bizarrely propped above his eyes on his forehead. 'I'm Smithies,' he said, 'and this is Miss Tandari. She'll be one of your teachers here.'

He gestured to a tall black woman standing to his left. She wore a floaty coral blue blouse and silver bangles which shimmered brightly against her skin.

'Welcome to Station X,' she said in a voice that was light and airy.

'Let's take you inside. Tandi, if you'd lead the way.'

A door opened into a small ante-porch and then out on to a wide corridor. Smithies stopped for a moment, pointing out to them an intricate tapestry hung on the wall. 'Made by one who was here before you,' he said, 'it's a map of the place as it was just after the war.' A twinkle flashed in his eye. Brodie continued walking and could see an impressive wooden stairway sweeping up to the right.

'We've basically adapted the inside of the house to meet our needs,' Miss Tandari explained as she walked. 'You'll see most of the rooms've been made into study spaces, except the music room which it seemed a shame to clutter up.' She led them to a large room with a massively high stained-glass ceiling covered with pictures of flowers. At the end was a tall stone fireplace with a bust of Winston Churchill on top. Miss Tandari patted the bust affectionately on his bald head. 'Obviously a great fan of Bletchley,' she said.

'You must remember,' Smithies added rather sombrely, 'this is a country home. It was never built to be a "Code and Cipher School" or "Black Chamber". Yet that's what it became just before World War Two and we're thrilled to say it's become so again.'

Miss Tandari led on. 'This is where your secret breaking adventure will begin. A place for you to use your power as you did in order to get yourself inside.'

'Mind you,' Smithies reminded them, calling over his shoulder, 'if you'd remembered our little clue from the very first piece of information you could've saved yourself a lot of time and got in rather more quickly. "Light is knowledge" after all.'

Brodie felt the colour rush across her face, straight to the roots of her hair. An awkward memory of a lamp on a bridge and a candle lantern burning brightly in the daytime stirred in her mind. She determined not to miss clues like that again.

They'd reached a large ballroom where several chairs were laid out boardroom style. Seated behind the table was a man who appeared to be wearing a pair of pyjama trousers and a rather crumpled shirt. He lifted his hand and tidied his unruly eyebrows with the heel of his thumb before offering a scowl in their direction.

'So,' said Smithies with a flourish. 'Now we're all here, let's get started.'

'All.' Brodie played the word over in her mind. All didn't seem to be very many. It was not stretching things to suggest this wasn't really what she'd expected but she sat down on the chair offered to her and tried her best to pay attention.

'I'd like to begin by thanking you for responding

to our call for help,' began Smithies. 'We've invited you here with two very clear purposes,' he said deliberately. 'Our first task is to train you. To make you masters of code and ciphers. To teach you all we know.

'Our second task is to test you.'

Brodie felt a little sick.

'To choose members for a Black Chamber Study Group entitled Veritas,' continued Smithies, 'who'll be given classified and highly confidential new information which will be used to work on a code that's baffled minds for centuries. A book of secrets. It's our serious hope to choose a team of people able to read it.'

Brodie felt the strange bubbling sensation in her stomach she'd got used to feeling now every time the unreadable book was mentioned. A chance to be in a team. She'd never been in a team before. She'd tried out once for the netball team. The teacher felt so sorry for her, she'd got the job of cutting up the oranges for half-time. But this was a *real* chance. To be part of a *real* team. At something she might actually be good at. She was surprised how much she wanted that now she was here.

'Now,' Smithies continued, as if speaking to a much bigger crowd. 'Although we'd like to include you all in the Study Group we'll need to be sure you're worthy of your place in the team. Myself, Miss Tandari and our learned colleague Oscar Ingham will be your teachers here.' He gestured to the man in the pyjama trousers then began to collect together some papers and notes from the table in front of him.

'So there's a chance we still might not make it, then?' hissed Hunter. 'Another chance we could get sent home.' This thought clearly worried him immensely. 'And the old geezer in pyjamas. What the crab apple's that all about?'

Tusia hissed back along the line. 'Maybe he just can't bring himself to get ready to face the day.'

'That's stupid.'

'Perhaps he thinks if he doesn't get dressed properly then the day hasn't really started.'

Brodie mulled this over and looked at Tusia with a deepening respect. 'You see *all that* because he's wearing pyjamas?' She hoped any tests they had wouldn't focus on working out things like that.

Tusia shrugged. 'Lots of people can't face the day,' she said knowingly. 'They just go about showing it in different ways.' She hesitated for a moment. 'Anyway, you can't blame the old guy if he's realised he has to try and teach *him*,' she added venomously, pointing along the line.

Hunter glowered and raised his hand attempting to

hide the fact he was whispering again, but Brodie batted his hand away. 'Shh,' she hissed. 'They'll hear. And we're supposed to be making a good impression.'

'Fair point,' winced Hunter.

Smithies had organised the papers and cleared his throat to speak again. 'Enough of the formalities. You'll be tired and hungry, and I for one have an appointment to keep.' He smiled and Brodie felt reassured. 'Take your time to make yourselves at home. Rest well. There's plenty of time to prepare for testing.'

'You'll be in Hut 8,' Miss Tandari explained, as Brodie began her private tour. 'Smithies lives off site in the village but you can always find me as I'm based in the mansion. Here's a map to refer to and I'll help you get your bearings.'

Starting beside Block B, Brodie could see a series of huts of different sizes and ages. Some were newly painted, but some were rather shabby. On the outside of each one was a number marked on the centre of a thick black name-plate. 'These huts were the heart of Bletchley,' Miss Tandari explained. 'In the war code-breakers were allocated to one particular hut. You worked there all the time. Each hut was responsible for different types of code-breaking.' Brodie nodded.

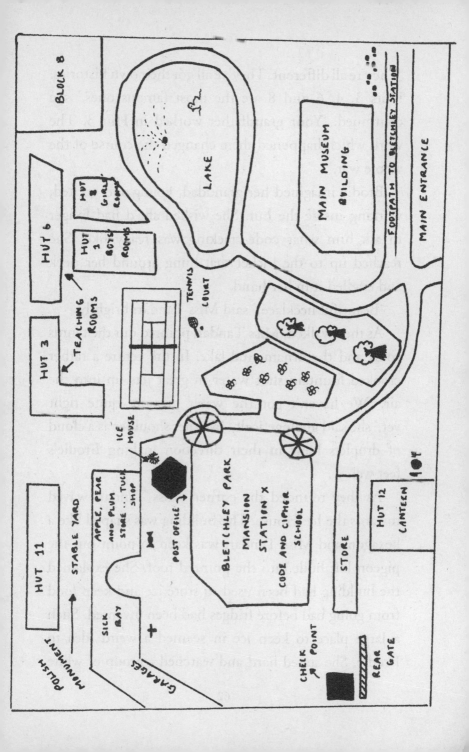

'They're all different. They've all got their own histories. Huts 3, 4, 6 and 8 are the most famous ones,' she continued. 'Your grandfather worked in Hut 3. The work which happened there changed the course of the whole war.'

Brodie imagined her granddad, young and excited, working inside the hut. She wished she'd had longer to ask him what code-cracking was really like. She reached up to the locket that hung around her neck and cradled it in her hand.

'Beautiful necklace,' said Miss Tandari brightly.

As they walked, Miss Tandari pointed out the tennis court and the ornamental lake. In the centre a rather crooked fountain shot water in great jets up into the air. 'We haven't got the water pressure quite right yet,' she said apologetically over her shoulder as a cloud of droplets blew in their direction making Brodie's feet wet.

As they rounded the corner, Miss Tandari waved towards the Ice House. The building was shaped like a hexagon and Miss Tandari was keen to point out the pigeon loft built into the pointed roof. She explained the building had been used to store ice and keep food from going bad before fridges had been invented. Such a large place to keep ice in seemed a weird idea to Brodie. She stared hard and watched a group of white birds circle above them then land on the roof.

'So Hut 8 then?' Miss Tandari said marching on, looking away from the pigeons. 'You'll find everything you need inside,' she added, and Brodie was not entirely sure she didn't see Miss Tandari wink, although on reflection it may have been a trick of the light.

She opened the door to the hut and entered a narrow corridor. She followed it until she found the room number marked at the top of her map. Room seven. She paused for a moment, unsure whether she should knock, and then thinking better of it, she swung the door wide and stepped in.

In retrospect it may have been better to knock.

Seated on a rush mat spread on the floor in the centre of the room, her legs crossed and her hands stretched up towards the ceiling, was Tusia. Her eyes were firmly closed and she was humming. From a CD player, balanced precariously in the corner, came the sound of songbirds and ocean waves and on the window sill a candle smelling strongly of lavender was burning.

Brodie coughed gently to announce her arrival.

Tusia didn't move.

'Hello again,' Brodie whispered nervously.

Tusia opened one eye.

'Looks like I'm your new room-mate.'

Tusia kept one eye firmly closed. 'One moment,' she said.

Brodie moved awkwardly from foot to foot as the sounds on the CD reached a crescendo and then died away. Tusia sighed deeply, opened her eyes and jumped to her feet.

'Great we're together, don't you think? After all the fun we had earlier. Did you enjoy your tour? I'd memorised the location of the buildings already so mine didn't take long. I've rearranged things here a bit though. Pulled the beds out to balance the shui in the room. The way it was all set out, our luck would've left the room before nightfall.'

Brodie knew she looked confused again. 'Shui?'

'Positivity. My mother swears by feng shui. We had a specialist over and he reordered the whole house. Had to knock down a chimney in my brother's room and turn the staircase round but Mum said it's worth every penny.' She patted the end of the unit. 'Anyway, this way you get a good view of the lake, but if you'd prefer the other bed, then I really don't mind.'

Brodie sat down on the end of the duvet.

'Here,' Tusia said, turning to a chest of drawers beneath the window. 'Apple and mango juice with omega three. Very restoring.'

Brodie thanked Tusia enthusiastically, although as

she gulped the drink down she was sure there was the faintest taste of fish.

She put her half-full glass down on the bedside table. 'So, anyway. Great place, isn't it?'

'Less rugged than I'm used to,' Tusia said. 'I live in Cornwall. They offered to fly me in but my family are against any form of air travel unless it's absolutely necessary. Kills the environment.'

Brodie smiled weakly.

'My father's fitted a catalytic converter to our camper van that allows it to drive using vegetable oil. It means the van can't go above forty miles an hour, and it smells a bit like a chip shop, but it got us here eventually.'

'Right.' Brodie glanced out of the window and saw Hunter being led by Mr Ingham on a walk past the lake. She laughed as he attempted an unsuccessful sidestep to avoid the spluttering fountain. 'This is great,' she said.

'There's a wardrobe and chest of drawers for your things,' Tusia said, 'and they've left you a complete uniform . . . although I hope yours looks better on than mine. Blue's not really my colour. I'm more of a summer person. I prefer yellows and oranges.' Brodie glanced down at the long stripy socks Tusia was wearing which reinforced that fact.

'Uniform?'

'Yeah.' Tusia pointed to a light blue blazer draped across the chair. Next to it was a long black skirt, several shirts and a blue and black tie. The blazer had 'Pembroke' embroidered across the pocket.

'Pembroke?' Brodie said quizzically.

'Yep. In the war, workers at Bletchley wore uniforms for an invented ship called *HMS Pembroke*. They've taken on the same idea now. If we wander round the station with a uniform on then chances are any members of the public who spot us will just think we're on a school trip. It'll look like we're pupils at a private school called Pembroke College. What d'you reckon?'

Brodie slipped on the blazer. It was in fact a perfect fit. She twirled round and Tusia nodded mockingly. 'Very classy,' she said.

The candle on the windowsill guttered a little and Brodie put the clothes down again across the chair. 'Guess I should unpack.' She looked over to Tusia's side of the room where a sea of photograph frames were arranged in height order.

'Some of my pets,' Tusia explained, 'and of course Mikhail Botvinnik. A supergrandmaster of chess if ever there was one.' Brodie tried not to look too puzzled and turned instead to peer at the photograph Tusia'd lifted in the air. 'Here's my mum and dad and brothers.' Tusia handed over a frame. It showed an eager group sitting at the top of a very high mountain. 'Ben Nevis,' Tusia said. 'Last summer. Before my brothers flew to Fiji. They're doing vital research there,' she explained before Brodie could mention carbon footprints. 'My dad always says mountains are there to be climbed.'

'Looks like a challenge,' Brodie said encouragingly.

'My family are into challenges.' Brodie felt this sounded like a statement of the obvious coming from a girl who'd willingly climbed on the roof. 'My parents teach me at home as my dad doesn't really believe in schools. He says they're full of irritating people, like that boy Hunter. People like him who think they can change the world and boss everyone round while they do it.' She sniffed. 'Now sit down and tell me all about yourself and then in about half an hour we can pop over to Hut 12 and get something to eat.' She paused for a moment. 'Come on then, tell me what your parents are like and what they think about you joining the Black Chamber.'

Brodie swallowed hard. Here they were, a few moments since meeting, at that point of a conversation which always came. She toyed mentally with the idea of pretending. Of just saying they were fine about it, but the way Tusia was looking at her, leaning forward, her eyes narrowed slightly, made her certain this was someone it'd be little use pretending with. 'My granddad was fine about it,' she said at last. 'My parents aren't around any more.'

'Oh.' Tusia fiddled with the edge of the photo frame. 'Look, I don't want to be nosey, so if you want to tell me that's fine, but if not, then that's fine too.'

Brodie suddenly wished she'd some sort of story to offer that made sense. But she'd never understood it herself.

Tusia returned the smile and put the photograph back on the bedside locker.

Brodie said nothing. There was, after all, nothing to say.

Smithies bit into his apple puff and a shower of icing sugar cascaded on to the table. He wiped the whipped cream from his top lip.

On the other side of the table, Friedman sliced his flapjack into four equal sections.

The Bletchley railway station café really did serve wonderful home baking just as the sign on the door suggested. The staff were also discreet. Generations of the same family had worked in the café over the years and being so closely placed to the mansion, workers had got used to turning a blind eye to secret meetings.

Smithies would've trusted Gordon, the main waiter, with his life.

'So,' Friedman could obviously barely contain himself, 'what are the children like?'

'Interesting.'

'The ones you wanted came?'

A cloud of icing sugar lifted from Smithies' fingers. 'We could've done with a few more but it'll be OK. It's quality that counts after all. There'll be three, I think, who'll make it.' He decided to be as economical with the truth as he could for now.

'And, her? She came?' Friedman touched the necklace he wore and the tiny golden key which hung there sparkled in the light.

Smithies nodded.

'And does she remind you? You know. Is she like her mother?'

'She's a peacemaker. I can tell already. But we can't allow ourselves to be distracted. We have to focus on why we've got them together. What they're here to do.' Smithies thought back to the conversation at Russell Square and the excitement he'd seen burn in Friedman's eyes. It was important to hone in on that, he knew it. Friedman was a dangerous man when distracted.

'But she looks like her?'

'She has her smile.'

Friedman gulped down the rest of his tea and Gordon appeared from behind the counter, teapot in hand, to pour a refill.

'And the adult members of Veritas? The interviews went well?'

'Ah yes. There was a slight issue with that.'

'So, who is there?' Friedman spoke like a child longing to know what presents he was going to get for his birthday.

'Oscar Ingham.'

'Sicknote. That old warhorse. Thought he'd snuffed it years ago.' Friedman leant forward. 'You really think he's up to it?'

'Of course. Of course. Barely troubled by his health at all now.' He lowered his eyes so as not to catch Friedman's gaze.

'And?'

'Sorry?'

'Well, who else is there?' Friedman was impatient.

'My secretary. Tandi Tandari. Came on exchange from Jamaica. The one with loads of adopted brothers and sisters. Is great with kids, remember?' He hesitated for a moment. 'She's really keen.'

'And that's it. You, your secretary and Sicknote. You've got to be kidding me.'

'It's the best we can do for the moment. It's a start at least.'

Friedman ran his hand along his chin dejectedly.

'Look, if you came up to the mansion and joined us, then we'd make progress more quickly.'

'You know I can't. I have to lie low. You know that. I can't risk being found. We stick to the plan. You work with Veritas and I work alone till it's safe.'

Smithies lifted the apple puff from the plate and downed the last section with the slowness of a man who was either savouring every mouthful or determined not to talk for a while.

'So what about the tasks?' Friedman asked eventually as Smithies added more milk to his tea.

The older man leant back in his chair. 'You know, I don't think the kids could be doing better.' It wasn't altogether true but he'd seen enough to be encouraged. 'It feels great to be dealing with a challenge again. Feels almost like the old days.'

A flicker of sadness flashed across the younger man's face. He pushed the remains of his flapjack around the plate with the prongs of his fork. 'So, you've given them the facsimile of the manuscript already? The children have a copy each?'

Smithies winked and there was a twinkle in his eye. 'I've *sort of* given it to them.'

'What d'you mean?

'It's like this,' he began.

'So, did you bring the facsimile of this unreadable book?' Tusia asked. 'They didn't give one to me so I guessed we must be sharing and they'd given it to you.'

'No,' said Brodie. 'Miss Tandari said everything we needed was in the room.'

'Well, she's wrong. If it was here, I'd have found it. I've sorted through everything and the only thing they left us was the uniform.'

'Maybe we should go and ask someone.' Brodie lifted the pile of clothes and went to place it in the wardrobe. As she opened the door, the belt placed on the top of the pile fell, unrolling on the ground like a snake. Tusia got up and lifted the belt from the floor.

'My life,' she said, stretching the belt between her open arms, 'how long is this thing? How wide did they think your waist was?'

Brodie put down the pile of clothes and reached for the other end of the belt. 'Even my great-aunt Agnes would get this round her waist,' she laughed, 'and she's a woman who's not to be messed with. You wouldn't want to challenge her to an arm wrestle, I can tell you.'

She curled the belt back into a loop.

'Hold on. Wait a bit.' Tusia grabbed her hand.

'What's that? On the belt?'

Brodie recoiled. 'Is it a spider? Get it off if it's a spider, cos I'm not good with spiders!'

The belt was once again in a snaking line at her feet.

'It's not a spider,' Tusia reassured.

Brodie reopened her eyes.

'It's letters, look.'

Spread evenly across the leather surface, picked out in gold stamping, was a series of shapes.

'This can't be coincidence,' Brodie said, banishing the thought of creepy-crawlies from her mind. 'But they don't make sense. They don't *say* anything.'

'It's a test,' said Tusia. 'Must be.'

'Another one? So soon?' Brodie had hardly recovered from the race against the stopwatch.

'Let me see.' Tusia's face creased with concentration. Laying the belt across the floor it was possible to clearly see the letters *IEOSCHUE*. 'Another language, d'you think?'

'Perhaps. I only know a bit of French. Stuff like "where's the cake shop?" It doesn't say that. You?'

'Russian of course. But that's all. And it's not Russian.'

Brodie ran her hand across each letter in turn. 'And why on a belt of all things? A belt for an impossibly large woman who'd obviously asked quite

73

often where the cake shop was!'

'Or,' Tusia's face softened, 'a belt especially selected to fit you, like the uniform.' Brodie could see a slither of a thought was worming its way into her brain. Something which felt like excitement bloomed in her tummy.

'But we've already said it's far too big for me.'

'If,' said Tusia, rubbing her hands together, 'you just wear it once around your waist. But what if I wrap it around until it does fit? Then what?'

Brodie was having difficulty following the line of thought.

'Look. I don't think the length of this super-belt which would fit a ten-tonne woman is a mistake,' pressed Tusia. 'It must all be part of *the test*.'

Brodie wished she wouldn't keep using that phrase.

'Miss Tandari said we'd everything we needed in the room. We must *need* the belt.' She picked it up from the floor and began to twist it around Brodie's waist. 'Help me,' she said urgently. 'See what happens to the letters.'

At first absolutely nothing happened to them. Then Tusia decided she was holding the belt upside down. 'Now look,' she said, peering at Brodie's waist. 'They're lining up, aren't they?'

It was true that across the double loop of belt the

letters now formed two rows, the letters set on top of each other.

I EOS
CHUE

'I'm still not getting this,' moaned Brodie, who was peering down at the letters.

'Let me read each row,' Tusia said, pressing the belt tight to Brodie's waist so it didn't fall.

'Got it yet?'

Tusia rocked back.

'D'you think it's one word? More?' Brodie wrinkled her forehead. 'I Eos Chue?'

Tusia just laughed.

'Maybe we read the columns,' Brodie blurted.

It was Tusia's turn to wrinkle her face in concentration. 'I Ce Ho Use?'

Brodie imagined she could see the message unscrambling in Tusia's brain. 'Well?' she pleaded.

'ICE HOUSE!' yelled Tusia. 'We've got to go to the Ice House,' she exclaimed.

'*Finally*,' said Brodie, unwrapping herself from the confines of the giant belt and breathing out. 'So let's go.'

Just then, the door banged open wide. 'What the cod and chips is this all about?' said Hunter, trailing his own 'message belt'. 'Why do they think *I've* eaten all the pies?'

Brodie let Tusia explain.

The door to the small hexagonal building to the right of the mansion was already ajar and Tusia led the way inside. On the floor was a small wooden trunk. The top of the trunk was patterned. Leaves and flowers carved somehow across the domed lid. There was a small leather handle and straps that ran across the trunk and fastened it shut. And a lock.

'Shall we?' whispered Hunter.

They knelt down beside the trunk.

'You do it, BB. Go on.'

Brodie turned the catch on the lock. She unfastened the leather straps. Then, very carefully, she rocked back the lid.

For a moment it looked like the trunk was filled with shimmering gold. A shiny fabric wrapped around a bundle hidden inside.

Brodie's hands were shaking and her stomach seemed to be pressing against the bottom of her lungs making it difficult to breathe.

She reached into the trunk and lifted the bundle. The fabric fell away. Underneath was a thick bound book. The red leather cover was soft, worn in places, unmarked by any writing or title apart from a small label of unreadable text in the corner. The pages were bulging against a thin cord tied round the leather. She slipped her fingers underneath the loop and loosened the knot. Then she uncurled the cord.

She could feel her pulse throbbing in her neck. Her nostrils were filled with the smell of wood and parchment. With the cord untied, the cover of the unread book flapped open.

This, then, was what her mother had spent years trying to read. The unsolved code her mother wanted to crack. The cipher that had broken full-grown men.

And she was holding it now, in her hands.

Mr Bray leant heavily on his walking stick and surveyed the pile of scattered photograph wallets that remained on the floor in front of the dresser. He took in a deep breath and then very carefully lowered himself down to his knees. It was nearly dark but he didn't want to put on the light. Having the light on would make everything too real.

He took the first packet of photographs in his hand. He didn't have to open it to remember the images inside. The details were written in an untidy scrawl across the label and the scenes themselves burnt on his memory.

He swallowed hard and rested the packet for a moment against his chest. He'd known this day would come and in a way it was all he'd longed for. That his granddaughter could carry on with the task he'd begun and his daughter had continued. Mr Bray tried to reassure himself. He knew it needed to happen. But he, more than anyone, knew the danger of breaking the rules.

He couldn't help being scared.

'It's beautiful,' said Brodie. 'Scary and strange, but beautiful somehow.'

The letters used for the writing were not like any Brodie knew. Even the pictures of flowers and plants weren't like anything she'd ever seen growing on earth. There was one whole section with pictures of women swimming in tubs or baths. The bit Brodie liked best was a map that folded out of the book, showing nine islands connected by causeways. On one island she could clearly make out what looked like a volcano and also a castle like the one sketched in her locket.

Brodie held the book in her hand and for a moment time stood still. There was something unsettling about it and she was suddenly peculiarly afraid, as if she'd peeped through a keyhole of a tightly locked room and seen something she shouldn't.

Brodie looked up at the others. It was growing cold and the light of the single bulb above them was flickering. 'Do we know what we're getting into?' she said at last.

Hunter frowned. 'Well,' he said, drawing out the word as if in an attempt to delay saying anything else. 'I'm still not really sure why they think we'll be able to help them read something that's never been read by anyone before. But they've certainly gone to a lot of trouble to get us here.'

'And why d'you think it'll matter if we read this?' asked Tusia.

'Ahh, now *that* I can answer,' said Hunter.

Brodie shuffled closer and Tusia, despite herself, leant in a little nearer.

'My parents told me about it before I came. People have been trying to read this manuscript for centuries.'

'So what it says is secret then?' added Brodie.

'Yeah, so secret no one has a clue what it means. But if you look at the pictures then this thing's about some weird unknown place. And it's the thought of that place which intrigues people. Maybe it's somewhere undiscovered.'

'You mean another planet?' Tusia asked.

'Maybe.' He paused. 'I think it's something even

weirder than that. A world inside our world. A place that exists alongside ours. That it's possible to find.'

Brodie retied the cord around the leather cover. 'People really think this book could be about an undiscovered place on earth and that all those weird pictures of things could exist there?'

'Exactly.' Hunter sat up straight. 'And those who believed the book's about a hidden place on earth have had a really hard time convincing others they may be right.'

'What d'you mean?'

'Well, anyone who's come close to thinking they've understood MS 408 has been paraded as a madman.'

'Like who?' Brodie was growing more nervous by the minute.

'Oh. Loads. Newbold's one they told me about. He was sure he'd found a hidden language in the writing after spending most of the 1920s looking at it but after his findings were published people tore his theories apart. He went insane.'

'Well, it won't matter if you try and read it then,' mumbled Tusia, 'seeing as you're mad already.'

Hunter pretended not to hear, but the suggestion had unnerved Brodie. 'Are we safe, d'you think?' she said quietly.

Hunter's face looked like he was trying to work out

a difficult sum. 'What d'you mean?'

'Well, looking at this manuscript? If it's driven people mad and others have done such a good job of destroying the theories about it, then are we safe messing around with it?' She was uncertain about whether to go on. 'And I'm not really sure they told us everything. You know. In the papers they gave us or up in the ballroom.'

Hunter seemed to be considering the idea. 'You think they're keeping stuff from us?' he said.

'I don't know,' Brodie said. It sounded silly to say it aloud. How could her granddad allow her to be involved in something that wasn't safe? But she wasn't sure he'd told her everything either. He'd said she would need to be brave. And somehow she wasn't convinced the story really added up.

'We have to give it a go, don't you think?' said Hunter quietly.

'I intend to give it more than *a go*,' smirked Tusia.

Hunter rolled his eyes.

'My parents believe this challenge is totally in my grasp. And I intend to prove them right.'

Brodie reached up and held the locket tight in her hand. She wished she felt so confident.

'It's got to be about finding the truth,' said Tusia as if she were a judge passing sentence. 'The group's called

Veritas after all. There has to be a truth behind what this manuscript says, however weird it looks and however badly people've failed before.' She peered down at the battered red cover, almost as if by staring long enough the truth would drift out to her.

'Yes,' Brodie said at last. 'The truth's important.' Something about how the words sounded in her head seemed to encourage her. Perhaps her mother had been close to finding the truth. Perhaps seeking the truth herself would bring her closer to her mum. She hoped so. She really did. This manuscript had a history interwoven with hers. That was what her granddad had said, and however difficult the path they were about to walk, she was determined to try her best. To pass the test and be chosen for the team that tried to break the secret of the unread book.

Kerrith Vernan tapped her newly polished fingernails on the edge of the oak desk then flicked the pages of her desk calendar with the end of her fountain pen. She folded her arms.

She couldn't shake off the nagging feeling that something was wrong. Everything was far too quiet.

Smithies' life was all about breaking secrets. He lived for the code. However much she detested the man she had to acknowledge that. Yet the person who'd made her life so miserable, just by being in it, had slipped from the office without even a murmur. It just didn't add up.

How could someone so consumed with secrets and the desire to discover truths simply glide away and work happily in a museum? She twisted the new diamond ring she'd bought herself around her little finger. It was a beautiful ring. Truly expensive. The man in the shop seemed surprised she was buying it simply because she wanted it. He presumed there was a reason for the purchase. And it was this thought that was nagging away at the back of Kerrith's mind. There *was* a reason she'd bought the ring. With Smithies gone she was now the most senior code-cracker on her level. The final barrier to her ultimate promotion to Level 5 removed. Of course she hadn't shared this information with the man in the jeweller's. He was there to sell her the ring not question her motives. But he'd been right. There *was* a reason. And there had to be a reason for Smithies' silence over his redeployment to Bletchley.

And whatever it took she was going to find out what it was.

5

The Blooming of the Corpse Flower

Brodie didn't sleep well. Her mind was filled with dreams where she was on a tiny island in the middle of a huge ocean. She stood on the edge of a lagoon and she wanted more than anything to walk forward into the water. She was sure there were steps leading down out of sight and she could hear a voice calling her. The ripples made hot circles around her feet. But she was scared.

The dream disturbed her but the lack of sleep was mostly due to the fact she'd never shared a room before.

Tusia chatted long after Brodie's eyelids were heavy with exhaustion but there seemed no way to shut her up and Brodie felt it rude not to answer. Then it seemed that even when Tusia was asleep she didn't stop talking. The muttering was low and incomprehensible and Brodie was sure there were frequent references to chess pieces. When Tusia finally pulled herself up to sitting and stretched her arms in the air to welcome the morning, Brodie groaned and pulled the pillow over her head.

'You OK, roomie?' Tusia said in a singsongy voice that sounded full of energy. Brodie merely grunted. 'Today's the start of something new and wonderful. How about a little yoga to set us up for the day? Or if you'd prefer we could give tai chi a go. I've a caftan I could lend you.'

Brodie wriggled further down the bed. 'I'm fine really. I just need five minutes.'

'Ahh, the effects of the sugar in the hot chocolate you drank before bedtime. A sure side effect is "grumpy mornings". If you stick to fruit juice or herbal tea you'd wake up so much more refreshed.'

'I'm not grumpy,' Brodie snapped and then smiled meekly over the edge of her pillow. 'OK, maybe a little.'

'Well, grumpy or not, it's our first full day and you and I have an appointment in the library.' Tusia snapped open her welcome pack and ran her finger down the printed list inside. 'Maths lesson, followed by Geography.'

'Oh joy,' Brodie moaned and let the pillow fall flat on her face again.

It was a simple scheme. Smithies explained normal lessons would be taught in the morning, in order to cover the home-schooled requirement of the plan, and in the afternoon there'd be sessions on code-cracking. Most of the lessons would take place in the mansion. Some sessions would be held in the huts.

There was only one rule. Whatever happened, don't engage in conversation with the general public.

Most visitors to the museum would see only what they expected to see and as long as the children were in their Pembroke uniform, they'd pass for a group on a school trip. It was, Smithies explained, the very best form of secrecy. The right-under-their-nose sort, which was rarely questioned and it was, he added, what made the process so exciting.

Miss Tandari taught them ordinary subjects, and for the most part did a very good job of it. She tried desperately to make the necessary work on primary factors and function machines seem interesting, and every now and then, when she felt the group was flagging, she bought them mini chocolate bars to boost their sugar levels, something Hunter was particularly grateful for but which Tusia refused in favour of yogurt-covered raisins.

Smithies and Ingham split the sessions on code-cracking while doubling as curators at the museum. Brodie couldn't believe there was so much to learn. They covered hidden messages written in lemon juice and revealed by heat; substitution ciphers and some crazy thing called the pigpen cipher. They even talked about 'disinformation' which could be added to codes to confuse those trying to crack them. *Everything* confused Brodie to begin with. And everything, it seemed, could be used to hide a secret message just as long as you knew where to look.

'But why d'you need code at all?' moaned Hunter after a particularly frustrating session on the Caesar Cipher.

Brodie saw a spark behind Ingham's eye. A fire growing. 'Power,' he said.

'You what?'

'Codes give power. They let me tell other people things I can keep secret from you. That gives me power over you.' He lifted his coffee mug to his lips and the chain attaching it to the radiator rattled. The children hadn't asked about the chain. It seemed rude.

'So if I use a code, that controls who knows what?' pressed Hunter.

Ingham put the mug down. He widened his

Invisible Ink...

- You write your message with lemon juice + vinegar

-Heat brings the invisible ink to life!

Wonder what ink was used on my socks?!!

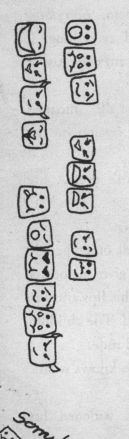

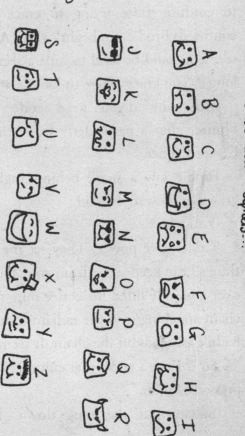

Substitution Ciphers...

Sorry!

hands in agreement. 'At this very place during World War Two, code-crackers, chosen just like you, intercepted codes sent by the enemy. Messages sent from generals to submarines or soldiers on the front line. The messages were sent over the radios and people here heard those messages. And they broke the codes they were written in.' He pulled himself up tall. 'People here at Station X knew what the enemy were saying to each other. They knew their secrets and because of that, they took their power. Churchill reckoned the Black Chamber here shortened the war by at least two years.' Ingham seemed to glow. Excitement blazed behind his eyes. 'Breaking codes is all about looking beyond what's written. The surface stuff isn't important. It's what's *under* the surface.

Brodie was going along with what he said but there were so many codes to learn about. So many ways to hide a secret. 'How do we know, though, what code something's written in? How d'you do that "breaking" thing in the first place?'

Ingham searched for the best ways to explain. 'Codes are like people,' he said. 'There's different types and different kinds. We see the outside of the person and we may think we know them. But it's looking from another angle, seeing things differently, that helps us really understand. What we see on the surface isn't what's inside.' He hesitated. 'Reading codes is like reading people. First impressions aren't important. They're just for fools.' His voice cracked a little. 'If you want to read codes you just have to learn to look carefully.'

His eyes sparkled even more brightly. Brodie no longer saw a man in pyjamas, irritated by having to work with children. She saw a man in love with the code. It was contagious.

Smithies kept up with how the group were doing via the internal mail system which had been used when Bletchley Park was a Black Chamber in the war. A series of overhead vacuum pipes carried messages contained in plastic screwtop containers that were passed into the pipe system at conveniently placed holes around the buildings. The noise of a container's arrival sounded very much like a sock being pulled down a plug hole, and it was this noise and the subsequent arrival of a message that announced the prospect of a test.

'Smithies says the time has come,' sniffed Ingham, rubbing his left knee which he'd earlier told them was causing him a fair degree of tendon pain. 'Personally I'm not sure you're up to testing yet.' He cast a glance in Hunter's direction. 'But if it means we get to move on to looking at MS 408 more quickly, then Smithies has my support.' Brodie saw that glimmer in his eyes again as if he were talking about the return of a long-lost friend. 'This message says you should be ready for the test the day after tomorrow.'

The morning of the test didn't begin well. By the time Brodie reached the breakfast table, Tusia and Hunter were in the middle of a full-blown row about earmuffs.

'I'm telling you they look ridiculous,' Tusia hissed across the table as Hunter smiled broadly at her from beneath a pair of red fluffy ear defenders.

'And I'm telling you I'm simply wearing them to drown you out. I've had enough of your moaning and whingeing.'

Brodie took a sharp intake of breath. If today was the day of the test and they were supposed to be working together then their chances of success were pretty close to zero.

'Please give it a break!' she pleaded, pouring herself a rather meagre bowlful of Sugar Puffs. 'Today's an important day.'

'Yeah, well, tell him that, if he can hear you behind all that fluff.'

'At least it's obvious why I can't hear you,' snapped

back Hunter. 'What's your excuse for mishearing everything that's ever said to you?'

Brodie slopped milk on her cereal. 'Can we *please* just try to get along?' she begged.

'Look, we're here to work miracles with the greatest unread code in the world,' Hunter continued in a voice that was far too loud. 'There's only so much miracle you can hope for.' He took a section of rather overdone toast, which was dripping with peanut butter, and pushed it eagerly into his mouth.

The rest of the meal passed in silence, apart from Hunter's chewing, and no one spoke either when they made their way over to the music room where the challenge was supposed to begin.

Tusia sat scowling on the floor, tracing patterns in the light cast by the beautiful glass ceiling above them. Hunter only removed his earmuffs when Smithies led Ingham and Miss Tandari into the room.

Smithies had obviously chosen a new tie for the occasion. He patted the mustard yellow fabric flat against his stomach before beginning to speak. 'So, this is it then. The moment of truth or, we hope, one of many such moments.' He laughed a little but there was an edge of nerves to his voice. 'You've worked hard on your training. The tutors have made pleasing reports about your progress.' Brodie looked along the line at Ingham whose face was flushing a little as if in an attempt to reject any association with notes of praise. 'Perhaps, and it's a big perhaps, we've begun to make code-crackers out of you.'

'Some of us were crackers to start with,' Hunter whispered behind the back of his hand to Tusia.

'Speak for yourself.'

Smithies coughed a little and then continued. 'But our purpose in bringing you here wasn't simply to train you, but to use you. Our Study Group lacks recruits and our task today is to choose those who'll swell our numbers and complete our team. We've set you a simple task. You'll be given no help from the adults here. But if you complete the task successfully, then you'll be part of Veritas.'

He reached then into his pocket and pulled out a long thin cord. Hanging from it were several tiny red ribbons. 'Your lifeline.' He smiled. 'A coded lifeline, in fact. Let me explain.'

Stuck to the wall was a long strip of paper with the letters of the alphabet printed on it. Smithies held the end of the cord at the start of the row of letters. Miss Tandari took the other end and pulled it straight. The first red ribbon fluttered under the letter 'I'.

'What the hot relish sauce is he doing?' whispered Hunter.

'Spelling,' Smithies laughed. 'Spelling out your chances.' He relaxed the cord and then held the first red-ribbon marker at the start of the alphabet line and stretched the cord again. The second ribbon fluttered beneath the letter 'N'. 'It's a rope code,' Smithies explained. 'Each ribbon marks a letter and the letters together spell out "*IN VERITAS*".'

'Nice,' said Tusia.

'It will be,' said Miss Tandari. 'And you will be,' she laughed. 'In Veritas, I mean. If you pass the test. And if you don't lose all the letters.'

Brodie felt a little sick.

'As you work on the test,' Ingham continued, 'you'll be asked to place the lifeline in the vacuum message system every time you hear a bell ring. The rope will travel down the system and to us.' He was enjoying this, Brodie could tell. 'We'll return the rope to you perhaps unchanged. Or perhaps with ribbons missing.'

Brodie didn't like the sound of this.

'We'll remove ribbons,' said Miss Tandari, 'if we feel you're making errors in the test. You have nine lives. Like a cat. If you complete the test but all the ribbons are removed – you fail. Keep the lives and you will really be "in Veritas".'

Smithies clapped his hands together purposefully as Brodie tried to process all she'd heard. 'Now before we begin, let me make two tiny reminders. Firstly, we will be watching you, so don't be put off.'

Brodie wasn't reassured by this comment.

'Secondly, remember nothing you've learnt before is without use.'

Brodie didn't find this last comment encouraging either. There was a lot they'd learnt before and retaining all of it in her head turned out to be a bit of a problem.

As she was contemplating this fact, Smithies put a small piece of paper on the table in front of them. He coiled the coded lifeline on top. 'Here it is, my eager ones. The final challenge. Pass this and you're part of the team.'

Then without even a backwards glance he led the way out of the music room with Miss Tandari and Ingham following behind him.

Tusia darted forward and grabbed the piece of paper. 'Shall I?' she said.

'Looks to me as if you already have,' Hunter murmured.

Brodie lifted the coded lifeline. Nine lives. Surely they'd be OK? She could not begin to explain how much she wanted this. How much she *needed* this.

Tusia began to read. '*To take a place amongst us, line*

95

the lower stitches straight with the fire then prepare for feasting in the place where the corpse awakes at two.

'Oh, that's gross,' snapped Tusia, recoiling and holding her hand across her mouth. 'What do they mean? Corpses awaking. That's just weird.'

'No more than anything else we've done here,' said Hunter, 'and before you panic it's not going to mean what we think it means, is it? That'd be too obvious. It might be disinformation. Or mean something else. Like not really dead people.'

'Good, because if it did then I wouldn't want anything to do with it,' said Tusia.

'Shame it doesn't then really,' Hunter said loftily.

Tusia didn't humour him with a reply.

'So, if not dead people, then what?' asked Brodie.

'I vote for getting a dictionary,' said Tusia. 'If we look the word up then there'll be alternative suggestions.'

'Do you think if she goes to get a dictionary we can have an alternative team-mate?' Hunter whispered.

This time Brodie didn't offer an answer.

It didn't take long for Tusia to nip across the hall to the library and retrieve two huge reference books. She left the door open as it was hot and the stained-glass window above them, covered with pictures of flowers, was making the room feel like a greenhouse. In the corridor, Brodie could see Smithies. He had a clipboard. Tusia seemed undeterred and raced back in, flicking through the pages of the dictionary, stopping at the Cs.

'OK, we've got the obvious one. Dead bodies. But apparently we're ignoring that, like I'm trying to ignore you.' She smiled smugly at Hunter before looking back again at the open page. 'Then there's "to corpse", which is to do with forgetting your lines if you're in a show. But I can't see how that one makes sense of the clue.'

Brodie frowned. 'Any more?' The rope of ribbons was heavy in her hand.

Tusia looked up. 'One,' she said. 'A corpse flower.' She ran her fingers across the page, skim-reading the information. Then she began to flick through the second book she'd brought, a heavy encyclopaedia, until she found the entry on corpse flowers. 'Says it's one of the ugliest flowers in the world. And worse than that, it's got a really disgusting smell.'

'Must remember to get you a bunch,' sniffed Hunter.

Tusia carried on reading. 'Apparently the flower only blooms when the plant's mature. And then not every year.' She snapped the encyclopaedia shut. 'And apparently, even when it does flower it's only for a few days. Five at most. It's pretty rare.'

'Bet I could track some down,' said Hunter, 'for the right person of course.'

Suddenly a bell rang.

Brodie's hand tightened on the coded lifeline. 'Already? We have to hand this thing in already?'

Two pink circles appeared on Tusia's cheeks. 'But we haven't done anything yet!'

'Except row,' muttered Brodie a little too quietly to be heard.

Brodie carried the lifeline as they hurried to the nearest hut. She opened the door to the vacuum tubing, coiled the cord inside a message container and shut the door. There was a familiar whirring noise and the container sped out of sight.

Brodie waited. The vacuum system thrummed above their heads. There was a popping noise. And then the sound of falling. The container dropped back down the tube.

'Well?' urged Hunter, as Brodie unscrewed the lid.

She held the cord outstretched.

Tusia gasped. 'Seven! Only seven ribbons. We've lost two lives already. Why?'

Brodie thought she knew but was too scared to say. 'What matters is we don't lose more.' She tried to sound calm but she wasn't sure she managed it. 'We need to focus on the problem and not stress about the "lives".' She was sure she failed to deliver that sentence as if she meant it.

Tusia looked back at the clue. 'OK. So we keep going. Do you think we're looking for a place somewhere at Station X where there's corpse flowers? The encyclopaedia says the smell's so gross we wouldn't be able to miss it. I reckon if there's a corpse flower around then finding where it blooms or *awakes* will be no problem.'

'OK.' Brodie twisted the lifeline round her wrist but with fewer ribbons it felt less comforting.

'Should be a piece of cake,' said Hunter. 'Come on.'

It seemed, however, he was wrong. A thorough search of the gardens left them despondent.

Eventually Hunter led the way back past Miss Tandari and towards the mansion. His stomach grumbled from hunger. He wasn't happy and his mood didn't improve when the bell rang again.

'Oh no. This can't be good,' said Brodie.

They hardly spoke as she pressed the lifeline into the vacuum system. They said nothing as the rope whirred through the air to return to them. Brodie couldn't speak at all when they saw the ribbons.

'Five,' groaned Hunter. 'Only five. This can't be happening.'

But it was.

'We've searched everywhere,' Hunter moaned, glancing up at the tapestry hanging in the passageway when they finally got back to the mansion. 'Look.'

Brodie stared up at the hand-stitched map of the Bletchley Park estate and agreed they'd searched every outside location shown on the needlework picture. She jabbed her finger at the various huts depicted on the scene. 'Do we try the inside places now?' she said. 'And look for an outside flower, inside?'

Tusia ran her fingers across the stitching. 'But the place's huge. And if we really have to search inside then what's the point of the clue about the flower?'

'What's the point of any of it?' moaned Hunter, scrabbling in his pocket for a rather crushed packet of Polos. 'I'm starving. We should stop to eat.'

'What and lose more lives?' blurted Tusia. 'I don't think so.'

Brodie was beginning to panic. 'The clue said we should prepare to feast,' she said, trying to cling on to any hope she could find. 'Maybe it's that simple. We go back to Hut 12. That's where there'd be a feast.'

'Hut 12's too obvious. And why the flower?' Tusia said, leaning her head against the tapestry.

'Look,' Brodie said at last. 'We're tired and hungry. Let's take the tapestry into the other room and lay it down on the floor so we can read it like a map.'

'OK. Maybe there's something we're missing,' added Tusia as she helped Brodie lower the hand-sewn map and carry it through to the music room.

'I tell you what I'm missing,' huffed Hunter. 'My lunch.'

'We don't have time for this!' shouted Tusia, waving the lifeline in his face. 'Five lives left, Hunter. That's all. And then it's over.'

The girls put the fabric map down on the music-room floor and weighted down the corners with their shoes and the huge reference books.

'OK, Station X,' said Brodie, lifting her head in exasperation to allow the sun from the window above to warm her face. 'Tell us where you want us to go before it's too late.'

Brodie closed her eyes and thought for a while. The light from the window danced on her face. Flashes of colour streamed through the stained glass. Brodie could still see the flowers with her eyes shut.

She opened her eyes.

'The glass.' She blinked to see more clearly. 'It's patterned, right?'

'Well done, Miss Observant. The glass skylight does have pattern on it. And the relevance of that is?' asked Hunter.

'And we're supposed to remember all we've learnt?'

'Yes.'

'And the thing we forgot when we were coming into the mansion for the very first time was about . . .'

'Light being knowledge,' Tusia interrupted, scrambling to her feet.

'Still not with you,' Hunter said, peering to see whatever Tusia was staring at in the skylight above them.

Tusia was now reaching for the encyclopaedia. 'Corpse flowers,' she said. 'Look. That stained glass in the skylight. It's of flowers. All sorts. But look. In the corner, there's a corpse flower.'

She thrust the book into Brodie's hand so she could see and true enough, the ugly flower depicted on the glass looked remarkably like the one sketched beside the definition.

'OK,' said Hunter, dragging out the word as if not entirely convinced. 'I can see the flower and that's all great. But how's that tell us where to meet?'

Brodie read the clue again. '*To take a place amongst us, line the lower stitches straight with the fire then prepare for feasting in the place where the corpse awakes at two.* So, if light is knowledge then maybe our answer is when the light shines through the corpse flower in the skylight at two.'

'OK,' Hunter said again, looking at the patterns

made on the floor through the glass. 'But how will light through the window give us a location? You want us to dig up the floor looking for corpse-flower bulbs? Cos the light's going to fall on the floor, right?'

Brodie rubbed her eyes to concentrate. 'We could hold a map,' she said. 'Under the light.'

Hunter seemed impressed but Tusia was shaking her head. 'But where would we hold it? Would you just wander around under the light? That way you could make the light fall anywhere you want to. That can't be what the clue means.'

Hunter looked down at his shoes. 'So maybe there's a fixed map. On the floor.'

'Well, there is now. I mean, not a fixed one. But this tapestry. There's your map.'

'So, where on the floor should it be?' yelped Tusia. 'Where do we put it?'

Hunter's face looked as if the suggestion he was saying in his head was not really very polite.

'Let's just see where the light falls at two o'clock if we line the map up with its edge against the wall,' offered Brodie, pushing up her sleeves to reveal both her watches. 'At least with this clue we aren't late.'

The hands on her Greenwich Mean Time watch revealed they had five minutes.

That was when the bell began to sound.

'You've got to be kidding me!' spluttered Hunter.

'We can't go now!' said Tusia. 'It's nearly two.'

Brodie was frantic. 'But we have to.'

Hunter grabbed the rope. 'I'll do it. You two sort the map!' He raced from the mansion.

Tusia and Brodie struggled with the tapestry. Brodie could feel her heart beating in her throat.

Minutes later Hunter threw the door back open.

'Well?' the girls yelled at him.

'Down to three,' he panted. 'Look.' The lifeline rope looked forlorn and nearly empty, three red ribbons flapping near the end.

'But why?' squealed Tusia. 'This must be right. The map and the light. I don't understand.'

Brodie stared down at the map while Hunter doubled over and tried to catch his breath. It was two o'clock. What had they done wrong?

When Hunter spoke his words came in gasps. 'The pattern from that corpse flower. It's settled. It doesn't look good.'

The three of them looked down. The pattern cast by the flower was right in the middle of the lake.

'That's why we lost the lives,' snapped back Tusia. 'I told you it was important where we put the map. You can't just put it anywhere.'

Hunter's face suggested he'd thought of another

unshared and impolite location.

'It's the wrong way round,' yelled Tusia, scanning through the clue again. She kicked her shoes from the corner of the tapestry and dragged the edges as if she were trying to train a badly behaved puppy on the end of a very short lead. 'Help me move it, then. Before it's too late. The clue says "*line the lower stitches straight with the fire*". It must mean we've got to get the bottom edge lined up with the grate, not the wall. The clue says so.'

Brodie and Hunter grabbed a corner each and pulled the tapestry round into position. Then they stood again. And the pattern stilled.

And the light from the coloured glass of the corpse flower settled now on the hand-sewn location of Hut 11.

Hunter straightened up. The coded rope hung down from his hand. They had three lives left.

'We can't do this,' mumbled Tandi, a pile of six red ribbons on the table in front of her. 'They're doing their best.'

'But they have to be better,' said Smithies. 'It's what we agreed.' His words were catching in his throat.

'But we'll lose them all,' moaned Tandi. 'It'll all have been for nothing.'

Smithies had been pacing by the window. He stopped. 'We agreed we'd find the best. The very best. Only those who are up to the task can stay. Working together, Tandi. That's always been the key.'

'Three of them. Three lives left. It could all be over,' she mumbled.

'I know.'

'And that's what you want?'

Something like anger flashed in his face. 'I want those who can cope with all there is to know,' Smithies said quietly. 'I want those who won't be scared when they know what we're really up against. And I want a team.'

'And if we lose all three?'

Smithies rested his hand on the pile of ribbons. He didn't say any more.

Hut 11 was small and dark. Brodie was sure she could see Ingham looking in at the window. She felt a prickle of fear.

There was a table in the centre but it was hardly fit for a banquet. Brodie looked closely. She saw graffiti had been etched into the soft wood with blades of some sort. The three of them circled the table slowly. Brodie let her fingers trace along the carved initials. 'Who do you think they were?' she said at last, letting her fingers slow across each shape and groove.

'Black Chamber members from the past. Real ones,' said Tusia. 'People who worked together on MS 408.'

'Well, maybe it was easy for them,' hissed Hunter.

Brodie let her hand rest. She pressed the nail of her finger into two pronounced carvings of the letters AB. Alex Bray. Could they be her mother's initials? Could she have carved them long ago as a child sitting with code-crackers at this table?

'Because they didn't have to work with you, Toots.'

Tusia scowled and then opened her mouth to answer.

Her words were drowned out by a bell.

'You do it, B,' said Hunter.

Brodie coiled the rope in her hand. It was lighter than before. She glanced at the window, then opened the hatch in the vacuum system, slipped the rope inside the container and closed the door. The container thumped in the tubing like an erratic heartbeat. No one spoke.

When Brodie opened the returned container her fingers were moist with sweat.

There was no need to say anything.

One solitary red ribbon fluttered on the end of the rope.

'I know why we're losing lives,' she said. 'And we

have to stop!' Her eyes stung with tears.

Hunter and Tusia said nothing.

'You just never let up. On and on, trying to prove which of you's the most clever, and the point is you both are, that's why you're both here.'

'Now hold on a minute,' interrupted Hunter. 'I'm always fair to you, BB. It's just her I can't stand.'

'Well "her" has a name. And it's not T or Toots. It's Tusia.'

Hunter flushed red but Tusia began to grin from ear to ear.

'And you're just as bad,' Brodie continued, causing the smile to evaporate quickly from Tusia's face. 'Hunter's OK and if you stopped for one moment trying to score points off him because he's a boy then you'd realise that. Don't you see?' she said, holding the rope as the single ribbon lifted and fell in the air. 'This must be where they worked! The code-crackers of the past. The Veritas team looking at MS 408. Working together, maybe all through the night, trying to make sense of a mystery. These are their names, look, carved here. If we join the Study Group we sort of take over from them. We sit where they sat. But it's not going to happen, is it? With the rowing and the moaning. That's why we're losing lives.' She lowered her hand once more to feel the shape of the initials on the table. She laid the rope beside it.

There was a long silence. The initials of Study Group members of the past stared up at them. The red ribbon fluttered.

Eventually Hunter drew a breath. 'Sorry, Tusia,' he said deliberately. 'I guess laughing at you was just too much fun. We should start again.'

'Yeah, well,' Tusia said slowly. 'We *should* be working together.' She tapped the initials on the table. 'Guess they were quite a team.'

In places the initials linked and looped together.

'Shape and space,' Tusia said. 'It's my thing. And I suppose being part of a team isn't. Or working with boys as a general rule.'

Hunter began to raise his hands as if to argue.

'But OK. I've got to try and see things differently. I'll give it a go.'

'Good,' said Brodie. 'We're a team. In this together. And we have one life left. So let's solve this puzzle.'

Hunter pulled the crumpled clue out of his pocket.

Tusia took the paper from him. She read the clue aloud for the third time.

'*To take a place amongst us, line the lower stitches straight with the fire then prepare for feasting in the place where the corpse awakes at two.*'

'We've covered everything except the feasting,' said Brodie.

'Yeah and that's the part I'm most looking forward to,' added Hunter, although there was really no need for him to confirm this.

'It says we have to prepare. Do you think we have to do some cooking?'

'I seriously hope not,' laughed Hunter. 'My rock cakes at school were so realistic they tasted like real rocks.'

'No. I'm sure we just have to get things ready for a feast. But in here? How can we do that?'

'We could lay the table,' suggested Tusia, peering round the room for anything that may do as a cover.

'Here,' said Hunter, scurrying to the corner of the room and returning with a large folded square of fabric. 'A tablecloth, do you think?'

'Maybe,' said Brodie, smoothing the fabric across the table as Tusia hurried over to help. 'It's a bit tatty. Hardly great for a feast.'

'It's all there is,' said Tusia.

'And it's full of holes,' added Hunter, slowing his hand over small circular tears in the fabric. 'But that's not a criticism,' he said quickly. 'Just an observation.'

Tusia stood up straight. 'Hold on. Look at the holes and the carving on the table. Can we let some of the initials show through the holes and spell out a message?'

Tusia dragged the tablecloth to the left a little and a new series of shapes peeped through the holes made.

'You write down letters we can see at any one time, B, and we'll try and make some words with them.'

Brodie grabbed her notebook and peered at the tablecloth and the initials that showed through the holes.

'Anything?'

After about twenty minutes of rejected combinations, Brodie was ready to give up.

'You can't give up now, BB,' Hunter pleaded. 'Not when it was all your idea about trying to get along. We've got to think around this. See it another way.'

Brodie wasn't so sure. She couldn't make any words at all from the showing letters.

Tusia suddenly stood bolt upright from the table. 'That's it.'

'Pardon?'

'The other way!' repeated Tusia. 'Hunter's right.'

'Look we don't have to go over the top with this friendship thing,' Hunter mumbled. 'B only wanted us to be polite to each other.'

Tusia waved her hand to stop him talking. 'I mean the cloth needs to go round the other way. Like the

111

tapestry. It's the wrong way round. Or in this case, *upside down*.' She pulled the cloth from the table like a magician performing a trick and then respread it across the wooden surface, teasing it straight so it hung with uniformity across the wood. 'Didn't Ingham bang on about seeing stuff beneath the surface. Didn't he go on and on about looking at things from different angles?'

Brodie nodded in agreement. 'It's what we've been taught. To see things differently!'

Tusia resmoothed the cloth flat against the wood. 'So now. This way round. What initials show through this time?'

Brodie called out the letters that appeared through the holes in the cloth. Two Es, two Ts, an S, O, V and R. She scribbled them down on her notes.

'Well?' said Hunter, peering over her shoulder. 'Can you read it? Can you make a word?

Brodie began to group the letters.

'What does it say?'

'Shh. I'm doing my best.' Brodie scribbled letters as she spoke.

TOE
ROT
STORE

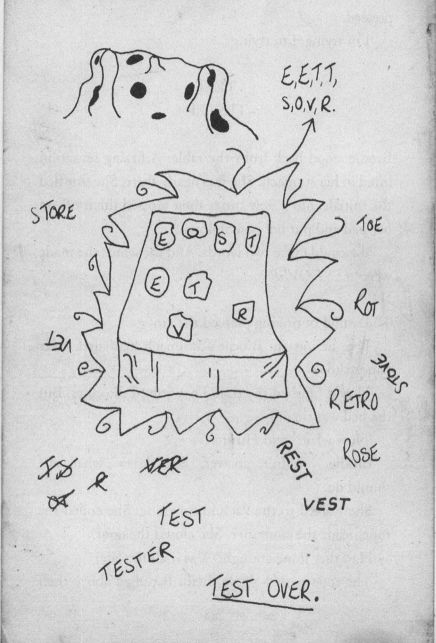

'We need to use all of the letters, surely,' Hunter pressed.

'I'm trying. I'm trying.'

TEST
TESTER

Brodie stood back from the table. A fizzing sensation lifted in her stomach. She was nearly there. She shuffled the initials into a new order then crossed them off on her pad and put her pencil down.

She could make two words. And the words she made were '*TEST OVER*'.

The sound of ringing pierced the air.

The fizzing in Brodie's stomach flattened. Her hands shook.

They'd finished the test. They solved the clues. But the bell was ringing.

'Now what?' said Hunter.

Brodie couldn't answer. She knew what she should do.

She walked to the vacuum opening. She coiled the rope inside the container. She closed the door.

Had they done enough? Was it all too late?

The rope rattled above them. It pulsed above their

114

heads. There was silence. Then the sound of falling.

Brodie looked at the others before she opened the door.

She took the rope.

Had they failed? She could barely look.

Slowly she uncoiled the loop. She held it high.

Nine red ribbons fluttered there. The coded message made it clear. They were 'in Veritas' at last. They were part of the team.

It took about ten minutes for the others to join them. Smithies led the way and Miss Tandari followed pushing a trolley laden with cakes and pastries, chocolates and pies. Ingham entered last, beaming despite himself, mug and chain firmly in his grasp.

'It was teamwork that did it,' said Smithies when everyone had quietened down enough to listen. Brodie thought for a moment he winked at her but she couldn't be entirely sure. 'And this hut's where the most special of teams met. The Second Study Group worked long and hard on the puzzle of MS 408. Many team members gave up their reputations trying to solve the code.'

Hunter munched noisily on a chocolate Danish before a glare from Miss Tandari made him rest it on his plate.

'You join us now as legitimate code-crackers, solvers of puzzles and enigmas, and we're honoured to have you as part of the team.' He raised a glass of lemonade into the air. 'We've no idea how this will all work out. But that's the exciting bit. We'll need our wits about us. And as Mr Jenkins has so aptly pointed out to us, an army marches on its stomach, so I suggest we all tuck in.'

Kerrith took her pair of designer glasses from the end of her nose and rested them on the pile of documents in front of her. It hadn't been easy to get hold of all the paperwork Smithies had spent his last few weeks in the Chamber looking at, but then she'd been very persuasive with the clerk in the records office.

She leant back on her chair. Shame then, that all her persistence had led her absolutely nowhere. Everything in front of her suggested Smithies had been researching home education laws and this made no sense whatsoever. Unless the man intended to set up a school inside Bletchley Park Museum the things he'd been reading were totally useless.

She rubbed her eyes with the heels of her hand, looking up only when her secretary knocked nervously on the door.

'I've traced them,' she said softly.

Kerrith pursed her lips.

The secretary held a small container of tablets in her hand. 'They were issued to a certain Oscar Ingham just over a month ago. Of course there's no records of his meeting with Smithies but finding them in Smithies' office a few days before he left would suggest this Oscar Ingham, whoever he is, paid Smithies a visit before he moved on to the museum.' She paused. 'Any help?'

Kerrith furrowed her brow. Oscar Ingham. The name seemed to enter her brain like a butterfly, flitting for a sensible place to settle. Somewhere, deep inside her memory, there was a feeling she should recognise the name. Oscar Ingham. No. She shook her head.

And then, just as the secretary was turning for the door, her head lowered, her shoulders hunched, Kerrith remembered.

She jumped up from her desk, knocking the stack of documents to the floor, and seizing her glasses, she scanned the spines of the books that lined the shelves on the wall.

'Miss Vernan? Are you OK?' The secretary's voice was pinched, her alarm obvious.

Kerrith didn't answer. She didn't speak until the book was open in her hands. Oscar Ingham. A classic code-breaker in his youth. The history books were glowing about his successes. Until. Kerrith could hardly focus on the words.

'Miss Vernan?'

But they were there. Clear and bold. *Oscar Ingham had been held in high esteem by all those in the Black Chamber until his growing obsession with the banned and highly controversial document MS 408.*

'Impossible,' hissed Kerrith, and she snapped the book closed. 'Impossible. But I've got to give it to Smithies. Totally inspired.'

'Miss Vernan?'

Kerrith placed the book back on the shelf and resettled her glasses on her nose. 'I know what Smithies is up to at Bletchley,' she said and her imperfect smile was broad and wide.

6

Elfin Urim

Brodie woke early, as the sun made rainbow patterns on the ceiling through the crystals Tusia had hung in front of the window. She resisted the temptation to roll over and snuggle down further beneath the covers and instead pulled herself up against the pillow and rubbed her eyes. The rainbows shattered into a thousand pieces in her head.

Tusia was exercising.

'You know if you stay in that position and the wind changes you'll get stuck,' Brodie laughed, imagining how her granddad would react if she began the morning with her head between her ankles.

'I'll have you know this is an excellent way of getting blood to flow to the brain, and we'll need as much brainpower as possible today. Normal lessons, cipher sessions and work with Veritas.'

Brodie nodded, a response she later realised Tusia probably couldn't see clearly from her position.

'You nervous?' came Tusia's voice from somewhere very close to the floor.

Brodie drew her knees up against her chest. 'Very,' she said deliberately. She guessed that's what it must feel like. Being part of a team.

Breakfast passed quickly, with Brodie managing to eat little more than a quarter of a Weetabix. She slopped milk down the front of her jumper and developed a fit of the hiccups while sipping her orange juice. None of this did much to calm her nerves.

Hut 11 seemed warmer than a few nights before. Some new smaller desks had been brought in and arranged like a giant horseshoe, with a seat and the long table in the middle and chairs arranged around the edge facing inwards. Brodie moved forward and sat down quickly between Tusia and Hunter, put her notebooks and bags down on the desk and her pen on top of them. In the centre of the horseshoe sat Smithies. On the table in front of him were various piles of books and folders. On top of these was a small wooden statue of an elephant. It reminded Brodie of the elephant from the front of the Veritas document she'd taken from the lamppost. Behind Smithies was a long blackboard resting on an easel. A haphazard selection of notes and photographs was tacked to it. Beside the easel was a huge candle like the sort Brodie had seen before inside a church.

Miss Tandari was seated beside Smithies and to her right sat Ingham. Today he was wearing a thick woollen scarf wrapped tightly around his throat and every now and then he sniffed loudly as if to remind everyone he was there.

Smithies glanced at Ingham disapprovingly before standing and beginning to speak. 'Well, well, well,' he said, wrinkling his nose, 'this is really it. Our inaugural meeting of the Third Study Group. Veritas reformed.' He laughed, unfolded his arms and rubbed his hands together. 'I'm sure, like me, you feel the hand of history upon your shoulders.'

Brodie tried to swallow but a rather large lump appeared to be blocking her throat. She wasn't sure about the hand of history but she could definitely feel her nerves jangling.

'It's taken a while, and an immense degree of selection and rejection, to narrow down the candidates to this and I have to say I'm excited. Extremely excited.'

Brodie wasn't sure that 'excited' was the word she'd use. 'Terrified' maybe.

Smithies hesitated. 'We'll know soon if we've

chosen well.'

He rubbed his hands together again and began to stride backwards and forwards in front of the blackboard, his tie, which Brodie noted was knotted a little too short, bouncing against his belly as he walked. Then he stopped and took a matchbox from his pocket. With a single strike he lit the candle. The flame swelled, flickering purple for a moment then settling into a blaze of gold. 'Everything I'm going to tell you today is important,' he began. 'But maybe most important is this light.' He pointed to where lines had been evenly spaced, stretched horizontally down the side of the candle. 'This light marks our progress. Twenty-five days to work on the task. Twenty-five days to find an answer.'

'Why the limit?' asked Hunter.

Smithies cast a look in Miss Tandari's direction. 'There's a season for everything,' said Smithies. 'And this will be our way of checking we're on task.'

'And when the candle burns down, sir. After twenty-five days. What then?'

Smithies' face showed he was thinking. 'We'll decide when that happens. Until then we work in secret as the candle burns.'

'About that, sir,' said Brodie. 'Why is it so important no one knows what we're doing?'

'Bletchley has a history of secrecy. Workers in the war went to their graves never telling their families they were part of the Black Chamber.'

'And that's the only reason?' pressed Brodie.

Smithies looked again at Miss Tandari. Then he tossed the spent match into the bin. 'Let's get on with our lessons, Miss Bray. It would be a shame to waste time now the candle has started to burn.'

Brodie watched the flame. The light cast grotesque shadows on the walls of the hut and they unnerved her.

'You know a little about the Station X Study Group Veritas,' went on Smithies, 'and how it was initially formed way back in the 1960s. You must remember it was referred to as the Second Study Group as a First Study Group had existed years before over the sea in the United States. It was the code-cracking partnership of Mr and Mrs Friedman who brought the quest to England and formed the Second Study Group. And it's our special honour to carry on their work.'

Brodie jotted down the name 'Friedman' and '1960s' in her notebook.

'Now the group's sole intention was to translate an encoded document which you've all seen now, although in copied form. The real manuscript is kept in another museum of sorts in America. The Friedmans and their team believed they'd be able to translate

MS 408. Yet after two years of unrelenting work and failure, they abandoned their task. They pledged if ever new evidence came to light about the manuscript, the group would re-form. I'm here to tell you,' his voice was casual but two pink circles bloomed on his cheeks, 'such evidence has been found.'

Brodie felt a twinge of excitement.

'We believe by using this new evidence we may force MS 408 to offer up its secrets. So . . .' Smithies paused dramatically, 'you've seen the manuscript. Now it's time for the new evidence.'

Brodie sat herself up straight in her chair and turned the page in her notebook. With a deliberate flourish of her pen she wrote the title, 'MS 408', then underlined it. She'd just reached the point of deciding whether to draw a small picture of a daisy next to the title when she realised Smithies had begun to talk again.

'The new evidence comes to us from a long-dead university professor.'

Brodie decided against the daisy picture.

'This,' went on Smithies, tapping the blackboard behind him and jabbing at a yellowed photograph of a tall man with a rather crooked nose, 'is a photograph of Professor Leo Van der Essen.'

'Leo,' muttered Hunter. 'That name's worse than Hunter.'

'Professor Van der Essen lived in Belgium. He worked in the university in a town called Louvain and was there during the time of the First World War. He was a specialist in myths and legends, you know, old traditional stories.'

'Oh, she knows,' laughed Hunter, jabbing Brodie in the ribs. 'That's just your meal of the day, isn't it? Stories about King Arthur and dragons and stuff. Just your thing.'

Brodie agreed enthusiastically as Smithies continued to explain. 'During that war the library was attacked and every book and document, folio and manuscript stored in the library was lost. The burning of Louvain was a terrible war crime. It enraged the world. Thousands have lost their lives in war, but when stories and books are destroyed, the memories and the cultures of those people die too.' Smithies paused again, as if allowing a moment for the weight of his words to settle.

'Professor Van der Essen escaped the burning and fled his homeland, staying a while in the town of Ghent, then made his way to England.'

'But how does Van der Essen connect with MS 408?' Hunter asked, shooting his hand into the air.

'Good question,' noted Smithies. 'A point I was moving on to. Van der Essen was close friends with the book collector Wilfrid Voynich. You remember he first discovered MS 408 in 1912, and that's why MS 408 is called the Voynich Manuscipt. Many believe Professor Van der Essen was in fact travelling with Voynich when he discovered the famous manuscript hidden away in the chest in Mondragone Castle in Italy.'

'Mondragone,' mused Brodie. 'Love that name.'

'Voynich never claimed to be able to read MS 408,' went on Smithies. 'He tried. He involved all sorts of people. But in the end he gave up and the manuscript was donated to Yale University. Voynich was after glory and fame. But the manuscript failed to give him that. His friend, Professor Van der Essen, on the other hand, was a quiet, more studious man. Voynich was into collecting, but for Professor Van der Essen it was all about the books and the stories they contained.'

'Sounds familiar,' said Hunter, catching Brodie's arm. 'Obsessing with story, I mean.'

'We can't be sure but there's perhaps the chance Professor Van der Essen knew more about MS 408 than he ever let on. The friendship between him and Voynich broke down and Van der Essen returned to Belgium. But there's always the chance, a small chance we admit, Van der Essen made his own find in the castle vaults of Mondragone. Perhaps he found the partner book of MS 408. The code-book that would allow us to read it. And perhaps, just perhaps he made sense of the manuscript but never told the world what he read.'

'Sorry,' Brodie said, raising her hand nervously into the air. 'I'm a bit lost.'

Smithies paused and ran his finger across his top lip as if searching for the right words to make it easy to understand. 'It's like this,' he explained. 'MS 408 is a book no one in the world can understand.'

'We'd got that bit,' groaned Hunter.

Smithies ignored him and ploughed on. 'We think MS 408 is in code. We think it tells a story no one can read because of the code.'

'I've been thinking about that,' said Tusia, now raising her hand. 'How do we know MS 408's in code? I mean, it could just be in a language everyone's forgotten. That no one speaks or reads now.'

This time Smithies looked impressed.

'Or maybe the book is like a sort of cookery book from a place far away and the guy who wrote it just made up weird signs and symbols to help him remember things and just never bothered to tell anyone the translation,' added Hunter.

Smithies clapped his hands. Sicknote was leaning forward in his chair, his sniffing forgotten. 'See, I told you they'd be good, Oscar. It's thinking like this that'll make them excellent code-crackers.' Smithies beamed.

'You could be right. Totally right. With either idea. But we have to make links if we're to make sense. And the link is *the hiding*.'

Brodie was sure her face showed she needed more explanation.

'When Voynich found the book MS 408 it was hidden. Hidden in a chest in a castle. Someone wanted that document kept safe and someone wanted it kept secret.'

'Sounds like that counts out the idea of a cookery book, then,' said Hunter dejectedly.

'The need to hide it suggests a need for secrecy, and the need for secrecy put together with a whole load of shapes and letters no one can read leads us to think MS 408 *must* be in code.'

Tusia nodded somewhat reluctantly.

'It's a theory we have to go with for now because it makes sense of what we know.'

Trying to keep up, Brodie edged forward on her seat.

'Now in order to make sense of the code we need to know what each symbol in the coded writing stands for. If we believe MS 408 is in code then there must exist, somewhere, a text showing what each symbol is and what it means. Like a sort of dictionary. You take a squiggle from MS 408 and look it up in this special book, which we now call the code-book, and we'd find out what the squiggle stood for.'

'Like looking up a word in a French/English dictionary?' called out Hunter.

'Exactly. Without the code-book MS 408 makes no sense. With the code-book then we'd be able to read it.' He smiled. 'But of course so would anybody else who found the code-book which leads us back to the idea of *hiding*.'

Brodie scribbled frantically in her notebook.

'Remember Professor Leo Van der Essen?'

'The Belgian guy? Obsessed with King Arthur? The one you said was friends with Voynich?' said Hunter.

'That's the one,' said Smithies, jabbing at his picture on the blackboard once again. 'Well, he hid something too. That's the link. But that's racing on with the story.' He paused as if trying to reorder his thoughts. 'Years after his travels with Voynich we know the Professor kept a certain book particularly safely in the university library of Louvain.'

'How on earth do we know that?' asked Tusia.

'Historical accounts,' explained Smithies. 'Writings about the time tell us that as the threat of war grew greater, Professor Van der Essen worried about a manuscript in his care.'

'And you think this manuscript was connected to MS 408?' said Tusia.

Smithies shrugged. 'Maybe. At least we do now, because of the new information we've received. We're making a leap based on their friendship and something we know happened after the fire of Louvain. But it seems quite likely Professor Van der Essen had a code-book for MS 408. And if we find *that* we can read the code.' He hesitated. 'But so of course could anyone else who found the code-book.'

'And what would be the problem with that?' asked Tusia, chewing hard on the end of her pen.

'It's back to the *hiding*,' pressed Smithies. 'Whoever wrote MS 408 must've wanted it to remain secret.'

'So who was the writer of MS 408?' Brodie asked, growing in confidence.

'We're not sure. Attempts at dating the pages suggest it was probably written in the early 1500s. As for who wrote it, we've no idea. But whoever it was obviously felt it important the information remained secret. That's why it's written in code.'

'Which only becomes a problem if the code-book is lost and then no one can decipher what was written. Even those supposed to read the code, can't do it without a code-book,' added Ingham.

'But you think this Professor Van der Essen had the code-book?' asked Hunter.

'Yes. And that initially he kept it at the University

of Louvain.'

'But he didn't tell anyone he had it?'

'Not directly,' said Smithies. 'Finding the code-book would enable anyone to read the secrets of MS 408 and so we think Van der Essen did all he could to protect it.'

'But hold on,' said Hunter, horror sweeping across his face. 'You said the library of Louvain was burnt to the ground in the war.'

'It was.'

'So the code-book the Professor was protecting would've been burnt too?'

'Correct.' Smithies nodded. 'So we believed. Then several years ago we discovered a report which explained what Van der Essen did on the night of the fire of Louvain.'

'What he did?'

Smithies ploughed on. 'Apparently he was away from home when the fire broke out. But he ran to his house and collected his family. He took no personal possessions with him as he escaped from the town. Except one. A single manuscript he had decided to withdraw from the shelves of the library.'

'The book that could be used to translate MS 408?'

'We can't be sure. It's a leap. But because of what Van der Essen did to save the book it seems a sensible leap to take.'

Brodie Bray :-) → 25 days!! Ö 🏠

??
↳
Friedman → 2nd Study Group → FAILED! → 1960's

America 🇺🇸

MS408 — every word in code...why?!

early 1500's

Just your Happy Meal

• Leo Van der Essen · Louvain   ♥ myth + legend

• All books ~~banned~~ burned during war...why?!
                              ↳ burned
↳ • Fled

Wilfred Voynich → found MS408 hidden in a trunk!
                                        ↳ why?

Mondragone Castle ♥   * donated to ~~Yale~~ Yale *

who from?
↑
LINK IN HIDING! 🎁
secrecy!

MS408 ??
?
↳
- cookery book? 📖
- old language?

codebook!!! 📦 ↳ Louvain?

Van der Essen?

Night of fire :- manuscript hidden in metal box!

WHERE IS IT NOW?!!

'So what'd Professor Van der Essen do with the book?'

'He *hid* it.' Smithies beamed.

'OK. I'm following this,' said Tusia. 'Two friends admit to finding one *hidden* book written in what looks like code. Then, years later one of the friends saves another book and *hides* it. And you think that *second* hidden book is the code-book to the first. Book two is the code-book to MS 408.'

Smithies could barely contain his excitement. 'See. They're really good, aren't they?'

Ingham looked happier than he had for quite a while.

'So where'd Professor Van der Essen hide this code-book then?' pressed Hunter.

'We don't know.'

Brodie felt the air of expectation burst like a bubble around her.

'All we do know,' Smithies continued, 'is that as the flames raged in the library, the Professor rescued just one book and hid it in a metal box. He ran away from Louvain and hid the box under the ground in a garden in Ghent.'

'And how d'you know that bit?' asked Tusia.

Smithies raised his hand. 'Glad you asked. Let's take nothing for granted here. Committees were formed to write about the destruction and rebuilding of the library. Van der Essen's story is included in the report issued in 1917.' He pointed to a stack of history books on the table and Brodie bristled with excitement.

'And the reports give us the name of the book he hid?' said Tusia. 'Let us know it's a code-book for MS 408?'

'Ahh, not exactly.' Smithies looked embarrassed. 'This makes it all the more intriguing! He does say there was a manuscript, but he doesn't explain why this manuscript of all of them was the one he was most keen to save. He talks about the metal box and it's almost as if the box itself was special. But if he went to all that trouble, the manuscript must have been worth hiding.'

'And this hidden book's still there?' said Hunter, dragging Smithies' attention back to the discussion. 'In some garden in Ghent. You expect us to go digging? Because as much as I'd love to help, digging's not really my thing. Earwigs. Worms,' he added by way of explanation. 'Not guests I'd invite to a party.'

'There'll be no digging,' Smithies said authoritatively. 'The report made the Professor's intentions quite clear. He intended to return to Ghent when the war was over. We believe he moved the secret code-book shortly before he died to a new and safer location.' He pointed once more to the history books, pre-empting Tusia's question about how they knew this.

Hunter visibly relaxed. 'So where's this new location?'

'With all due respect, if we knew the answer to that question we'd have found the book and translated the manuscript by now.' Smithies paused and traced a finger across his brow. 'For years it seemed the code-book was lost. No more mention of it in the history books, you see. The trail, as they say, ran cold. Until a few months ago when a letter was discovered. A letter written by Professor Van der Essen. He died in February 1963 and he'd left the letter in the care of his solicitors for release in the fiftieth year after the date of his death.'

'How'd we get hold of the letter?'

'The solicitors had instructions it was to be passed on to the Study Group at Bletchley. They had a name. Friedman. And of course it was the use of the name Friedman and the instructions to the solicitor to pass the letter on to the Study Group at Bletchley that let us link all the ideas together.'

Brodie looked down at her notes. She'd written down Friedman earlier. He was an American. He'd come over to England to form the Second Study Group to try and read MS 408.

Smithies straightened up and marked out the links with his fingers like a child counting, trying to make everything clear. 'First, two friends find a hidden book; second, one friend hides another book protecting it from fire; third, fifty years later, a letter arrives for a Study Group that were trying to read the first coded book. You see,' Smithies paused, and Brodie tried to show that she did, 'it's all about making links.'

'So when exactly,' begged Hunter, 'are you going to get around to telling us what this mystery letter passed on by the solicitor says?'

Smithies began to pace. 'The letter contains a puzzle. We believe if we can solve that puzzle, then we'll be able to find the location of the missing code-book and therefore read the secrets of MS 408.'

'Complicated, but really cool,' let out Tusia. 'Like the very best chess matches.'

'So,' Smithies said pulling his stomach in. 'My task today is to share with you what's known. What we've discovered so far. And it's *your* job to listen and *decide for yourself* what's important to retain and what information from everything I share with you could hold the answers.'

Brodie thought this sounded like quite a task.

'In the tradition of the best code-crackers,' Smithies said briskly, 'help yourself to a mint imperial as they're passed around. Nothing makes the mind sharper than a good old-fashioned mint.'

Brodie popped the offered mint into her mouth and took a deep breath. Hunter snuffled three into his mouth and popped a few spare into his pocket for later. In the corner the flame from the candle blazed.

'A copy of Van der Essen's letter,' Smithies passed out sections of paper. Brodie laid hers flat in front of her as Miss Tandari read the script aloud.

To the worthy alchemist of words,

It is my dying wish that you seek the

Phoenix of power,

in her cloak of Elfin Urim,

she who is wrongly considered to fly

lower than the rightful dragon.

Search 1st on the dawning of the 25th.

Such a task requires 14 from the one the world

rejected,

Professor

Arthur Van Der Essen

Brodie's hand shot into the air. 'I thought the Professor's name was Leo, sir.'

Smithies nodded appreciatively. 'Well done, Miss Bray. Well done. You've indeed shown an eye for detail that'll be very useful to us.'

Hunter smiled at her reassuringly.

'Our first clue *is* the use of the word Arthur.' Smithies tapped the photograph on the blackboard behind him. 'It's obviously not a mistake. A slip-up with numbers, a misspelling of unusual words, they could all be errors. But the wrong name.' He shook his head. 'That's got to be deliberate. And if it's deliberate it's got to be a clue.'

'A clue to what?' asked Tusia.

'The puzzle,' said Smithies. 'The Professor must be hiding secret information by using that name.'

'It's all about the *hiding*,' said Hunter.

Smithies smiled. 'So what was he hiding? In order to understand that we have to think about what we know about the Professor.'

'Well, not that much, except he had a weird name,' said Hunter.

'Ooh, I know, I know,' blurted Brodie, hardly able to sit still on her chair. 'What you said about him being into myths and legends. That could be a clue, right? I mean, maybe he wants us to make a

The Firebird Code...

"To the worthy Alchemist of words...

It is my dying wish that you seek the phoenix of power in her cloak of Elfin Urim; she who is wrongly considered to fly lower than the rightful dragon

Search FIRST on the dawning of the TWENTY FIFTH

Such a task requires FOURTEEN from the one the world rejected.

Professor Arthur van der Essen

from the envelope -
the wax seal

That's why it's a
Firebird Code! Keep
up Hunter!!

It was a firebird, not
a marine animal!

link with the stories of *King Arthur*.'

'But it could be any other famous Arthur?' asked Tusia.

Smithies agreed. 'It could. But in order to solve the puzzle we're trying always to make links. And I think Brodie might be right. It's a sensible guess to make. But we have to find other details to back it up if we're going to go with that link completely. And if you look closely they might be there.' He smiled reassuringly in Brodie's direction. 'The idea the puzzle leads us to ancient stories seems quite logical.'

'Why?' Tusia's brow was now furrowed into thick lines of concentration.

'Because,' Smithies said, 'if we're to crack Van der Essen's puzzle we need to find something called a "key". Not a literal key,' he said, miming the turning of a door key in a lock, 'but a text that's been used as the starting point to turn the message into code. With this puzzling letter from Van der Essen was a series of numbers. I've reprinted them for you on the back of your copies of the letter. We'll call them the "handle with care" numbers because for some reason we don't understand, Van der Essen wrote those words above them.' Brodie flicked her piece of paper over and sure enough, under the words 'handle with care' was a series of thirteen numbers in a line that looked like an

140

overlong mobile phone number.

Hunter read aloud. 'Handle with care: 41, 33, 57, 2, 24, 40, 3, 52, 23, 24, 23, 39, 29.'

'We believe,' Smithies said with a sigh, 'that the Professor has left us a poem or story code. They were used extensively during the war so it seems to make sense.'

Brodie wondered at this point if very much of what she heard was making total sense.

Smithies continued. 'If we find the right piece of writing, and the right section in that story, we'll be able to substitute letters from the story or poem in the place of these "handle with care numbers" here, and eventually understand his message. And perhaps if we solve this puzzle we'll be led to the location of the code-book that will allow us to read MS 408. Perhaps. It's like links in a very long chain.'

It all seemed rather overwhelming and for the briefest of moments Brodie thought fondly of lessons on long division back home with Miss Carter. She gave herself a shake and sat up straight. 'There seems a lot of "perhaps",' she said quietly.

Ingham beamed. 'That's the beauty of it all.' His eyes seemed to be looking far away, his face open and unlined as if he was for once incredibly relaxed. 'The beauty of it all is in the lack of certainty. The possibilities. The links we can try to make. It's like building a house out of cards. All about balance and skill and at any time the house could come tumbling down. But if we manage to build. If we manage to connect the whole thing together, then . . .' He didn't finish his sentence.

'So you think,' Hunter said at last, crunching the remains of his last mint imperial, 'that the piece of writing we need to understand Van der Essen's letter could be a story or poem about King Arthur?'

Smithies beamed. 'Exactly, Mr Jenkins. You've got it exactly.'

Tusia had begun to underline some of the words in her copy of the letter. 'But there must be hundreds of things written about King Arthur,' she said in a rather dejected tone.

'There's thousands,' Smithies laughed. 'Written in English and in other languages. The field of possibilities is endless.' And here he waited. 'But we believe the Professor left us other clues in his letter.'

He turned his back on the waiting audience and jabbed the blackboard with the end of a long stick he'd obviously brought along for such a purpose. 'Elfin Urim,' he said theatrically. 'Any ideas what they are?'

Brodie looked along the line of listeners. 'They're lights, aren't they?' she said quietly. 'Lights made by elves. Something magical. And beautiful.'

Smithies clapped his hands in appreciation. 'Spot on, Miss Bray. There's debate, but we generally accept the term to mean jewelled lights made by otherworldly figures. And it's this line about the "elfin Urim" that confirms for us we're right to think the use of the name Arthur points us to *King Arthur*.'

'Why?' Tusia said, this time her voice sounding a little strained.

'"Elfin Urim" is a phrase used in the stories of King Arthur. It crops up in the poems about him by the poet Alfred Lord Tennyson.' At this point, at Smithies' suggestion, Ingham limped to the end of the table and lifted a pile of dusty, green hardback volumes and began to pass them along the line. Brodie took hers and flicked through the pages.

'The poetry of Tennyson,' Smithies continued. 'A copy for each of you.'

'Great,' whispered Hunter. 'I needed something to lean my notes on.'

Brodie didn't like to remind him that any books of stories or poems made her excited.

'Five hundred and six pages no less,' Hunter muttered behind his hand. 'That's even if you exclude the index.'

Tusia's hand shot up into the air. 'And the coded

message could've been written using any part of his poems?' she asked in a voice now about an octave higher than usual.

'Quite right, Miss Petulova. Although of course, in our work so far on the code we've focused on the Arthur poems and in particular his use of the words "elfin Urim". And that section involves the giving of the sword Excalibur to the king, by the Lady of the Lake. It's the first chapter of Tennyson's really long poem *Idylls of the King*. This bit's called "The coming of Arthur". Here.' He directed them to a section of the poem by jabbing the stick once more at the blackboard. The picture of Professor Van der Essen flapped a little against the stand and it looked for a moment as if the old man was winking. 'If someone would be so kind as to read this portion aloud,' Smithies said, waving his hand in offer.

Miss Tandari rustled her pages and began to read. It was a descriptive section all about how the bright 'elfin Urim' on Arthur's sword blinded people who looked at it.

Brodie slipped a page of notepaper in the book to mark the section as Smithies continued to explain.

'So, we think the poem that's been used to make the code may be Tennyson's and we're pretty sure the section we need refers to Arthur's magic sword, but,' and at this point two small pink circles lifted again on his cheeks, 'in all honesty we are, as of this moment, completely stuck. Since Van der Essen's message came into our possession, try as we might to arrange letters against the "handle with care" numbers, all we've discovered is,' he appeared to search for a technical phrase that'd cover what he meant, 'absolutely nothing.'

'Our problem is being sure we're using the right section of the poem,' Ingham called out. 'We risk wasting time if we don't do things correctly.'

'Indeed, indeed,' Smithies said despondently. 'That's why you're all here.' He drew himself up straight. 'It's true our efforts have focused on Tennyson. But maybe we should look elsewhere.'

Brodie traced the embossed writing on the poem book with the tip of her finger as Hunter shuffled restlessly beside her.

'What about the numbers written in the letter?' Hunter said at last, as if referring to familiar friends, and turning back to his copy of Professor Van der Essen's puzzling message. 'Not the "handle with care" ones. But the numbers he's actually written in the letter. First and twenty-fifth? Why'd he do that?'

'To show dates, maybe?' Smithies said tentatively as if he knew he was grasping at straws. 'We believe them to be dates. We're unsure what else they could be.'

Brodie reread the letter.

To the worthy Alchemists of words,
It is my dying wish that you seek the phoenix of
power, in her cloak of elfin Urim;
she who is wrongly considered to fly lower than the
rightful dragon.
Search 1st on the dawning of the 25th.
Such a task requires 14 from the one the world
rejected.
Professor Arthur Van der Essen.

'And there's a number fourteen too,' said Brodie looking at her notebook where she'd copied the digits into capitals. 'What's that for?'

'No idea at all,' Smithies said apologetically. 'Really no idea at all. We're in this together now. Your idea's as valid as mine. Your idea's as needed as mine. We need you to think sideways, upside down, inside out,' he urged. Brodie thought back to the contorted positions Tusia managed to make while she exercised. 'Nothing about this will be easy. We have to be prepared to work. To stretch our brains and see things from any angle we can to try and make sense of what we see. But if we do make sense of this puzzle then . . .'

146

he widened his hands and what looked like a tear glistened in his eye. 'Then we could discover great and wonderful secrets.'

Brodie looked down again at the letter in Van der Essen's handwriting rested now on the top of the poem book. Was it likely she was really a worthy alchemist of words? And were there unworthy code-breakers out there puzzling over codes like this?

'Mr Smithies,' she said, at last breaking the heavy silence that'd fallen. 'What do you think the phoenix is?'

'It's the thing we search for, Miss Bray,' Smithies said. 'The ultimate solution to the code. The ending of our quest. If we find Van der Essen's phoenix then perhaps we stand a chance of finding the code-book that'll enable us to read MS 408.' He hesitated. 'And the thing we know about the phoenix is it's a thing of great beauty and immense power. And it's reborn in fire. A bird of flame. A firebird. We search something of power that was the single survivor of the burning of Louvain. We need to solve Professor Van der Essen's Firebird Code and find it.' He patted his stomach and smiled but the smile was strained and flickered only fleetingly across his eyes. 'And like all things worthy of a quest, we will not rest until we do.'

Kerrith couldn't rest. She tapped her blood-red nails

against the table, drilling away the seconds.

Now she needed proof. Tangible proof Smithies was playing with fire. If she could be the one to bring him in then there'd be no reward out of reach. No honour out of the question. An office on level five would be hers for the taking. Now all she had to do was reel him in. Catch Smithies red-handed and the prize would be hers.

Smithies stood in front of the candle. The flame stretched and grew, casting more shadows on the wall.

'You didn't tell them.'

Smithies turned to face Miss Tandari. 'How could I?'

'But I thought after the testing. I thought we agreed.'

'There's three of them, Tandi. After everything there's just three. And they're bright and they're keen and they want to do this.'

'But they don't know everything.'

'I *will* tell them.'

'When?'

Smithies looked at the flame. Wax ran like a tear and pooled at the base. 'It's safer this way.'

'Safer, maybe. But is it *right*?'

Smithies turned to look again into the flame.

The Most Precious of Gifts

It was Brodie who'd insisted they take out every single book in the library that contained any reference to Arthur. A quick search on the library computer listed books that contained mention of 'Arthur's Famous Cheese Pizzas' and a cartoon character for children who was apparently the world's most famous aardvark. When they'd narrowed the search to books making reference to King Arthur they were still left with a pile of over twenty volumes.

'Do you realise this little lot contains over thirteen thousand pages?' Hunter said from beneath the pile balanced precariously across his arms.

'Then the answer must be in here somewhere,' snapped Brodie, who didn't want to start feeling negative about the search before they'd even begun it.

'I don't know why you think it isn't Tennyson,' said Tusia.

'Because they've checked him out already,' Brodie explained, 'and it's too easy. Surely if this Professor is going to go to such great lengths to encode his message then he'd have been cleverer than that.'

Hunter snorted. 'I think hiding a message in five hundred pages of poetry about an ancient king is clever enough.'

'Yes, well. Maybe. But I just think we should look at all the possibilities we can. If the words needed for the code were in a poem by Tennyson, Smithies would've found it by now and they wouldn't have sent for us. We're supposed to look at things with new eyes, remember?'

The three of them made their way towards the lake and the ornamental fountain. Brodie selected a dry patch of grass on the highest part of the bank and slumped herself down, spreading her books out in an organised row in front of her. The other two sat beside her, Hunter balancing for a moment on his stack of books as if it were a chair, before a quick glare from Brodie made him mutter an apology and drop on the grass beside her.

Brodie drew a large notebook out of her bag. Keeping a logbook of their work had been Miss

Tandari's idea. She'd explained that just like Voynich had been a collector they should all be one too. Collectors of ideas! They'd been told to note down anything – any thoughts, any connections, any links – and Brodie loved the suggestion. Writing notes helped her think. Helped her shuffle things into order. 'So,' she said purposefully, 'any clue about how we should begin to try and solve this problem?'

Hunter took a yo-yo out of his pocket and flicked it backwards and forwards, catching it with his open hand.

'Start with the message and try and focus on the unusual words,' said Tusia.

'You'd be perfect for looking at the *unusual*,' Hunter laughed, emphasising the final word and then ducking as Tusia hit out her arm at him. 'You'd certainly know about all things strange.' He winced a little and then added apologetically, seeing Brodie's frown, that he was only joking.

'OK,' said Brodie, trying to regain control. 'What struck you as unusual in the letter?' She made quick notes on the paper.

'Well, the numbers for a start,' said Hunter, back on familiar territory. 'I know Smithies says they're dates, but I'm really not so sure.'

'What else could they be?'

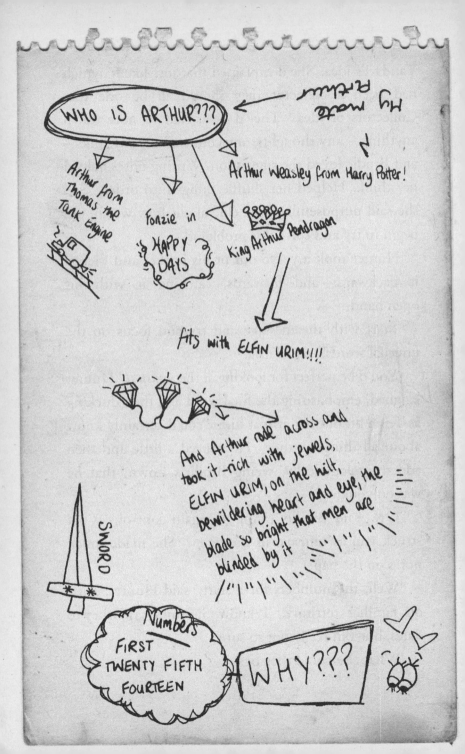

The yo-yo flicked high into the air. 'Numbers for an address. Page numbers maybe. Even the number of letters important to the code.'

Brodie jotted down the suggestion.

'And the phoenix in a cloak,' said Tusia, pulling her Pembroke blazer tight around her shoulders. 'When do you ever see a bird wearing a cloak? That's odd, don't you think?'

Brodie added the idea to the list.

'And what about "the one the world rejected"? Who could that mean?' Tusia asked.

'Madmen. Criminals. The insane,' Hunter said, grimacing and rocking backwards and forwards.

'So maybe we want a piece of writing about Arthur written by a madman,' Brodie said, looking sheepishly at the pile of stories. 'Was Tennyson mad?'

'I've heard there's an eighty-two per cent chance all poets are mad.'

'Fair enough. But,' Brodie flicked open the first book on the pile, 'they're not all criminals. Look,' she said, snapping the book shut and lifting it in the air. 'This book was written by Thomas Malory. I think I've read somewhere Tennyson based his poems about Arthur on Malory's story.'

'So he copied them?' Hunter said indignantly.

'No. Not copied. Just borrowed. The best bits

anyway. And,' she said, trying to hide her excitement, 'I'm pretty sure I've read somewhere else that Malory wrote a lot of his stories while he was in prison. That's *"rejected by the world"* surely.'

'So we should look at Malory's version?' Hunter said, scooping the pile of other versions to his side with a rather eager grin.

'Maybe let's start there. Find all the references to Arthur's sword in *Morte d'Arthur* by Malory.'

'Why the sword bits?' said Tusia looking confused.

'Because of the *elfin Urim*. That bit in Van der Essen's letter must've been talking about the otherworldy lights on the sword. So it makes sense to start with the stuff about the sword.'

'Sounds good to me,' Hunter said, kicking off his shoes and tying the end of the yo-yo string around a button on Tusia's blazer. 'It's as good a place as any. So,' he passed the book over, 'why don't you do the looking and I do the writing down when you've found them,' he added with a flourish and then lay down on the grass, his head resting on his arms. 'Let me know when you need me and I'll be right there.'

'And what exactly will *you* do while Tusia and I look?'

'I've got this to read,' he said, pulling a rather squat flat book from his trouser pocket. 'It's on substitution codes. When code-writers use other things for letters. Like numbers. Sicknote lent it to me. Look,' he added defensively, 'stories are your thing and I'm more into numbers.' Brodie couldn't stop herself rolling her eyes. 'So I'll do some research about codes and when we've found the right bit of poem then we'll be set to go.'

It was not the sort of help Brodie had banked on, but it made sense. The sessions with Ingham had left her more than a little shaky about swapping letters for numbers.

However, after a while, when the sun was beginning to slip behind the mansion and the air was growing cooler, she and Tusia had to admit defeat.

'We don't have to give up though,' said Hunter, staggering once again under the weight of the books. 'You know I think much more clearly after my dinner. Something may come to me when we've eaten.'

Brodie didn't hold out much hope today's dinner would provide Hunter with inspiration and on the way to get food she couldn't help look at the candle in Hut 11. The wick had burnt down, leaving fifteen days. It was taunting them, she was sure.

'It took everyone else who worked on the problem years to get to where we are now,' said Hunter later on through a mouthful of reheated cabbage. 'We mustn't be despondent, BB.'

The Firebird Code

Things that stood out...

① The [name] Arthur ⟶ KING ARTHUR 👑

② The [numbers]
     1st ⟶ 🏅 = position?
     25th ⟶ 🏠 = address?
     14th ⟶ [24 JUNE] = date?

③ "Phoenix in a cloak"

? - Bird with a coat on?
    dressed up? covered up?
    in disguise?
       hidden?

PHOENIX

④ "Him the world rejected" ⟶ X

Criminal (Why?) — Outsider
      Madman
   Disease

             Was he mad?

[Tennyson] → Was he a criminal?

★ Who else wrote about King Arthur?

⑤ Rightful dragon

- How does this fit?!

- What is a rightful dragon?

Thomas Malory!

He was in prison

Brodie couldn't help it. Suppose they had only the time the candle burnt to solve this thing? Supposing, when the flame had died, it was all over?

'I just don't think I'm very good at waiting,' she said, passing Hunter the tomato ketchup and watching as he spurted a particularly large splodge of it on to his plate. 'I just like to know the answers.'

Tusia smiled. 'Isn't that what code-cracking's like? Waiting and waiting for a breakthrough.'

'Maybe,' Brodie answered thoughtfully. But if it was, she wasn't sure she liked it.

Breakthrough, when it eventually arrived, came from a very unusual source.

Miss Tandari stood at the front of the room, her eyes narrowing and her smooth skin wrinkled around the brow. For a moment she looked unwilling to meet the gaze of those who waited for her to speak. But Miss Tandari wasn't embarrassed. She was angry.

Brodie put down her pen.

At the front of the room, next to Miss Tandari, and looking as if she were willing the ground to open up beneath her, stood Tusia.

'It's just not good enough,' Miss Tandari said so quietly it was almost impossible to hear.

Tusia stared defiantly forward. 'But it's normal

157

lessons, miss. And surely you understand our priority . . .' she paused a little, '*my* priority, is to focus all my attention on what really matters here. Code-cracking. We've only got two days left according to that candle!'

Miss Tandari seemed to visibly bristle, her lips narrowing into thin dark lines. 'But it's my job, Tusia,' she said and Brodie couldn't help but notice she seemed to spit the name from her mouth, 'to make sure that while you're in the glorious position of being here at Station X, you do not miss out on normal learning.'

Tusia made an odd face and folded her arms across her chest. 'But what good honestly, miss, is all this stuff on percentages and ratios? Why don't we leave all that sort of thing to Hunter? I mean, he actually understands what you're talking about.' She paused for a moment to draw breath. 'I mean, really. For me it's a waste of time. A waste of energy. I could be working on the code. Two days, miss. Don't you understand?'

Miss Tandari pulled her shoulders up. She was tall anyway but now she seemed suddenly to fill an awful amount of space. She placed her hands on her hips and breathed in deeply. 'Tusia,' she said, and this time there could be absolutely no doubt about the spitting, 'your work in sessions the last few days has been abysmal.

You've lacked focus and care and to be perfectly frank with you, your efforts are sloppy and substandard.' She shook the exercise book she was holding in her hand and Brodie saw clearly a sprawl of marking in bright red ink across Tusia's work.

Tusia was embarrassed. Brodie could tell that from the way she was wailing and throwing her arms about, something Brodie found more than a little distracting! Hunter, though, was obviously enjoying the telling-off just a little too much.

'I'm afraid, young lady, you've got to realise you can't ignore the importance of everyday learning for the sake of the glamour of the code,' she added sternly. 'Who are we to count out what may be the very thing we need to learn? Whatever the time limits, we have to pay attention to details. Now,' she pressed her fingers together almost as if in prayer, 'take a seat, Miss Petulova, and take note. Don't ignore the seemingly ordinary or you may pay a heavy price for your neglect.'

Tusia muttered something under her breath as she walked back to her seat.

Brodie didn't hear what it was.

She was busy scribbling a note and passing it across the table to Hunter.

Hunter looked up as soon as he read it.

The note said simply: *I've got it!*

They decided to meet in the music room.

Hunter stood by the fireplace leaning his weight on the large stone bust of Winston Churchill. In the past Brodie had told him off for being disrespectful, but now she simply didn't have the time. She was buzzing with excitement.

Between them they'd carried all the books they'd taken from the library and the logbook now crammed with notes and doodles. The books and notes lay strewn across the patterned carpet as Brodie paced backwards and forwards rubbing her hands together.

'It's so obvious. I don't know why I didn't see it before. Anyone who was really looking should've seen it from miles.'

Tusia was sitting cross-legged on the floor, her arms outstretched across the books. 'Any time you could just explain and let us in on the secret we'd be grateful,' she said, gazing up as Brodie continued to pace.

'Yes, BB. If you really don't mind it'd be wonderful if you could share.'

'OK. OK.' Brodie cleared her throat. She at last stood still, closed her eyes and tried to focus her thoughts. 'Let's recap what we know,' she said authoritatively, sounding a lot like Smithies.

'Number one: we're looking for a poem. A story

about Arthur that'll serve as the key to the coded message that Van der Essen left for us. His message about the phoenix. What we call our Firebird Code.'

'We know all that,' Tusia said impatiently.

'But what part of the stories and poems have we been focusing on?' asked Brodie, still taking on the mantle of teacher.

Hunter lunged forward dramatically, his hand thrust sharply in the air. 'Bits about the sword,' he said, sweeping his hand behind him before bowing low to the ground. 'The wonderful Excalibur.'

'Exactly,' said Brodie. 'And what do we know about the sword, apart from the elfin Urim on it, of course?'

'That it's rather special,' said Tusia. 'Could kill lots of people. Sort of nasty really.' She wrinkled her face into the one she normally wore when Hunter was tucking into a particularly juicy hamburger or bacon sandwich at lunchtime.

'Absolutely.' Brodie grimaced. 'Nasty sword really. Used for awful things.'

'Yeah. But that's what swords do, B. Kill people,' said Hunter, shadow-fencing once more before steadying himself with one hand pressed tightly around Churchill's nose.

'Yes,' went on Brodie. 'I know. Everything we've read,' she gestured at the sea of books spread around where Tusia sat, 'goes on about the "power of the sword" and the "might of the weapon". But,' at this point she could barely hide her excitement, 'the sword wasn't the most important thing the Lady of the Lake gave Arthur, was it?'

Tusia looked puzzled and Hunter let go of Churchill's nose and patted the dome of the plaster head apologetically. 'Wasn't it?'

'No.' She giggled and one of her paces looked, just for a second, a little more like a skip. 'Look, in the Malory version, after Arthur is given the sword and is told how wonderful it is, Merlin asks him what he values most. The scabbard or the sword?'

'Scabbard?'

'Yeah, you know,' Brodie said, directing her answer down towards Tusia. 'The cover thing you keep a sword in.'

'Like its case?'

'Exactly. Or,' and she laughed a bit at this, 'its cloak.'

'Like the cloak of the phoenix in the Professor's letter?'

'Exactly. Just like that.'

'And?' Hunter looked confused.

'Well, that's the incredible bit. The thing we were missing. And it came to me when Miss Tandari was going off on one to Tusia about making choices and not always going for the most glamorous thing.'

Tusia's face coloured at the reminder. 'So?'

'Well, Arthur chose the sword. He went for the thing *inside* the case. Said that was the most important thing.'

'Sounds sensible to me,' Hunter said. 'A king in battle would find a sword kind of useful, wouldn't he?'

'Yes. He would. He would. But,' Brodie swung round to face him, 'Merlin said he'd made the wrong choice. The obvious, but wrong one. It was the *container* that mattered. Merlin said the scabbard was worth ten of the sword.'

'Really?' Tusia's forehead was furrowed into lines.

'Yes. Because the scabbard *looked* more ordinary, but it wasn't.'

'So what's so great about this sword case then?' asked Hunter who obviously needed more convincing.

'Well, so the story goes, the scabbard could make you invincible.'

'Like no one could see you?' Hunter replied.

'Not *invisible*. *Invincible*,' Brodie said, trying to keep the exasperation out of her voice. 'It meant all the time Arthur had it, he couldn't be hurt. Not even shed a drop of blood.'

'Now that makes me think the scabbard is *infinitely* more valuable than the sword,' Hunter added dramatically.

'But Arthur died, right?' Tusia asked, from her new position on her knees. 'So the scabbard can't have worked.'

'He was badly injured *eventually*. In a terrible battle. But, and here's the important bit, he'd lost the scabbard by then.'

'Lost it? That was careless.'

'Had it stolen actually. By this evil woman Morgan Le Fay. And after that, Arthur was vulnerable.'

'And so he died?'

'Sort of,' said Brodie.

'Ermm, how can you sort of die, B?'

Brodie was trying to keep track of her thoughts. 'People thought he was dead but the story says he was taken off to Avalon. To this amazing place where he was going to be healed.'

'I like the sound of Avalon.' Hunter grinned. 'With the making-you-whole-again thing. Sounds great.'

'Yeah. But the point is, we've been just like Arthur. Focusing on the sword. All the poems we've read, all the sections of the story we've explored. They've been about the sword. And we should've been looking for sections about the scabbard.'

Tusia leant back on her heels. 'So, let me see if I've got this right,' she said slowly. 'We go back to the

It's not all about the sword!

- King Arthur 👑 gets powerful sword EXCALIBUR

from the Lady in the Lake 〜🐟

- Merlin warns him it's the scabbard that is the most important.

SWORD   but   SCABBARD

↓   ↓

Harms and   Makes you
kills people   invincible!

↓   ↓

Good in battle ✓   Brilliant!! ✓✓✓

Merlin said

SCABBARD = case, ~~suit~~ covering, pouch, container, cloak ✓✓✓

↓

like the "phoenix in the cloak"!!

FIREBIRD CODE ←

beginning, through all these books and texts, and this time we go looking for a scabbard, not a sword.'

Brodie tried to look encouraging.

'And that will take us how long exactly?' said Hunter, resting his elbow now on the statue's head. 'I hate to mention the old candle clock, but last time we looked there were only two sections left to burn.'

'I know. I know,' spluttered Brodie. 'So we focus and we try to be systematic. And we take it one step at a time.'

'But we should start with the Malory, though, don't you think, as he was the one the world rejected and all that.'

Brodie nodded. 'Yep. I think we start with Malory.'

Tusia leant down and scooped up the copy of the *Morte d'Arthur* by Thomas Malory which was beginning to look well thumbed around the edges.

Hunter reached forward and grabbed at the copy. 'Let's get looking.' As he lifted his hand, a smudged, black, stamped design turned quickly from sight before the text of the story began.

Tusia looked aggrieved. 'You do realise there are twenty-five chapters in Book One alone, and it'd be much better if we took about eight chapters each. For the sake of fairness, don't you think?' she added, as if aware she was being stared at.

'Pardon?'

'About eight each. An equal split.'

'No. Not that. I mean, the twenty-five chapters. What d'you mean?' Brodie said now, taking her turn to grab at the red leather volume and flick through the pages.

'Didn't you notice?'

'Notice what?' she said, the pages slapping the air.

'Well, Malory's work is arranged into what he calls "books". Each book's arranged into chapters and the first "book" of what Malory wrote's got *twenty-five chapters*.' She smiled. 'Shape and space. My thing. Remember? How things are arranged.'

Brodie tried to take it in. As far as she was concerned Malory's work was just a story. A long, complicated and wonderful story. It never seemed important to think about how it was set out. Suddenly, as if reading her mind, Hunter hurried forward. 'Where's the copy of the coded letter?'

Brodie scrabbled for the notes they'd made during Smithies' session on the code. She knew her grin stretched from ear to ear. She jabbed the page with her finger. 'You're right, Hunter. You said the numbers weren't dates, and they're not. They're references. Look.'

She traced her fingers across the capitalised words. 'FIRST. TWENTY-FIFTH. First "book".

Twenty-fifth "chapter". Well?'

Tusia had the copy of Malory and was turning the pages furiously. 'Here. It's here,' she said, holding it out in front of her so the three of them could see more clearly. 'Book One. Chapter Twenty-five.'

'And?' Brodie said, barely able to focus her eyes on the print in front of them. 'What's it about?'

Tusia read the title of the section slowly. *'How Arthur by the mean of Merlin gat Excalibur his sword of the Lady of the Lake.'*

'And the scabbard. Does it talk about the scabbard?'

Hunter thumped the page with the palm of his hand.

'There, look. There. It's the bit of the story you knew.' He grinned broadly, and read the words aloud. *'You are most unwise, said Merlin, for the scabbard is worth ten of the sword. For whiles you have the scabbard upon you, ye shall never lose no blood, be ye never so sore wounded; therefore keep well the scabbard always with you.'*

Brodie clapped her hands together. 'So that's it then. That's it. We've found a section about the scabbard in the *twenty-fifth chapter* of the *first book* written by the man rejected by the world. We've done it. We've really done it. We've found the section of writing that must have the key to the Firebird Code somewhere in it.'

Hunter was still frowning and pointing at the paper with his finger, his lips twitching as if he were counting in his head.

'Even better than that,' he said. 'We've got even closer.'

Brodie waited for him to go on.

'We've found the section of story. I'm sure. The cloak of the phoenix, or the scabbard of the sword. It all makes sense. So now we have to try and use the "handle with care" numbers and somehow fit them with this bit of writing. That must be the thing we need to do next.'

'OK,' agreed Brodie.

'But the bit of writing we've found is a fairly long section and the "handle with care" numbers Van der Essen gave us could fit with any of the words in this section.'

Brodie tried hard not to look too crestfallen. 'But we can narrow it down. If we give ourselves enough time.'

'We don't need to.' Hunter pushed out his chest with pride. 'We've done it already.'

Brodie clung on to Tusia's arm.

'Think about the message from the Professor. About how much we know.' He read Van der Essen's letter aloud.

To the worthy Alchemists of words, It is my dying wish that you seek the phoenix of power, in her cloak of elfin Urim; she who is wrongly considered to fly lower than the rightful dragon. Search 1st on the dawning of the 25th. Such a task requires 14 from the one the world rejected.

'We've covered the first and the twenty-fifth. But what about the other number in what he wrote?' said Hunter slowly. '*Number fourteen*. It must refer to the most vital fourteen words that we need to solve the code. Logical, don't you think?'

'Of all these words in the passage, how'd we know which fourteen he wants us to use?' Tusia asked.

'We go with the most important. That's been the message all along. Remembering what's really important.' Hunter underlined groups of words.

'Yes. So?'

'So the most important words *must be* these. And these fourteen words are the key to the code,' said Hunter and he placed his notes down on the floor and then stood to speak the words aloud like an actor on a stage and Brodie felt her stomach twist inside her as she listened.

'*For whiles you have the scabbard upon you ye shall never lose no blood.*'

To Do:

Find section of Morte D'Arthur
by Malory that's about the
SWORD and SCABBARD.

REMEMBER—

→ Book 1   Chapter 25   14 words

Numbers = Books and CHAPTERS...and WORDS in them!!
Not addresses or dates!

Find 14 most important words...

Book 1, Chapter 25......

You are most unwise, said Merlin, for the
scabbard is worth ten of the swords. For
whiles you have the scabbard upon you, ye
shall never lose no blood, be ye never so sore
wounded; therefore keep well the scabbard
always with you.

"For whilst you have the scabbard upon you, !
ye shall never lose no blood."
   !!   !!!

* * *

Kerrith leant against the counter top and tried to avoid the display of cakes beneath the glass. 'Skinny cappuccino,' she said.

Gordon chose not to correct her lack of the word 'please'.

Kerrith took the offered Styrofoam cup and curled her lip in disgust.

'Staying long in Bletchley?' Gordon asked, trying to keep the irritation from his voice.

'Just a couple of days,' she said without meeting his gaze. 'What I have in mind will only take a couple of days.'

8

A Flightless Bird

'What will you do when the candle burns out?' Miss Tandari's question was hardly louder than a whisper.

Smithies pressed his finger into the pool of wax on the table. It was cold. 'I'm not sure,' he said.

'The children think it will be over,' she said.

'Maybe it will.'

'You can't mean that. Not after all the work you did to get them here.'

'You made me promise to be careful. A time limit is being careful.'

'But what if they can do this?'

'What if they can't?'

Miss Tandari folded her arms. 'What was she like? Brodie's mother, I mean?'

Smithies turned from the candle. 'She wouldn't give

up. Even when Robbie and I thought we should, she wouldn't give up. And . . .' He couldn't finish the sentence. Instead he took his wallet from his pocket and pulled out a folded strip of paper. Along the line of the paper tiny holes had been punched. 'She sent me this, you know, just before she died. I have no idea why. But the holes and the light coming through gave me the idea. The invitations I sent to the children to be here. Light through the darkness. It seemed a good idea.'

'It is a good idea.'

'I know. But it's dangerous and eventually the light runs out. Eventually, even if you don't want it to, there comes a time to stop.'

For the first time in weeks Brodie enjoyed her dinner. She took extra helpings of apple crumble and even a rather unpleasant crunch of what felt very much like a large section of apple core couldn't prevent her finishing the second bowl.

Tusia leant forward so as to be sure her words would not be lost on anyone else. 'When are we going to tell Smithies we've found the key to the code?'

'Surely, before we tell him anything, we've got to break the whole secret,' spluttered Hunter, interrupting her train of thought. 'It's time for the "handle with care" numbers now. Where the fun starts.' He stirred frantically at a mug of hot chocolate in which the chocolate seemed to be neither hot nor in fact real chocolate and was instead floating in great cloudy lumps on the top of the mug, looking a lot like miniature dumplings.

Tusia sat back in her chair. 'You want us to actually crack the code. Try and find out how the words fit that enormous series of numbers he gave us and read what the code says. Before we tell anyone in charge.'

'It's hardly enormous,' mumbled Hunter, who was now wearing splashes of chocolate on his upper lip. 'Just thirteen.' He grabbed her logbook and scribbled them down. 'Here, look. "*Handle with care: 41, 33, 57, 2, 24, 40, 3, 52, 23, 24, 23, 39, 29*". See?'

Brodie peered at Hunter. How could he possibly remember them? She couldn't help being impressed or suddenly aware that the second bowl of apple crumble was sitting a little heavily in her stomach.

'There must be literally hundreds of ways the letters could be substituted for these "handle with care" numbers though,' said Tusia. 'We've found the important words in the poem, but it doesn't mean we'll be able to work out how the numbers and the words we've found fit together.'

'I know, I know,' said Brodie, 'and if you think we

should tell him what we know now then I'll go along with whatever you decide. But if we keep going it'd mean we'd gone the whole way, and how pleased would the Group be with that? It'd justify all their hard work with us. Prove we'd learnt something. Before the candle burns out completely.'

Tusia took a moment to answer. 'How about we try and work it out? But,' Tusia sounded forceful, as if in a desperate attempt to at least think of herself in charge, 'we give ourselves a time limit. Ten o'clock tonight. If we haven't done it then we'll tell what we know.'

'Midnight?' Brodie said coyly. 'That leaves just a few hours left for the candle to burn. If we haven't done it by *midnight* then we go straight to Smithies in the morning and we show him what we've worked out already.'

'Having some sort of feast?' laughed Miss Tandari who was taking her turn at staffing the sweet counter after locking up the museum for the night. 'Don't forget to brush your teeth after all that sherbet and chocolate.'

Hunter led the way back to the huts, his arms weighed down this time with a bag full of edible goodies. Tusia threw her blazer around his head as they reached Hut 8. 'Oh yes, such a clever disguise,'

Hunter moaned from behind the sleeves which flapped against his nose.

'Well, you know we're not supposed to go into each other's rooms. They stressed that in the welcome pack information,' Tusia reprimanded. 'Now watch the step.'

Watching the step was in fact impossible from beneath the folds of fabric and Hunter performed a magnificent flying leap as he tripped up the stairs. Once inside, Brodie stacked the Malory, their logbooks and lots and lots of pieces of paper on the chest of drawers which Tusia had positioned at a crazy angle just inside the door.

'There to trap the good luck,' explained Brodie as Hunter reeled from stubbing his foot on the base.

'Fantastic plan,' he groaned through gritted teeth.

Brodie tried her best to look apologetic while nervously opening a packet of Polos. 'OK. Let's think this through. We're pretty sure we've found the fourteen special words in the poem by Malory. *For whiles you have the scabbard upon you ye shall never lose no blood.* Somehow, we have to use those words and the string of "handle with care" numbers that were with Van der Essen's letter, to crack the code.' She copied the numbers from her logbook on to a clean page next to the special words about the scabbard they'd found.

41, 33, 57, 2, 24, 40, 3, 52, 23, 24, 23, 39, 29. It sounded almost easy in her head. 'Numbers are your thing, Hunter. Where d'we start?'

Initially Hunter seemed reluctant to take control of the session but after nearly three hours had passed and the clock on the windowsill was creeping nearer to eleven, and the best Brodie had come up with was a code that included the words 'hamster' and 'beetroot', he coughed to clear his throat and swept his rather too long fringe away from his eyes.

'You've got to be more systematic,' he said, in an obvious attempt not to sound too frustrated while glancing down at the discarded piles of screwed-up paper now littering the floor like overstuffed snowflakes. 'Substitution codes are a thing of beauty and you really have to take more care.'

Brodie considered herself well and truly told off and scribbled out the words 'hamster' and 'beetroot' from her pad.

'If we think logically,' Hunter added, 'which after all seems sensible to do if we're solving a code, then what we hope to find, when we've cracked this code, is the name of a location.'

'A place name then. Where we'll find the "phoenix" . . . whatever Van der Essen has hidden for us and written the code to protect.'

'Exactly,' said Hunter, rewarding Tusia's suggestion with a broad smile. 'And so although in code-cracking you should obviously consider every possibility, you should at least have some sense of what you're aiming for and then when the code throws up something that may make sense, you know you're on the right lines.'

Brodie looked down at the floor.

'Look, BB,' said Hunter, standing up suddenly and swinging his arms by his side. 'Think back to what we've learnt.'

It was trying to use all Ingham had taught them that'd led Brodie to the words 'hamster' and 'beetroot'. She tore out the page from her notebook and tried hard to focus on Hunter's instructions.

'Let's think this through step by step,' he said. 'We think we've found the key to the code. A phrase from a poem. The fourteen words Van der Essen wanted us to focus on.' He turned to write it this time on a large piece of paper he'd tacked to the wardrobe. *'For whiles you have the scabbard upon you ye shall never lose no blood.'*

'And finding that part was exciting,' said Tusia.

Hunter tutted a little and continued. 'We've fourteen words and they all contain letters.'

'Can see why Station X chose you as a super-brain,' Brodie mocked.

Hunter tutted once more. 'Now the next thing we've got to deal with is a series of thirteen "handle with care" numbers which Van der Essen wrote on the back of his message.'

Brodie pulled her most impressed face as Hunter scribbled the line of numbers this time on to the big sheet of paper. *41, 33, 57, 2, 24, 40, 3, 52, 23, 24, 23, 39, 29.*

'Now,' Hunter went on. 'Each of these numbers must represent a letter in our phrase about the scabbard. In a really simple code the letter A is given the number 1 and the letter B is given the number 2. So, if I wanted to write BALL, for example, my code would read: 2, 1, 12, 12.'

'OK,' said Brodie. 'Nice and simple.'

'Yes. But so simple we wouldn't need a special sentence hidden in part of a poem to write the code, would we?'

Tusia shook her head. 'No. A would always be 1, B always 2, I guess.'

'Exactly. A poem code works because the letters in the chosen phrase give the numbers and if I don't know the phrase then I've absolutely no chance of breaking the code.'

'So how do you think the letters in the phrase about the scabbard are numbered?'

'I'm getting to that, Toots,' said Hunter, with the tiniest note of irritation in his voice. 'This poem system was used all the time in the Second World War. You take the phrase and you give the letter A the number 1. But, and here it gets more tricky, if there's more than one A then the next one gets a number 2, and the third a number 3. Eventually, when you've used up all the As you can start to number the Bs. The first of those would get a 4 in this example.'

'And what happens if there are no Bs?'

'Good question. The letter C would be 4, or the letter D.'

'So the numbers are totally dependent on the letters in the phrase then?' said Brodie, trying not to sound too panicked.

'Totally. And the chances for making a mistake are huge. But Van der Essen had a long time to check his code so I don't think there'll be many mistakes.'

Brodie took a toffee from the shrinking pile of sweets and began to chew.

'If we try this system,' said Hunter, 'first we have to number the letters. The letter A in "*have*" should be number 1 because that's the first time A is used. Then the As in "*scabbard*" are 2 and 3. Do you see?'

Brodie tried to show she did. 'We should all have a go at doing the numbering and compare answers just to make sure we don't slip up.'

As it was, Hunter finished so much faster than the others, Brodie suggested they trust him and use his numbers. Tusia didn't attempt to disagree.

F o r   w h i l e s   y o u   h a v e
18, 32, 41,   54, 19, 23, 24, 11, 44,   55, 33, 49,   20, 1, 52, 12

t h e   s c a b b a r d   u p o n   y o u
48, 21, 13   45, 8, 2, 5, 6, 3, 42, 9   50, 40, 34, 29   56, 35, 51

y e   s h a l l   n e v e r   l o s e
57, 14   46, 22, 4, 25, 26   30, 15, 53, 16, 43   27, 36, 47, 17

n o   b l o o d
31, 37   7, 28, 38, 39, 10

'We're nearly there,' Hunter said. 'We're really nearly there.'

Hunter's excitement was contagious. 'So what now?' Brodie asked.

'Now, we simply decipher the code.'

Tusia giggled but Brodie was sure this was due to a combination of exhaustion and her unusually massive intake of sugar by way of the Sherbet Dips.

Hunter took the series of 'handle with care' numbers and read them aloud again. '41, 33, 57, 2, 24, 40, 3,

52, 23, 24, 23, 39, 29. So, the first number in our code,' he continued, 'is 41.' He traced his finger along the line of letters from the scabbard phrase they'd just been numbering. 'And the number 41 matches the letter R in our phrase. The first letter of the location is R.'

Brodie jotted it down.

'The next "handle with care" number is 33. That,' he said, 'gives us the letter O.'

Brodie added an O after the R.

Tusia blew a rather large violet bubble-gum bubble which hung for a moment in the air and then popped all over her nose. Brodie looked down and tried to make it seem she hadn't noticed.

For a moment Brodie thought she might've stumbled on the word 'Rottweiler', but then she remembered they were looking for a place name and decided not to share that discovery with the others anyway.

Outside it'd begun to rain slightly and the sound of the drops against the windows kept a gentle rhythm as they worked.

It was after midnight. Her eyes were heavy and the combination of apple crumble, Curly Wurlies and a whole packet of Starbursts was making her feel more than a little unwell.

Hunter showed no sign of giving up. He was scribbling as if trying to scratch through the paper stuck to the wardrobe in front of him, muttering numbers as he wrote.

At last he lowered his pencil.

'I've done it,' he said and his voice shook a little, maybe from exhaustion but more likely from delight.

Brodie swallowed and the pen she was holding fell from her fingers. Every number of the code now had a letter written below it and the words that had been hidden by the code said:

41 33 57 2 24 40 3 52 23 24 23 39 29
R O Y A L P A V I L I O N

'So we should go and tell Smithies,' Brodie said, stretching and standing up from the floor, her knees cracking a little as she stood. 'Right away.'

Tusia looked down at her watch. 'It's half past one in the morning.' They'd long since exceeded their self-imposed deadline, but not one of them had mentioned it.

'And the man's made his life about trying to crack this code and we've done it. I don't think he'll mind what time it is. Not with less than one day left on that candle clock of his.'

'I'm with Brodie,' said Hunter. 'He's got a right to know.'

Cracking the Firebird Code!

"For whiles you have the scabbard upon you, ye shall never lose no blood."

(14) most important words from Book (1), Chapter (25)   pass us a mint!

To DO: Number the letters, like in a poem code

F o r   w h i l e s   y o u
18 32 41   54 19 23 24 11 44   55 33 49

h a v e   t h e   s c a b b a r d
20 1 52 12   48 21 13   45 8 2 5 6 3 42 9

u p o n   y o u,   y e   s h a l l
50 40 34 29   56 35 51   57 14   46 22 4 25 26

n e v e r   l o s e   n o b l o o d.
30 15 53 16 43   27 36 47 17   31 37 7 28 38 34 10

Eat your own sweets!!

19, 4, 48 → hat ◼   45, 50, 31 → sun ☼

5, 42, 34, 4, 23, 11 → Brodie!

Rottweiler Raya
KRaya
Royalp

The Solution

	41	33	57	2	24
	R	O	Y	A	L

40	3	52	23	24	23	39	29
P	A	V	I	L	I	O	N

Tusia blocked the doorway, her arms on her hips. 'Hold on a minute. Let's just think this through.'

Brodie was really of the opinion they'd done enough thinking and in fact it'd be better just to get a move on, but something about the way Tusia looked at them made her hesitate.

'Smithies doesn't stay at the mansion overnight, does he?' Tusia said, as if she were explaining the fact to a group of small children. 'They told us that in our tour. He has a house in the village, so even if we went up to the mansion we wouldn't be able to find him.'

Brodie slumped despondently on to the foot of the bed. 'Oh great. I'd forgotten. So what d'we do then? Morning's years away. The candle will be nearly out by then.'

Tusia flickered her eyes in thought. 'OK. What about this? We could use the internal mail system. Leave him a note to say we've cracked the code and we know where the "phoenix" is hidden and then he'll be all set to meet us tomorrow. And that way it'll have been worth staying up half the night working. What do you think?'

Brodie rubbed the back of her neck. She felt there was a very real possibility that with all that looking down at pieces of paper she'd never fully regain the movement of her head! 'I say yes,' she mumbled. 'To at least make the pain and the headache worth it!'

It was still raining. 'Suppose it isn't open?' Hunter called as he ran towards Hut 11.

'We'll worry about that if it's locked. I thought the idea was the hut was always open so you could pass on information in an emergency. Ingham did explain that,' Tusia said in her best teacher voice.

The door to the hut was indeed unlocked and after a small degree of struggling, when Hunter realised he was turning the handle the wrong way, the door opened and they were able to push inside out of the rain.

The hut was lit in a pale yellow glow. The candle was nearly spent; the flame weak and fragile. Above their heads the internal mail vacuum system hummed gently like a sleeping animal snoring.

'This Royal Pavilion,' Brodie said as they positioned themselves below the opening in the pillar. 'Where do you think that is?' It was the first time they'd questioned the answer they'd found.

'No idea,' said Hunter. 'But I'm sure Smithies will know. We just have to get him the information.'

'What shall I put on the note then?' Brodie asked, glad at least they could leave some of the problem for the adults.

It took a while and several rejected versions before they finally agreed. Brodie wrote it down and after they all signed their names at the bottom, Hunter folded the page and slipped it carefully inside a waiting tube.

Mr Smithies. We've managed to find the location of Van der Essen's phoenix. It's in a Royal Pavilion. Does this make sense?

There was a gentle popping noise and then a rather inelegant slurp as the message and its tube was sucked into the overhead system and began to rattle away from them unseen across the piping in the ceiling.

'So that's it then,' said Hunter decisively. 'Problem well and truly solved.'

'Absolutely,' said Brodie.

It was a shame really, that after all their hard work, their problems were in fact only just about to start.

'There's been a break-in,' Mr Ingham declared over the row of breakfast cereals.

Brodie's glass of orange juice spilled a giant tear into her bowl of cornflakes.

'A breach in security. In the early hours of the morning. Smithies is going demented.'

Hunter kicked Brodie sharply under the table, causing the final remnants of juice to splash on to her toast.

'We have to go and check,' Tusia hissed behind her hand, dragging Brodie by the arm.

They hurried towards the door and across the lawn, past the ornamental fountain whose spray this time Hunter managed at least partially to avoid.

'Who do you think it was?' Brodie called, her question coming in gulping spurts.

'A break-in from anyone can't be good,' returned Hunter, bending slightly to the left to escape the second sweep of the fountain.

'Not good at all,' added Tusia, who was trailing some distance behind mainly because the Doc Martens boots she'd chosen to wear were flapping open and she was tripping on the laces. 'Not good at all.'

When they reached Hut 11 the door was open and the children could make out Smithies deep in conversation with Miss Tandari. There was no flame on the candle – all trace of light now drowned by a pool of hardened wax.

'Mr Smithies! Mr Smithies!' Brodie called, trying her best to catch his attention.

Miss Tandari hurried out of the shadows, her face set in deep lines. 'Now's not a good time,' she hissed. 'You need to get back to your huts. Keep a low profile. The last thing we want is to draw attention to this and get the police involved. There's not much damage, only to the internal mailing system. Discretion is vital.'

'But we need to speak to . . .'

Miss Tandari's eyes were deep dark pools. She was not to be argued with. Brodie backed away as Miss Tandari turned and hurried into the hut.

'It's no good,' said Hunter as the door swung shut and the inside was cut off from view. 'We have to get Smithies' attention somehow.' He paused and then his face cracked into an eager smile. 'You two wait here. I'll be right back.'

It took about two minutes before he returned.

'So he really rides a unicycle?' Tusia gasped as Hunter emerged awkwardly from around the corner, the single wheel of the unicycle still severely buckled from the first-day encounter. 'He's really the most unusual person I've ever met.'

Brodie thought this was a little rich coming from a girl who kept league tables of Russian chess matches on her wall, but decided not to argue.

Hunter cycled perilously up to the high window and then, balancing his weight on the sill, he tapped rigorously. 'The guy's got to take notice from here,' he called over his shoulder. 'He's just got to.'

It was not at all likely that Smithies would notice Hunter, who was balancing precariously outside the window, if it weren't for the fact that the unicycle's wheel slipped from under him and left him suspended in midair, his face pressed sideways against the glass, before he crashed spread-eagled to the ground.

'Rather unfortunate timing, Mr Jenkins. We're in the middle of a crisis.' Smithies hurried from the hut, his face etched into worry lines and his left eye twitching a little.

Over Hunter's pain-dominated mutterings Brodie managed to blurt out about the message in the mail and a note they'd sent. Smithies stopped short, his left eye twitching so rapidly it looked as if it were dancing.

'A note,' he said, 'about the Firebird Code?'

'We've cracked it, sir,' Brodie said. 'We wanted to let you know.'

The colour seemed to ebb from the old man's face, his eyes stilled and for a moment it seemed to Brodie that he'd cry. Then he shook himself and his words were just a whisper. 'Let's get you three up to the billiard room. You've some explaining to do.'

Once Hunter was propped in the corner of the room on a rather moth-eaten sofa, Brodie talked through everything they'd discovered. Mr Smithies clapped his hands together in an obvious attempt to contain his excitement. 'Absolutely brilliant. Absolutely marvellous.'

From his persistent moans in the corner, Hunter

was finding it hard to agree.

'Have some water, boy,' Smithies said. 'You'll feel fine in a moment, I'm sure. And besides,' he added with a giggle, 'you'll have to be. The five of us are off to Brighton.'

'Brighton, sir?' said Brodie.

'Yes, Brighton. It all fits! The Royal Pavilion's a palace built in the middle of the seaside town and the prince who lived there created the whole place to look like a sort of fantasy world. By the time he became king he could hardly tell fantasy from reality. It all works perfectly with Van der Essen's choice of the story of Arthur. A king who wanted to bring about a new way of living. Perfect. Absolutely perfect. And of course the dragon reference in Van der Essen's letter fits too. The Royal Pavilion is absolutely teeming with dragons!'

Brodie tried not to look too scared.

'Not real ones of course. Ornamental dragons.' He looked like a child thinking about Christmas. 'What better place to hide something of such importance than a palace? Twenty-four-hour security, restricted access. It's all perfect. Now,' he said taking what appeared to be his first breath in many minutes. 'You need to go quickly and collect your code work so on the train I can make sure everything you've explained is true. It's important we keep our visit as low key as possible. A school trip to the Royal Pavilion. What could be suspicious about that?' At once his eyes darkened and the excitement which had lit his face seemed to fade. 'Tusia, take this to Ingham. He'll understand.'

Smithies thrust a small wooden model of an elephant into Tusia's hand.

'Mr Ingham will understand?' she mumbled.

'Jumbo Rush,' replied Smithies, his eyes dark. 'A code while we're away.' He caught his breath. 'When the workers of Station X were in a tricky situation during the war and they really needed to be vigilant, they got out this elephant as a visual reminder to take care. An elephant never forgets, you see.'

'Never forgets,' mumbled Tusia, making it sound a little as if she were taking an oath and had been instructed to repeat snatches of everything said to her.

'Yes. All the members of Veritas need to remain focused, even Ingham if we leave him in charge of the museum,' Smithies added forcibly. 'Because of the break-in here it looks highly likely your deciphering's been intercepted. If that's the case then a new race against the clock's on the cards.'

Hunter pulled himself up to sitting and wobbled a little before speaking. Brodie noted an egg-like lump appearing on his forehead. 'Who do you think is after the code solution, sir?' he said faintly.

Mr Smithies frowned. 'I shall explain everything on the train.'

Kerrith Vernan sat in the foyer of the penthouse boardroom suite sipping nervously at her cup of cappuccino. She'd met the Director of Level Five of the Black Chamber on only two previous occasions and her nerves were causing the bone china cup to shake a little in her hand, light flashing from the diamond on her ring.

When the phone rang the noise shattered the silence. The receptionist lifted the receiver and cradled it against her ear. She listened for a moment then replaced the handset. 'You can go through now.'

The office was oval in shape. The wooden floor was spread with a deep carpet on the centre of which was embroidered an elaborate crest. In front of three long picture-windows were two flags. One was the Union flag and the other the flag of the Chamber. In front of these was an ornately carved wooden desk and behind the desk, in a high-backed leather chair, sat the Director. He looked up as Kerrith approached.

He was not a large man. In many ways the grandeur of his office overwhelmed him. His shoulders were hunched and his shirt loose around the collar as if it'd been chosen for someone bigger. But his eyes revealed a resolve that wouldn't weaken.

Kerrith mumbled an introduction and the Director leant back in his chair. 'I know who you are, Miss Vernan,' he said pointedly. 'What I need to know is how reliable your information is.'

Kerrith coughed quietly into her hand. 'Totally reliable, sir,' she said.

'And there can be absolutely no doubt?'

'None at all, sir.'

'And Van der Essen's phoenix? What'd you suppose this is?'

Kerrith considered her answer. 'Since our activities in Belgium, we know Van der Essen was a professor interested in MS 408.'

The Director's voice showed he'd understood this point. 'But the phoenix?'

'We're not sure, sir. But whatever it is, those has-been halfwits seemed keen to find it. It must be of interest.'

The Director swivelled round in the chair, surveying the scene from the window. He sighed as if he were considering his options, then moved round on the chair once more to face her. 'I suppose for someone as new to the Chamber as you, it's hard to understand the risk we face if news leaks out.' He ran his finger momentarily around the back of his collar and loosened his tie. 'Here,' he said, standing and walking towards a set of shelves along one wall of the room. 'Perhaps this will make it clear.'

On the shelf was a small bronze figurine of a horse and rider rearing up in battle. The Director locked his hand around the head of the rider and tilted the figurine back in his hand. To the left of the shelving a picture of a pastoral scene glided, almost imperceptibly, to the left. There was a click. The Director slid the picture further like a door to reveal a small cupboard with a keypad on the door. He tapped the keys and the door itself clicked open.

Inside was a small leather-bound folder tied closed with a red ribbon. He took it out and waited a while, the folder in his hand.

'This is a record of all the crazy and dangerous theories that've existed about MS 408,' he said and his words were hushed. 'It's a record of careers lost and reputations ruined. A warning to us all,' he added.

Kerrith was unsure how to answer.

'There are some who believe MS 408 is a book of great meaning, a text that will reveal a great secret. There are many who see it as a guidebook to another world in our own if we can only work out the code in which the secrets are recorded.'

'And you don't believe that?' Kerrith asked, her desire for answers overtaking her need for politeness.

'There are no worlds within worlds, Miss Vernan. There's only what we see around us. What we know to be fact. Chasing after the end of the rainbow is a childish dream. One we should leave behind.' He stood himself up taller. 'Our job on Level Five is to clarify tangible, believable truths, not try and catch or bottle shadows.' He sniffed as if the folder he held was reeking an unbearable smell. 'They're all listed here, you know. Newbold and Levitov; that meddling Fabyan woman; even Ingham, Friedman and Bray. Their crazy notions about MS 408 stored for posterity. But that's where they should remain. Locked away, forgotten, and discredited for the lies they are.'

Kerrith tried to smile.

'If what you tell me is true and Smithies really has been working on trying to translate the manuscript, then he must be stopped. For centuries we've worked to eliminate any study or publication of documents that support belief in fancies and not tangible facts.' He twisted a silver ring on his finger bearing the mark Kerrith had seen stamped on the copies of MS 408. The same emblem on the carpet. The Director saw her watching. 'History bears record to the lives of great men and women who've done their best to prevent these stories and imaginings being given life,' he said. 'I value your commitment to the cause, Miss Vernan. It will not go unacknowledged.' His hand stilled on the ring and then moved to press once more on the cover of the document he held. 'If the ideas contained in this folder were given public airing there'd be mass panic. Public order would be at risk. If the theories were proved to be true our understanding of what's real in our world would change.'

Kerrith felt her heart quicken a little. 'You're sure the theories are untrue?' she asked.

The Director rocked back his head to laugh. Then his eyes darkened, almost pityingly. 'It doesn't matter whether they're true or not,' he said, and each word was spoken carefully as if he were afraid his words would betray him. 'What matters is that we on Level Five are in control. We are the keepers of secrets, the guardians of mystery.' He put the folder back in the confines of the secret cupboard and swung the picture back across the door. 'As members of Level Five, working for the Ministry of Information, we're in the business of ensuring belief in what can be seen and tested. We're not here to chase dreams and myths.'

Kerrith felt her brow furrow into lines.

The Director inclined his head to study her. 'You

were under the impression Level Five had another purpose?' he asked.

'I just thought—'

He didn't let her finish. 'It's not important what you thought, Miss Vernan. You are, at the moment, a Level Four employee. What matters is what I think. And I'm here to tell you whatever mysteries are contained in the pages of MS 408 that's what they are to remain. Mysteries.' He walked back to his desk and sat down again, spreading his hands across the polished rosewood before looking up. 'I'm exceptionally grateful to you for bringing this matter to my attention. You shall of course be amply rewarded for your services.'

Kerrith felt her grin widen.

'But first we must catch those responsible for meddling.' He hesitated for only a moment. 'Smithies should've known better.'

He glanced at his watch. 'You should take the pavilion yourself. Catch the team before it can do any public damage. I shall send agents out to the homes of the children to explain the termination of this ridiculous schooling system Smithies has had the audacity to launch. If we work quickly the whole matter can be wrapped up in hours.' He sighed again. 'Make sure there are no mistakes,' he added sharply.

Kerrith lowered her head.

'I'm not surprised about the pavilion by the way,' he said. 'We had our suspicions in the 1970s and there was an incident we hoped would mean the end of the matter. We can't be entirely sure we dealt with it fully. So, whatever you do, make sure they don't leave with any documentation that could give them answers. Tell them whatever they'll believe to make them leave it behind. Use your powers of deception, for if ever there was a time they were needed, it's now.'

Kerrith's hand poised on the handle of the door.

'And one other thing,' the Director called. 'Be careful of the girl. Tell her anything that'll stop her. But be sure never to share the truth. I'm trusting you with a great task, Agent Vernan.'

Kerrith mumbled a thank you, but as she clicked the door behind her she knew she'd barely begun. She was going to bring Smithies down. Smithies and his team of children.

Ambition to be the very best pulsed in her veins. And children had been trusted with the secrets of MS 408 when Smithies had never trusted her.

It was time for payback. And she was going to enjoy every moment.

Beyond the Thunder Dragons

'You're telling me this isn't an official Study Group?' Brodie felt her stomach tighten with fear.

'Not unofficial, exactly,' Smithies said, pushing his glasses up on to his forehead in an obviously futile attempt to allow him to focus on the problem. 'Just not government backed, or government approved, or . . .' he hesitated for a moment, 'to be entirely precise, not government known about.' He was clearly agitated.

'So,' Tusia said, trying to bring Smithies back round to the question in hand. 'Does that mean what we're doing, learning about codes, is something we shouldn't be doing?'

Smithies closed the door of the train carriage and leant against it. 'There's lots of interpretations of the word "should". It's very easy to make generalisations.'

'Mr Smithies.' Hunter was speaking now, his lumpy forehead shining with the deepest of purple bruises. 'Just tell us please, if the government found out we're being trained in codes and ciphers and we're trying to translate the Voynich Manuscript, would that be a bad thing?'

It was Miss Tandari who answered. 'Yes, it'd be bad. Very bad.'

'We knew it,' yelped Brodie. 'We said you weren't telling us everything! How can you not have told us? Why's it so bad?'

Miss Tandari looked over to Smithies as if seeking permission to go on. He nodded. 'The government has no belief in the old way of code-cracking and they certainly don't believe children should be involved.'

'But you did?'

'We *do*,' Miss Tandari added emphasis to her use of the present tense. 'But there are rules.'

'What rules?'

'Any work on MS 408's been a source of great embarrassment to the government. There was some awful incident in the nineties where a worker in the Black Chamber claimed to come very close to finding a solution. There was a big rumpus, and of course the theory about the manuscript turned out to be completely flawed.'

'It wasn't Friedman's fault,' Smithies interjected. 'He made an understandable error and paid dearly for his mistake.'

'Who's Friedman?' asked Brodie. The name seemed familiar. 'And what do you mean "paid dearly"?'

'Friedman's the grandson of the American Friedmans. The ones who set up the First Study Group on MS 408. Interest in the manuscript's in his blood. Like it's in all of yours.' Just for a second a shadow swept across Smithies' face.

'And the "paid dearly" bit?' Brodie pressed again, sensing Smithies had hoped not to answer this part of her question.

The old man continued, his voice a little shaky. 'He lost his job, was banished from the Chamber.' He raised his hands in defeat. 'And then we all paid, as MS 408 became officially "Off Limits". Slapping a D notice on the document meant no one could go near it. It's banned. Against the rules to try and read it.' He paused. 'So you can see that setting up a school and Study Group to look at the secrets of the manuscript wouldn't go down well with the powers that be.'

Brodie felt a wave of urgency. A burning sensation in the back of her throat. 'Do you really think the manuscript has a secret worth breaking all the rules for?'

Smithies' eyes were the cool, opaque green of agate stone. He looked suddenly incredibly sad. 'People have searched for centuries to find the meaning of the manuscript,' he whispered. 'And some of those searchers have paid with their lives. It seems to me the document must contain some secret those in power are keen to keep undiscovered. And there are those,' he added, 'who fought against the very worst that history had to offer to keep the manuscript safe. Van der Essen rescued what he knew from the flames of war. Surely we owe it to him and those who followed him, to find out what secret was worth so much.' He twisted his hands together and Brodie thought for the first time how old he looked, how frail. 'But,' Smithies added with a smile, 'I never intended you all to be involved in some race against the authorities. It's why we didn't tell you. If this is all too much, if we're expecting more than you can give, then we can go home. It's up to you.'

Something in the way Smithies said 'home' made Brodie believe he wasn't talking about Bletchley. He was saying it could all be over. Finished. This could be the end.

She looked around the carriage at Hunter, his face bruised and his eyes narrowed, and at Tusia, her hands folded in her lap as if she was waiting for someone else to decide for them. For someone to tell them what was best to do.

Outside, against the moving window of the train, it'd begun to rain.

The car which pulled up in front of the house had the sort of darkened windows Brodie's grandfather associated with film stars. The sort that allowed those inside to look out but made it impossible to look in. Mr Bray craned his head around the curtain and watched as a tall willowy-looking man, wearing a suit buttoned high to a mandarin collar at the neck, slid out of the car. The man's shoes were sharp and pointed at the toe, reminding Mr Bray of the child catcher from *Chitty Chitty Bang Bang*. The woman with him was by all polite forms of measure a large woman. She had a hard-looking face Mr Bray instantly took a dislike to. He welcomed the visitors graciously into his home though, and poured them two glasses of home-made lemonade.

Mr Bray was a very patient man but as the visitors spoke it was as much as he could do not to take the paper parasol he'd placed in his own glass of lemonade and crumple it between his fingers.

When the man in the suit had finished speaking, Mr Bray coughed politely into his hand. 'It's very kind of you,' he said through teeth barely separated, 'to alert me to the educational needs of my granddaughter. I appreciate the time you've taken explaining the home schooling rules to me.' He coughed again. 'I have to say though, I'm more than happy with the arrangements at Station X. Brodie's getting a far more meaningful education than she ever got in the school down the road, what with their obsession with levels and targets. If the government had left them alone and allowed teachers to do their job, it would've been a far happier place.' He put his now empty glass down on the table and the paper parasol rocked gently backwards and forwards beside it. 'So thank you very much for your time, but Brodie will be staying right where she is.'

As far as Mr Bray was concerned the conversation was at an end. His guests had other ideas. 'It's disappointing,' the man in the sharp suit said. 'We thought maybe we could reason with you, Mr Bray. After all, I'm surprised after what happened to her mother, you want Brodie having anything to do with MS 408.' He straightened the cuffs of his sleeves and pushed his lips together into the shape of an unsettling smile. 'How much of the truth does your granddaughter really know?' he asked.

Mr Bray sat straighter in the chair. 'I'll thank you

not to talk of my daughter,' he said, without lifting his head.

The man in the suit simply nodded. 'Very well, Mr Bray. Consider the matter closed.' He got up then and turned as if to make for the door. 'But I should warn you it's not the only thing that will remain closed.' His laugh was thin. He pulled out a folder from a shiny black briefcase, withdrew a single sheet of paper and put it down on the table with the careful precision of a surgeon.

It'd been a while since Mr Bray had had dealings with official documents, but it didn't take him long to work out what this was. Nor did it take him long to crush the paper parasol in his hand, or reach for his bicycle clips.

'I'll go and get some food from the buffet car,' Smithies said at last. 'Brodie, will you help me carry things?'

Brodie knew from the way his brow was furrowing this was not a rhetorical question and only for a second did she consider arguing.

'So?' he said as they negotiated walking in the moving carriage. 'Do you want to end it now?'

Brodie shrugged her shoulders. 'It doesn't seem right,' she said, 'breaking the rules to try and break the code.'

He smiled as if her confusion made sense to him. 'Brodie,' he said with a sigh, 'do you know the story of Plato's cave?'

Brodie shook her head. The look on Smithies' face suggested it wouldn't be a simple story. She waited.

'The Greek philosopher Plato told a story long ago, about a cave. People were born and raised in the cave and they were held prisoner there all their lives. They were forced to stare at a wall, looking only at shadows that moved across the stone.'

Brodie didn't think much of the story so far.

'One day, for a reason we don't quite understand, one of the prisoners was freed. He was allowed out of the cave and into the world and there he saw things he'd never seen before, the beauty of the sun and the flowers and the trees.'

She had to admit the story was improving.

'The escaped prisoner returned to the cave to tell others of the brilliant things he'd seen.'

'And?'

'They didn't believe him. They said he was mad.'

'Oh.'

'Not the happy ending you were hoping for?'

Brodie shook her head again.

'The point is, Brodie, he got to see the trees and the flowers and the sun. And if those he told didn't believe him then it didn't make what he saw not true. It just meant they hadn't seen them too. I expect you're wondering why I've told you this story.'

The thought had crossed her mind.

Smithies leant forward. 'Because I think, Brodie, that you and I, and the others in Veritas are like the prisoner who escaped from the cave.'

'You do?'

'We've got a chance to see things how they really are, and perhaps there'll be those who won't agree with us taking a look. But it doesn't make it wrong for us to do so.' He paused. 'I don't want you to do anything you're not happy with. But we've come this close to making an important discovery.' He held his hands fractions away from each other as if he were about to clap. 'Do you really want to stop now?'

Brodie didn't know what to say.

'You know all the best reformers in the land have opposed laws they haven't agreed with in an attempt to bring about change. If the government's wrong we should make a stand.' He smiled. 'I believe MS 408 has secrets worth sharing, and I know your mother believed that too. The law says children can't be taught code-cracking. It's a bad law. The law says MS 408 need never be translated. It's a bad law. But if we are to break the code, Brodie, we have to break the rules.' He waited for a moment before he went on. 'But I'll understand your decision if you want to give up.'

'You will?'

'Of course. I was foolish to expect you to believe in the project as much as I do. As much as your grandparents and your mother did.'

'But . . .'

He raised his hand as if to demonstrate he hadn't finished speaking. 'Your granddad, Hunter's parents, Tusia's. They all agreed to your involvement, but that's not enough any more. I suppose I just hoped it'd matter more *to you*. The truth, I mean.'

'It does!'

His eyebrow twitched.

Brodie made a study of the train carpet. There was a rather nasty Ribena stain below her toes. 'But if we carry on, the officials from the government, or whoever, will stop us, won't they? You've said that.'

Smithies shook his head. 'I've said they'll try and stop us. There's a difference.'

Brodie was getting tired of the way Smithies insisted on precision. She supposed that's what made him a good code-cracker. She was surprised to find, when she looked up, he'd carried on speaking.

'Look, Brodie. You're absolutely right. We should've

explained "Veritas" was not only a secret from the general public, but from the government itself. We should've explained we'd no official backing. That what you were really involved in was a secret inside a secret. But we didn't. Now you can, as I think you want to, leave the train at the next station and return to the life you left behind, or . . .' and here he hesitated for a moment, 'you can choose to go on and face the consequences. Perhaps we'll get there first. Perhaps the Ministry officials won't catch us and we'll find whatever was hidden by the mark of the Firebird and a truth the government's scared to let us find. But whatever you decide, know I'm grateful to you.'

'Grateful?'

'Before Veritas re-formed, before the work at Station X, I believed the thrill of the code was over. Now I'm in a race to find a manuscript hidden in a palace. I've escaped from the cave. The excitement of the code doesn't get much better than that.'

Brodie looked down at the floor, a lump forming thick in her throat.

Outside the window, trees flashed past in a blur. She closed her eyes and tried to steady herself. There were three more minutes left until the station. Smithies walked slowly back to the carriage.

* * *

Friedman sat alone in the Bletchley Park railway station café. Outside it'd just begun to rain. The water ran in rivulets down the windowpane. He looked at his watch. Smithies was late. He slurped a mouthful of tea. The undissolved sugar was gritty on his tongue.

Behind the counter, Gordon reset the telephone receiver on the cradle. He rubbed his head. Working near Bletchley was getting to him. He needed a break. A change of scene. Still, the message had been clear and he knew the man on the end of the telephone line would make good his payment. He was good with tipping too, so it was best to go with the flow. He wiped his hands purposefully down the front of his apron then took an apple cream puff from the chiller cabinet and slipped it on to a plate.

Once Gordon reached him, the seated man looked up, surprise written on his face. Gordon cleared his throat nervously before putting the apple cream puff down on the table. 'Your friend says to tell you they only serve cakes as good as these at the Prince Regent's home in Brighton.'

Friedman's brow creased into lines. 'Excuse me?'

'Your friend said to tell you they only serve cakes this good at the Prince Regent's home in Brighton.'

Gordon wondered, after the man rose from the table and ran from the café, whether it would be entirely inappropriate to replace the apple cream puff in the chiller cabinet. The man, after all, had never even touched it.

'I think we should go on.' Brodie stood in the doorway to the carriage, her arms keeping the sliding doors separate.

Smithies made his relief obvious with a sigh.

'I mean it seems a bit mad to give up now.'

Hunter smiled and then winced as his forehead obviously caused him immense pain. 'So you're not worried about the government officials who may be chasing us?' he asked cautiously.

'Course I am! We may not be fast enough for them. So we must make sure we are.'

Tusia laughed. 'Nice one, sister.'

'We must stay focused and determined and whatever happens we must get to the phoenix before they do.'

Hunter clapped his hands. 'So we're back in the race then?'

Brodie nodded. 'We're back in the race.' She pulled the carriage doors closed behind her and looked first to Smithies and then to Miss Tandari, who were both beaming broadly. 'So who's going to tell us about the Pavilion?'

* * *

Miss Tandari did the explaining. Built by the demand of the Prince, the Pavilion looked like an Indian building from the outside, but once inside the decoration was mainly Chinese. According to Miss Tandari, the Prince had never been to either China or India and neither had his architects or builders, but what they created was a palace by the sea which from outside was topped with minarets and domes, and inside was packed with, as Smithies had already told them, statues, pictures and carvings of mythical beasts. 'Ideal place for a phoenix,' added Miss Tandari. 'We just have to use our wits and the original letter from Van der Essen to find it.'

They ran all the way from Brighton station. The town was bustling with people and it seemed odd to Brodie that so many of them walked past the Royal Pavilion without even giving it a second glance, as if it wasn't really there.

'Like the scabbard,' panted Smithies. 'People just take the building for granted but if you step back and consider, it's really a remarkable thing.'

The palace was long and surrounded by gardens but not far from the main road. It was a creamy stone colour with high French windows along the side topped with patterned stone fretwork. An Indian castle dropped into an English town. What struck

The Royal Pavilion

Built by demand of the Prince

Looks Indian from the outside, but inside decoration is mainly Chinese

The Prince, his architects and his builders had never been to India or China!

Statues, pictures & carvings of mythical beasts

* Used as a hospital for Indian soldiers during WW1

The Music Room was shut for 11 years after an arson attack in 1975!

Brodie most were the domes. One huge central dome was ringed with petal-shaped windows like a belt around its middle, and to either side were smaller domes ornately decorated.

'Not bad for a seaside retreat?' Smithies smiled, hurrying them towards the main door. 'Although you can see why many people thought the place was vulgar and over the top.'

Brodie thought it was simply beautiful.

Smithies gathered the group together just outside the main door. 'Now remember. We're on a school visit. Researching the Prince. Don't draw attention to yourself but don't miss any details – however small. Think about Van der Essen's letter. We're looking for

The phoenix of power
In her cloak of elfin Urim
She who is wrongly considered to
Fly lower than the rightful dragon.'

Brodie wrinkled her nose and repeated the phrase in her head. Then she followed the others towards the pavilion entrance.

'You know, I've been thinking about part of the code,' said Tusia shuffling to the front. 'The whole *flying lower* bit. It's to do with use of space, right. And it must mean the idea phoenixes fly lower than dragons is wrong, if you know what I mean.'

Brodie chewed this over. 'I guess that's what it means. *Wrongly considered to fly lower* and all that. But that's weird.'

'Why?' pressed Hunter.

'Because in the ancient myths of China there's a rule,' she said. 'I've read about it.'

'What haven't you read about?' Hunter jibed before frowning when Smithies glared.

'In the ancient stories a dragon represents males and the phoenix a female. And in tradition males are more important than females.'

'Well, it's hard to argue.'

Now Tusia glared at Hunter and for good measure dug him hard in the ribs. '*Ancient tradition*,' she said, emphasising her words.

'Anyway, a dragon should always fly higher than a phoenix. That's the rule of the story.'

Miss Tandari held her hand up and caused them all to halt. 'You're probably right, Brodie. I mean about the legend. But the designers of the Pavilion weren't really clear on all the rules about China and its traditions. None of them had ever been to Asia and there's rumour they did all sorts of crazy things like copy Chinese phrases from packing-cases down at the docks instead of checking out what they said.' She laughed. 'They literally copied things like "this way up" and "handle with care" and then painted them beautifully in Chinese characters on the walls of this place. They'll have got things wrong, that's for sure. They might not have known dragons were supposed to fly higher than firebirds. But they certainly tried to make things look good here, for anyone who didn't know the rules.'

'Let's see how good,' said Smithies, taking charge of the tickets, and stuffing the offered souvenir guidebook into a large brown paper bag. Miss Tandari led the three of them through an octagonal hallway into the main entrance hall.

'Look,' gestured Hunter. 'There really are dragons everywhere.' On the wall, either side of a gilt-framed mirror, were raised white panels on which dragons coiled protectively, and in small glass windows high above the doorway olive green dragons were framed by the painted golden rays of the sun.

'The Prince certainly liked his mythical beasts,' laughed Smithies.

'And bright colours,' added Tusia who'd made her way to the front and was heading out into what the signs told them was the 'long gallery'. 'My mum would have a field day in here.'

Brodie tried to take it all in. Pink walls painted with pictures of blue bamboo; statues of Chinese court officials; tiny golden bells hanging all along the top of the wall and great skylights painted with pictures. 'That's Lei Gong, the Chinese God of Thunder,' said Brodie, craning her neck to see more clearly the stained glass of the skylight above her. 'I think I've read in Chinese myth he always had two thunder dragons with him. Look.'

Hunter glanced up. 'Your obsession with stories may come in handy here.'

There were few other visitors, it being quite late in the afternoon. An elderly woman with a folded pink umbrella was giving an over-wordy lecture to a group of bored-looking tourists. They were bunched round a large mantel clock in the form of Cupid driving through clouds in a chariot, being pulled along by butterflies. Smithies led the way quickly past them, hurrying through the gallery as if mere speed alone would help them find what they looked for. When they came to the banqueting room though, his feet slowed to a stop. Brodie had been impressed by the ballroom at Bletchley. The long gallery in the Pavilion was certainly quite stunning.

But the Banqueting Room was something else.

A long table ran down the centre of the room,

groaning under the weight of plates and golden cutlery. On the window side, the room was decked with gold and red curtains topped with figurines of golden dragons. Huge pictures of Chinese art framed with burnt gold hung on the walls and the ceiling arced above them. The rest of the walls were covered with patterned golden paper showing dragons and stars and planets. But it was the chandeliers hung from the ceiling that caused Brodie to wobble a little as she looked. Appearing to fly free beneath a canopy of leaves was an enormous silver and gold dragon. In its claws hung a crystal chandelier so large Brodie was sure it'd be possible for a grown man to hide in the falls of crystal and not be seen. Around the light, six more dragons reared upwards. Each held another light in their mouth, shaped like overlapping tongues of flame.

'Now that's surely what you call elfin Urim,' said Tusia. 'Amazing use of the space in here.'

It was a while before Brodie tore her gaze away from the central light and looked around the rest of the room. It was then she saw them.

Suspended in the four corners of the massive hall were four more spectacular lights, each hanging from a glittering star of crystal and gold. Yet above each star, carrying the light on a silver collar tight around her neck, tail spread in flight and wings wide, was a golden phoenix.

Brodie could barely speak. 'Look. Look.' She jabbed at Hunter's arm and he switched his gaze from the central chandelier to the edge of the room. 'Do you see?' she said. 'A firebird in flight.'

She looked back at the dragon chandelier weighed down by the crystal and the gold. Then back at the firebirds as they flew high towards the ceiling, their outstretched beaks almost touching the painted canopy above them.

Suddenly she was aware of someone twitching excitedly beside her.

'It's wrong,' Tusia yelped. 'The lights are wrong.'

The others gathered closer. Brodie was just getting herself ready to deflect Tusia's moaning about the amount of money which had obviously been splashed around to pay for the amazing chandeliers. Surely even Tusia understood princes were allowed to spend money.

'I mean the position of the light is wrong.'

'You think there's a better way to hang chandeliers other than from the ceiling?' said Hunter quizzically.

'It's what I said about "flying lower". Remember? When we were just coming in and we talked about how the designers might have got things wrong.'

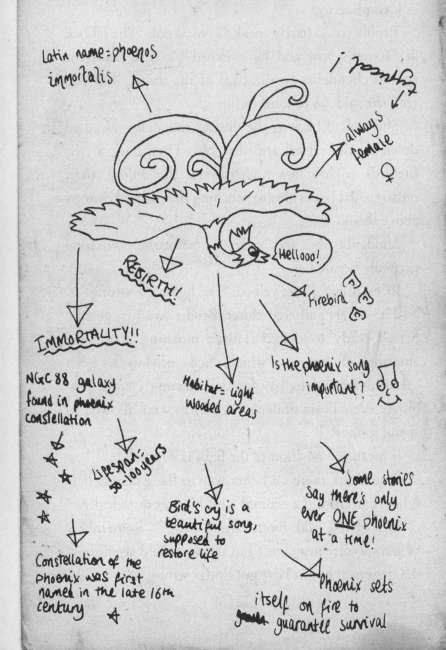

'And B was going on about her story and boys being more important than girls.'

Brodie knew Hunter was teasing but she was too intrigued to let him get to her.

'Yes, Brodie was going on about a story. And the story said the dragon has to fly higher than the phoenix. She said that was the rule of the story. And in here . . .' Tusia pointed up again at the impressive chandeliers. 'Here the phoenixes are flying higher.'

'And?' mumbled Hunter.

'So the clue said *she who is wrongly considered to fly lower than the rightful dragon.* We said it's talking about where the dragon and the phoenix fly.'

'And?'

'And in here the dragon isn't right. You see? It's a play on words. The *rightful dragon* isn't right. It's too low down and the phoenix is too high.'

'You think the light's connected to the clue?' said Hunter.

'It could be. I mean, it's a mistake, the position of the lights.' Tusia turned to face Miss Tandari. 'You said the designers of the Pavilion hadn't been to India or China. They might've included pictures and ideas from the myths they heard and not quite got the details right. But Van der Essen. He was a myth master. You told us that. He was a specialist in ancient stories and so he'd have known the lights in this room were wrong.'

'And so,' cut in Brodie, catching Tusia's train of thought, 'perhaps he wanted us to see the light and connect it to the clue.'

'OK,' said Hunter. 'So we make the connection. Now what?'

Brodie bit the inside of her lip. She tried to take the jumble of ideas bouncing in her head and line them up. 'The "phoenix" we seek is somewhere in the Pavilion. And if we follow the clue from these lights then it's high up. Above the dragons? Somewhere it shouldn't be.'

'Exactly!' Tusia couldn't have looked more relieved.

'You think Van der Essen hid whatever we're looking for in one of the phoenix chandeliers?' asked Hunter.

Brodie didn't. 'It's got to be safe and hidden but not somewhere people are going to look just by chance. But, it's got to be higher than all the dragons we see.'

'But there are dragons painted all over the place. You think the phoenix has got to be higher than all of them?' Hunter asked, visibly bracing himself for another jab in the ribs.

Brodie wasn't sure. It was a guess. But the position of the phoenix lights flying higher than the dragon made the guess seem sensible.

Notes on the "rightful dragon"

Latin name: draco.

Habitat = varied!
Mountains + caverns
or underwater

5 types of dragon

- European
- Near
- Middle Eastern
- Indian
- Oriental

Flys higher than a phoenix

Dragon slayers aim for the soft underbelly of the dragon

Draco = dragon = 4 legs
Wyvern dragon = 2 legs
Not a 'real' dragon

Lifespan:
More than 400 years!

Can dragons breathe fire?!

What does "rightful" mean?!
- In charge?
- In control?
- True??

'So where in this place is higher than all the dragons?' said Tandi.

'The sky itself?' said Hunter, who was obviously struggling to stick with the idea.

'Well,' began Tusia, who'd been busy flicking through the Pavilion guidebook, 'what about in a room with a picture of the sky painted on the ceiling?'

'Yes,' answered Smithies, who was still looking at the chandeliers and had missed Tusia's hunt through the guidebook. 'If only we knew if there was such a room.'

Tusia flapped the open book in front of him. 'There is, look,' she said. 'The saloon.'

Tusia was right. The ceiling of the saloon was domed and high and on its surface were painted swirling clouds against a cotton blue. A floor-to-ceiling gilt-edged mirror reflected back the many painted silk hangings which lined the walls, on top of silvered wallpaper. The room was round and crowded with furniture, an oval table supported by golden dolphins and several chairs covered with green buttoned satin.

'In here then,' Smithies said frantically. 'You think the Professor hid the phoenix here in a room with a painted sky?'

Brodie looked around. 'Maybe?' she said desperately.

A guard sitting in the corner on an upright wooden chair nodded acknowledgement to them and, as if in an attempt to cover for their rather rushed entry to the room, Smithies smiled and engaged him in conversation. 'Nice room,' he said. 'Very nice ceiling.'

The guard smiled knowledgeably. 'Certainly is, sir.' He stood up and puffed out his chest. 'This room was the centre of the original design of the Pavilion when it was merely called the Marine Pavilion.'

'Yes, fascinating,' snapped Smithies, in a way suggesting it was anything but.

His impatience seemed to be lost on the guard, who'd obviously had little chance to share his information with anybody yet that day and needed to demonstrate his knowledge.

'See, not many people know you're standing now underneath the very central dome of the Pavilion.' He glanced up at the sky pattern above him in such a way as to suggest he was responsible for placing the huge dome structure there himself.

'And we can go up into this domed room then?' asked Smithies, a look of concentration stretching across his face.

The guard paced back and forth in front of the fireplace. 'No, sir. There's no room in the dome of the Pavilion.'

227

Brodie stepped forward. 'But I saw windows in the dome when I was outside.'

'An observant one you've got yourself there,' smiled the guard. 'Not a lot of people notice that. Or even ask.'

'So was there a room then, once?' asked Tusia.

The guard was warming to his audience. 'Story goes there was to be a terraced room up there. The most splendid room in all the palace.'

'But there never was?'

The guard shook his head. 'Our Prince was a one for the good things in life. By the time he was King he weighed twenty-three stone!' He drew in a breath in a dramatic whistle. 'He was so large he took to wearing corsets on his thighs as well as his stomach and without his corset, his belly reached down to his knees.'

Brodie was just trying to rid her mind of such a revolting image when Smithies spoke again. 'And the relevance of this detail is what exactly?'

'Well, because the King became so large, going upstairs became impossible for him. So the room in the dome of the building never got finished. Not proper like.'

A thought was formulating in Brodie's mind. Half formed at the moment like a wisp of cloud. 'So there's a half-finished room above this false sky?' she said.

The guard's radio began to crackle and he drew it from his belt holster like a cowboy drawing a gun and began to fiddle with the knobs on the top. The crackling continued unabated and a woman's voice blared out.

'And this room? Or half-room?' Miss Tandari asked anxiously. 'How'd you get up there? If you could.'

The guard hesitated, distracted by his radio. 'Well, not a lot of people know there's a fair bit of this pavilion that's hidden. Kept from view, you see. Servant's corridors, tunnels. And . . .' The female screeched over the airwaves again. 'Sorry. If you just let me take this.'

Brodie looked frantically at Smithies as the guard lifted the radio to his ear. The female voice continued.

'Please. If you don't mind,' said Smithies, his eyes now so wide Brodie was sure they'd tumble from their sockets. 'We'd reach this half-finished room how exactly?'

The guard lowered his radio. 'Stairs,' he said. 'Hidden stairs.'

'Brilliant!' yelped Tusia, who then stuffed her hand into her mouth in an attempt to look more discreet.

The group turned and was hurrying from the saloon when the guard called to them. 'My radio,' he said, 'front desk just called me on my radio, so as I could let you know the other teacher from your school has just arrived.'

Brodie's blood seemed to run like cold water through her body.

A vein on Smithies' forehead began to pulse.

Hunter let out a quiet moan.

'Front desk says Miss Vernan is glad you managed to make it down here so quickly.' Smithies eyes darkened as the guard added, 'And she's brought some friends and they're looking forward to catching up with you.'

Smithies stumbled to a halt. The guidebook fell from his fingers. 'Of all those in the Chamber. Of all those who'd want to stop us,' he said darkly. 'I should've guessed it'd be her.'

10

Above a Painted Sky

'There's nothing for it. We'll have to face her.' Smithies' face was grave and his brow was creased into deep worry lines.

'What, and give up the search?' Hunter gasped.

'But if we continue, and are successful, then we lead her straight to the phoenix, and she'll take it from us and we'll never know the truth Van der Essen wanted us to know.'

'We could split up,' Miss Tandari whispered nervously. 'Some of us stall her while the rest keep searching.'

Smithies looked behind him down the long gallery. It was empty but he could hear voices. People getting nearer. 'You lot go,' he said and there was a sorrow mixed with steely determination in his eyes. 'You find the phoenix and I'll hold Kerrith back.'

Miss Tandari reached out for his arm. 'You're sure?'

'This was always about the power of youth, wasn't it?' Smithies said wistfully. 'Now go. Before it's too late.'

Brodie turned but Tusia stood rooted to the spot. 'I'll stay,' she said. 'I can help make things safer for the rest of you. Provide a distraction. A Petulova speciality,' she added.

Before the others could argue she began to make a wailing noise. A sort of guttural gasping. Then she bent herself in two, clutching at her stomach. 'Panic attack,' she squeaked, winking beneath the fall of auburn hair. 'Need help. Lots of help.'

Smithies swung into action. 'Give her space, please. Lots of space. Poor girl can't breathe.' And taking her cue from his outstretched hand, Miss Tandari grabbed Brodie and Hunter by the arm, ducked below the view of the guard and began to run.

Behind them Brodie could hear continued wailing, the guard calling frantically into his radio for assistance and new voices in the saloon.

With a glance over her shoulder Brodie saw Tusia sprawled across the Axminister carpet. She was breathing fast into a brown paper bag Smithies had thrust into her hands. And she was positioned perfectly, across the open doorway, cleverly preventing anyone

232

from getting past her into the room beyond.

'Shape and space,' Brodie called to Hunter. 'It's "her thing".'

Hunter nodded, leading the way.

'We've only a few moments,' Miss Tandari gasped as they ran. 'Vernan won't want to break with her story about being a teacher from Pembroke or the guards'll be suspicious. So she's trapped for a while. But Smithies won't be able to hold her back for long. Everything depends on speed.'

The three of them stormed down the long gallery, beneath the skylight picture of the thunder dragons. A curling stairway, with bamboo balustrades, took them to the second level past a room painted poppy red, before they came to another long gallery whose walls were painted vivid azure blue. There were no windows but two huge daylights painted with swooping dragons and large winged bats. One wall was lined with doorways. Beside each panelled door stretched tall blue marble columns topped with wooden statues of fierce mythical beasts which Brodie sensed were keeping guard.

Miss Tandari stopped, panting, and pressed her hand to her side.

'The doors,' said Hunter urgently. 'Maybe one of these doors leads to the secret stairs.'

Miss Tandari looked along the line of wall. Above each doorway, painted in scarlet, were Chinese characters. Snatches of Chinese writing. She rubbed her temples, her eyes narrowed in concentration.

'So which one?' Brodie hissed, wondering desperately if Tusia's distraction was still holding Vernan back. 'How d'we know which door?'

'We try them,' said Miss Tandari, lurching forward.

'Hold on,' called Hunter, grabbing her arm. 'Wait. Look.' He pointed up at the Chinese writing above the doors. 'It's wrong,' he muttered, 'like the phoenix flying too high.'

'What d'you mean?' asked Brodie, hopping from one foot to the other and not at all encouraged by the look of concentration on Hunter's face.

'My parents made me study Chinese writing once, in an attempt to distract me from my maths obsession. It didn't work,' he said proudly. 'Do you have any idea how many different figures there are in ancient Chinese writings?' he said.

Brodie's hopping was getting rather vigorous. 'Ermm. If this reminiscing isn't going to get us up to the roof room then . . .'

Hunter nodded an apology. 'Yep. Sorry. Anyway, I didn't learn much but I picked up enough to know the characters are wrong.' He wrinkled his forehead.

'You'd expect the phrases above the doors to say something clever or suggest a good luck wish, but these don't.'

Miss Tandari widened her eyes in understanding but Brodie still had no idea what he meant.

'You *said* the designers just copied Chinese writing they saw on boxes down at the docks,' he blurted in Miss Tandari's direction. 'Phrases they saw which actually meant things like "be careful" or "don't drop this".'

Brodie pushed her fingers into her hair in a wave of frustration. 'Both of you, please. We don't have time for this. Which door?'

Hunter stumbled forward. 'Not that one,' he said decisively. 'The phrase above it says "This Way Up".'

上朝面此

He led the way down the corridor in an awkward run.

'That one says "White Tea" so not that one.'

茶白

He rejected others and kept running. Then he stopped and Brodie crashed into the back of him. 'This one,' he said purposefully.

'You're sure?' Brodie pleaded, stepping over the viewing rope that kept visitors back and making for the door.

'Absolutely,' said Hunter, following Brodie over the rope. 'It's because of the numbers.'

'What?' Brodie was sure she couldn't be more confused.

'The "handle with care" numbers. We never worked out why he put that, did we? Why Van der Essen put that phrase above the list of numbers we needed for the code. Well, now we know. *Handle With Care*. That's exactly what that Chinese writing says above that lintel.'

放輕心小

Once behind the door Miss Tandari leant against it in an obvious attempt to catch her breath. It was dark and the lack of vibrant colours after the opulence of the gallery took a moment to get used to.

'This is it,' whispered Brodie, stepping forward. 'This is really it.'

In front of them a spiral wooden staircase twisted

upwards, curling out of sight. The walls were bare, unpainted plaster, and the stairwell was cold. Brodie drank in the smell of damp and neglect.

'Certainly not a public staircase,' whispered Hunter, reaching out for the chipped wooden handrail. 'No wonder it was a secret. We're going up, right?'

Miss Tandari looked a little nervous.

Brodie led the way, stepping cautiously on the rickety treads, each creaking footstep ringing out in the silence. 'How high do you think these stairs will take us?' she called to Hunter behind her.

'Just higher than the phoenix,' he said.

Hunter counted the steps aloud and when they reached the top, Brodie pushed cautiously against a closed door that barred their way. It swung open with a groan.

Beyond the door was a small room. The walls were papered with thick brown patterned paper torn and stripped away in places to reveal the bare and crumbling plaster. There was a rough opening for a fireplace but no mantle or surround. The ceiling was low and covered in clumpy patches of mildew and there was no sign at all they were standing inside the dome of an elegant royal palace. 'The guard was right about it not being finished,' Hunter said, making his way across the room to where a tarpaulin covered a stack of used and broken planks of wood. 'What a complete mess. What's this all for?' he said, prodding the stack of wood with his toes. 'Looks like they're about to build a fire.'

'We should be careful,' mumbled Miss Tandari, who was still catching her breath. 'I'm not sure how safe the flooring is.'

Brodie followed Hunter to the centre of the room and then towards a doorway in the left-hand corner. It creaked open as she pushed. 'Look,' she gasped. 'You can see the rest of Brighton.' The doorway opened on to a small section of floorboards and, set into the flaking curved wall, a large petal-shaped window through which Brodie could see the tall towers of the minarets and the other domes of the roof. Beyond the palace she could see the city.

Hunter joined her at the window. 'Great view,' he said, peering closely through the mottled glass.

'But be careful not to be seen,' Miss Tandari called. 'We'll make things worse.'

Brodie stepped back from the window and, turning to the left, pushed open another doorway. 'Look. There's loads of doors all leading from each other and circling the room.' The others joined her as she led the way around, past the petal-shaped windows and back towards the stairs. 'What a crazy layout. I suppose the builders intended to extend outside to make a terrace which went round the dome,' she suggested. 'Until the Prince got too fat and they gave up on that idea. Instead all they have is a corridor around the edge of the room, broken up with lots of doors.'

Miss Tandari considered this as they searched.

'There's nothing here, is there?' said Hunter at last, as if choosing the words none of them wanted to use. 'No furniture, nothing except doors and wood.' He drew in another breath. 'There's certainly no phoenix.'

Brodie stood once more in the central room. They couldn't be wrong. They'd read the clues and everything led them here. Everything.

'I'm confused,' she said slowly. 'There must be more.'

'But we've tried every door on the circuit and all they reveal's a fantastic view of the palace and the town.'

Something about what Hunter said grated in Brodie's brain. Wasn't this whole search about looking beyond the obvious? Turning away from the spectacular? Wasn't it about the practicality of the scabbard and not the splendour of the sword?

'Try again,' she said. 'Try again. We're missing something.'

They circled the room once more, pushing one door after another, and then Brodie stopped. 'Here,' she said. 'This one.' The last doorway, out of the loop of the others, set back to the right of the main room. One door untried.

She reached out for the handle and then the air exploded with noise.

There were footsteps on the stairs. Heavy. Fast. And getting nearer.

Brodie pushed open the door and the three of them bundled into the room beyond. The room was crowded with furniture. Two chairs. A packing-box containing a broken headless statue, and a cast-iron surround for a fire propped precariously against the wall. Stretched across the ceiling was a thick wooden beam and from the beam hung a rusty metal pulley.

'Quick,' gasped Brodie, hardly able to breathe. 'She'll find us. We need to hide.'

'But there *is* nowhere,' yelped Hunter. 'The only way out's back down the stairs and that means being seen.' He rubbed his face with his hands. 'What do we do? Just wait here for her to open each door in turn until she finds us?'

'OK. Don't panic,' Miss Tandari said briskly. 'Think of your strengths.'

Well, no numbers were going to help them out of this mess. And there were no stories to turn to. Brodie tried to breathe and wondered what use Tusia's special awareness would've been to them if she hadn't flung herself down as a sacrifice.

Then it hit her. Special awareness. Spatial awareness. Awareness of space.

Why was there a pulley hung over the floor in a rooftop room? Why would it be there if not to lower something down?

The stairs were not the only way out.

She sank to her knees and ran her hands across the dusty floor.

The footsteps were getting closer. Whoever it was had almost reached the top of the stairs. In seconds they'd be close enough to see them.

It was nearly over. The code-cracking and the searching wasted. All for nothing.

'Brodie,' hissed Hunter, aghast at her crouched position on the floor. 'This isn't the time for praying.'

'I'm not praying. I'm looking,' she whispered urgently. 'Help me look.'

Miss Tandari and Hunter fell to their knees beside her. 'What are we looking for?' begged Miss Tandari.

'A trapdoor,' said Brodie. 'There must be an opening. To get things up and down on the pulley.'

Her hands scratched through the dust. Her nails digging into the wood.

And then she found it. A small metal ring sunk into

the boards. The handle of a hidden door.

She swung the door open and the three of them tumbled through the opening, pulling the trapdoor shut behind them. She could feel her blood pounding in her ears. The air was cold around them. Icy cold. And the fall below them stretched unseen into unbroken darkness.

They'd landed on a thin wooden ledge inside a void. Below they could see the curving roof space of the saloon. Beside that, as Brodie's eyes grew accustomed to the lack of light, she could just make out, right in front of where they crouched, a rope hanging freely down towards the ground, its end disappearing out of sight. It was attached to a sharp claw-like hook and Brodie supposed when the pulley was used the end of the rope was unleashed from the claw and tied to the pulley.

'Do you think the rope goes all the way to the ground?' she whispered, the breath catching in her throat as she spoke.

'If it does, that's about fifty foot down,' said Hunter and there was a tremor in his voice.

Miss Tandari sat silent, hunched between them, her knees pulled tight against her chest as if she were preparing to perform some sort of forward roll, yet her head was pressed back hard against the wall, her eyes

242

cast upwards. When she spoke her words were barely recognisable as human. 'What we must not do is panic,' she said. Beads of sweat on her brow showed she was finding it difficult to take her own advice. 'Not very good with heights,' she mumbled at last, and Brodie tried to shuffle closer to her.

Above them, Brodie could hear Vernan's footsteps. And she was obviously not alone. At least two other people were with her. With every footstep, a cloud of dust leaked through the cracks in the floorboards and covered their heads. Brodie's nose twitched. She tried to swallow a sneeze and her eyes began to burn.

'Please don't let them find us,' she pleaded silently in her head.

There was a scraping noise. Metal against wood. Brodie guessed Vernan was dragging a chair across the room. Then the sound of china breaking. A shattering of porcelain on the floor above them – the broken statue, she presumed – and new clouds of dust rained between the cracks. Brodie pressed her fist into her mouth as the urge to sneeze grew stronger.

Would it end like this? In a roof space, in the half-light. Hidden and afraid.

She reached out her free arm to steady herself against the ledge and her hand brushed something cold.

She ran the tips of her fingers across it. Metal? A

metal box? And then something else. Something warm.

A single feather. Glowing in the half-light. A warm scarlet glow.

Brodie ignored the pacing footsteps above her and scrambled along the ledge. The rope for the pulley caught on her leg. But she didn't stop. She reached out her hand again.

Her fingers curled around the feather.

Then, with the other hand, she lifted the metal box from the ledge and blew the coating of dust from the surface.

The box was the size of a book. Tarnished silver with golden engraving on the top and each side. Her heart pushed against her ribs. Her fingers trembled.

Engraved on the lid of the box, difficult to see in the half-light, but as welcome as a familiar friend, she could just make out the shape of a bird. A firebird.

Hunter and Miss Tandari smiled silent understanding.

Brodie closed her eyes and drew the feather and the box in tight against her chest. She'd found the phoenix.

Her breathing slowed. Her muscles loosened and as she lifted her head she was aware of a shaft of light, bright and strong and bathing her in a delicious warmth.

It took Brodie several seconds to realise that, above her, the trapdoor had swung open wide.

The feather tumbled from her fingers and fell down into the void.

A hand reached into the half-light, feeling for connection. Brodie tried not to breathe; not a single breath to give away their location. The hand stopped moving. The fingers long and still. A scrabbling sound above. Then a face filled the hole of the trap, and violet eyes pierced the gloom.

Brodie's breath burned in her chest.

She could feel Miss Tandari trembling beside her.

There was only one way out, and that was metres beneath them, at the end of a rope. They were simply seconds away from being seen.

What happened next became a blur, a confusion of noise and movement and fear. More voices in the room of the tower. Shouting and the sound of scuffling. A woman pulled back from the opening as if rescued from her impending fall. 'Madam. Madam. You must leave now. This part of the building is strictly prohibited.'

Then an angry shout. 'You don't understand. You don't understand!' Next, a struggle. A fallen chair. The crash of the trapdoor, closing.

'We've got to use the rope,' Hunter hissed.

'Are you sure it'll take our weight?' asked Miss Tandari.

'We've got no choice. Either we get down to the bottom, or we've got to hand over what we've found to the Pavilion guards or whoever followed us from the Chamber.'

'The rope then,' said Brodie. 'There's nothing for it.'

Leaning back into the recess of the shelf, she took off her blazer and pushed the silver box into one of the sleeves. Then she tied the end of the sleeves together around her waist, like a belt.

'Is the phoenix secure?' Hunter whispered.

Brodie tapped her waist to check.

'You two go first,' Hunter said. Brodie made as if to argue. 'Come on. My parents raised me to be polite.' He waved his hand elaborately. 'After you.'

Miss Tandari moved closer to the rope.

'Nice and carefully,' said Hunter. 'And don't look down.'

Brodie watched as Miss Tandari curled her arm and leg around the rope and swung slowly free of her perch on the shelf. Hand under hand she began to climb down, her legs wrapped tight around the rope, the bracelets on her arms glinting in the half-light.

'You next,' Hunter said to Brodie. 'I should be last.'
Brodie could hear his voice tremble a little.

The shouting above them grew to a crescendo. There was the sound of glass smashing and falling like rain on the boards above their heads.

It was as Hunter swung himself at last on to the rope, there was a scrabbling at the trapdoor again. Brodie scrambled lower, hand under hand, her legs burning against the rope. She could see Miss Tandari still climbing just below her. She could hear Hunter's voice calling from above. The three of them hanging in line one above the other.

And then, with an ominous creak, the trapdoor swung back once more on its hinges.

It was hard to know how far she'd climbed, how near she was to the bottom, when the rope began to sway erratically, side to side. Hands half seen through the light high up near the trapdoor scratched at the fixings above her, tugged at the metal claw, attempting to loosen the rope on which they hung.

Brodie couldn't see the ground. She couldn't breathe. The weight of the silver box cut a line against her side. Through the darkness a voice sliced the air.

'We'll find you. This isn't over.'

Colours kaleidoscoped. And Brodie fell, tumbling and sprawling, winging the air like a newborn bird tossed from the nest.

The ground came up to meet her.

Way above her, Hunter hung like a weight on a plumb line as the rope swung and twisted. Then the rope tumbled free of the claw. Hunter crashed to the floor, his arms splayed. And the unloosed rope coiled like a snake across his body.

Brodie blinked and the space she was in flickered into focus. A long white-walled corridor, stretching towards the light.

'Hunter?'

He was still.

She scrambled to her knees.

'Hunter?'

'Have I died?' His eyes flickered open.

'No. Not quite,' Brodie laughed in relief.

Miss Tandari knelt beside them. 'We're going to get you out of here, just as soon as we can.'

Hunter tried to smile and failed. He tried to sit and swooned back down against the ground, the red feather bent and crumpled beneath his arm.

'A bit wobbly,' he mumbled. 'From that height, I reckon there was slightly more than a fifty-three per cent chance of death. Seems I came off lightly, BB.'

Brodie rubbed his arm reassuringly.

'The phoenix?' he said at last.

'Safe,' she said. She held up the box still tucked in the sleeve of her blazer.

This time Hunter managed a glimmer of a smile.

'Do you think you can manage to stand?' Miss Tandari asked, casting a nervous look up above her.

Hunter grimaced. 'Not sure my foot should be stuck at that angle.'

Brodie tried not to look.

'I think I've sprained my ankle,' Hunter moaned, sinking his body back to the ground.

Brodie's stomach turned. 'So what do we do?'

'You'll have to try and escape with the phoenix, Brodie,' said Miss Tandari.

'What?'

'I'll need time to get Hunter out of here, and time isn't something we have. Any moment, Vernan and the others'll work out where we've fallen. Hunter and I can stall any guards here and spin some story to keep them back, but you,' she said and her eyes were steely, 'you'll have to take the phoenix.'

Brodie tightened her grasp on the precious container.

'The work you do now's important, Brodie,' said Miss Tandari. 'It's what all the training and the learning was for.'

Brodie tried hard to smile in return but her mouth

wouldn't move to make the shape she wanted.

'Now,' said Miss Tandari, 'we've obviously landed in some sort of servants' corridor. You need to follow the corridor till it leads you back into the state rooms. Then you need to make for the music room.'

'The what?'

'The music room. To the north of the palace. According to what I've read, there's a secret tunnel there that leads out under the gardens and to the building that used to be the Prince's stables. If you make it through the tunnel you'll be free. And,' she added seriously, 'the phoenix will be safe.'

Brodie nodded weakly.

Hunter stretched out his hand. 'You can do it, Brodie,' he whispered, and the way he said her name as if he might never see her again made her want to cry.

11

From Ashes to Ashes

The corridor was narrow, lined with large white tiles, cold and spartan. Brodie counted them as she passed, as she knew Hunter would've done. To make the walk easier and escape more certain. It didn't help.

At last she came to a small anteroom and the colours of the state rooms of the Pavilion blazed ahead of her. She hurried into another gallery lined with high cream marble pillars with golden snakes curled round them. A sign told her it was the 'music room gallery'. Her heart thumped. It was difficult to breathe.

At the end of the gallery was a door.

The door was open.

Brodie clutched the phoenix close to her chest and stumbled inside.

And then, the door swung closed behind her.

'Well, well, well.' The voice was slow and metered and accompanied by loud, rhythmic clapping. 'Then there was one.'

Brodie's heart was forcing itself against her ribs as if it was trying to make its escape without her.

'At the very end I must take my prize from a child,' the voice continued from behind her. 'I think the Director would like that.'

Brodie turned and there, blocking her escape through the now closed door, was a woman dressed in high black boots and a short pleated skirt. Her tight-fitting red blouse was the same colour as her polished fingernails. Her dark hair was pulled back into a tight ponytail, straining the skin around her eyes. Thin blood-red lips cracked into a smile and on her hand a diamond ring glinted.

She stopped clapping and moved further into the centre of the room, her arms stretched wide as if welcoming a guest to her home. 'Magnificent, don't you think? Of all the rooms in this palace, this must be, of all of them, the most impressive.'

Brodie's heart was still jumping in her chest. Yet she couldn't help but look up at the splendour around her.

The room was huge and even more ornately decorated than the Banqueting Room. A golden domed ceiling held nine lotus-shaped chandeliers. Painted dragons supported scarlet canvases against the walls. Carved, silvered, flying dragons carried blue silk satin window draperies, fringed with golden tassels. A blue carpet was spread with dragons. On the far wall, pipes of an organ were set against red and gold, while on the wall facing the windows a mirror stretched above a marble fireplace, bouncing the light around the room, catching the dragons in flight.

'One hundred and eighty-five dragons,' laughed the woman. 'Your friend Hunter, with his ridiculous obsession with numbers, would like that fact.'

'You know about Hunter?' Brodie said slowly.

'My dear child. I know everything. I've the power to read your mail, scrutinise your computer use and watch you from cameras in the sky. I'm all-seeing. It's my job to know.' Her violet eyes flashed in the light. 'I'll agree it took us a while to catch on. A crafty old thing, Smithies. Deception of the very best sort. Right beneath our noses. But it hasn't taken us long to catch up.' She flexed her hands and her knuckles cracked. 'I know about Tusia and her glorious chess wins. I know about Miss Tandari and her complicated family. I know about the washed-up has-been Smithies recruited to work alongside him.' She waited. 'And I know about you.'

Brodie looked away.

The woman's voice was measured. 'All that happened to your mother. So sad. Such a shame with you not even knowing your father. Cruel to be without both parents. Still,' she paused, 'I suppose there was always your granddad. Him and his romantic love of the code. I expect he was glad to get rid of you, that's why he let you leave and be part of the madness.' She laughed. 'Such a burden you must've been to him. I bet he could hardly wait to see you go.'

Brodie clutched the silver box closer to her chest. She felt her pulse racing in her ears.

'But your little tussles with danger are over now, Brodie. Code-cracking is no pursuit for has-beens or children. There are rules. And rules need to be obeyed. It won't be long before the guards arrive and by then you'll have handed me what you found and the whole sorry mess will be over. That,' she added sharply, 'is how this story will end.'

The woman began to pace, the heels of her black boots leaving impressions in the carpet. When she spoke again her voice was almost gentle. 'Hand me whatever precious gift Van der Essen left hidden here and I'll let you go.'

Brodie tried to breathe.

The woman spoke again. 'Give it to me, Brodie.'

Brodie's breath burned at the base of her throat.

Then in a voice she wasn't even really sure belonged to her, she said, 'No.'

The woman's violet eyes flashed wild. 'You seem to think there's a choice.' Her smile was thin. 'Give it to me.'

Brodie reached up and grasped the locket from her grandfather in the cup of her hand. Things looked bad, but it wasn't over yet. Somehow she knew she shouldn't give in. She'd stand her ground as her granddad had done, as her grandmother had done, and as she knew her mother would've done. Whoever this woman was, and whatever she stood for, Brodie knew deep down that passing Van der Essen's phoenix to her would be wrong. Smithies had explained how much Van der Essen had done to protect the secret of MS 408. He'd saved the code-book from the fire of war; he'd protected the phoenix under a cloak of code. And he'd wanted worthy code-breakers to find her. Over the last few weeks that's what Brodie hoped she'd become. A worthy alchemist of codes. And she had the phoenix in her hands. Now nothing would make her give it up. She let the locket fall free against her skin. 'I've got to look after the phoenix,' she said. 'You can't have it.'

The woman merely smiled. Then she folded her arms across her chest and waited. 'I think it's time, Brodie, I filled you in on a few details you appear not to grasp. Once I've finished perhaps you'll see things my way.'

She looked down at the ground, tracing a circle with the toe of her boot.

'As soon as we join the Chamber they tell us about MS 408. They warn us about its pull, its power. It works like a drug, a virus, you know, that gets into your blood and before you know it, it's taken over. The need to read the unreadable. The need to make sense of madness.' She hesitated for a moment. 'And that's the only place MS 408 can lead, Brodie. To madness. The manuscript destroys all who touch it. That's why we wrote the rules. I'm simply here to protect you from working on a mystery that can only lead to unhappiness.' She paused as if allowing time for her words to run through a filter. 'Smithies was wrong to involve you. Children. Vulnerable children. Selling you a dream. A promise of discovery. It cost Friedman his job, Ingham his health. And for your mother,' she waited for a moment, 'the cost was her life.'

'What are you talking about?' Brodie gasped.

The woman's brow was furrowed, feigning concern. 'Brodie, your mother wouldn't leave the lure of the code behind. She travelled to Belgium to pursue a worthless dream, the stuff of fairytale and myth. Have you never wondered how she lost her life?'

'She was killed in a car crash.'

The woman looked the way teachers do when a child offers an answer so badly incorrect they're unsure how to respond.

'It had nothing to do with MS 408,' Brodie blurted. 'It was a terrible accident.'

Still the woman said nothing. She traced a circle once more with her toe. Then she looked up. 'The manuscript offers nothing but false dreams, Brodie. Now it's time to give it up.' Her voice tightened. 'Pass me Van der Essen's phoenix so we can end this.'

Brodie could barely breathe.

'Pursuing a solution for MS 408 can only end in sorrow, Brodie. You've been tricked into thinking there's some great secret to discover. That's a lie. The book's a fake. Whatever you've found is just another playing piece in the game. An elaborate game. One that's already cost your mother's life.' She stepped forward and Brodie could feel her breath against her skin. The heavy scent of lotus flower swirled around her. 'Hand me what you found.'

Brodie's mind was in free-fall. The manuscript a fake? Tricked? Fooled into caring? Into trying? All for nothing. The ground was sliding like wet sand under her feet but something kept her from falling. She felt the picture of the castle inside the locket burning

257

against her skin. As if the castle built of sand was standing tall in the waves as they lapped around it. The castle refused to fall. And she was holding on to it.

'Perhaps it's all a terrible game,' she said. 'But I've got the phoenix.' She swallowed. 'I'm not going to give it to you.'

'Nice speech, little girl,' the woman laughed and a bead of spit bubbled on her blood-red lip. 'But this is no time for bravery. The game's over and this time I've won. I've got what Smithies wants and he'll walk away the loser.'

She lunged towards Brodie and the silver box she clutched to her chest.

Brodie stumbled backwards. The long metal box tumbled from her fingers as her arm grazed against the jagged wing of an ornate dragon that reared up beside the window. And like a bell ringing out in the silence, there was the sound of metal on stone as the box crashed against the wall.

It bounced on the ground, its lid flung open.

There, resting in the folds of fabric lining, inside the box, was what the search was all about. The codes, the secrets, the quest.

Brodie knew what it was as soon as she saw it.

Ash.

Tears of blackened scraps lay like petals on the fabric

and the smell of ancient burning rose in the air. A piece drifted on to the woman's hand. She reached with the fingers of her other hand, pale ghost letters from the kiss of the ash still visible against the skin. At her touch they turned to dust and blew away.

Friedman looked closely at the map in the guidebook and tapped his hand nervously on the front desk. The Dome, a building set behind the Royal Pavilion, had been built by the Prince Regent as a stable for his horses. Now the building was a museum and the exhibitions on Chinese art and Brighton's picture postcards were drawing many visitors. Friedman had no interest in the exhibits though.

'Excuse me,' he said in hushed tones to the rather bored-looking tour guide who was staffing the front desk. She turned her head sharply to the side, her lips pursed. 'Erm, would you be so kind as to show me the entrance to the secret tunnel?'

The tour guide continued to frown, the ring through her nose wobbling a little, and the tattoo of a mermaid on her neck creasing so it looked as if she were swimming. 'I'm sorry, mate. Tunnel's strictly out of bounds. Health and safety issues regarding the structure so it's closed to the public.'

Friedman clenched his hand into a fist yet tried to

make his voice sound relaxed. 'Yes. I appreciate it's closed to the public. I was just wondering if you could show me where it is.' He smiled what he hoped was his most enthusiastic smile. 'The other guide over there wouldn't show me either but I thought you looked so much more daring.' He cast his gaze in the direction of a fairly elderly-looking guide wearing a matching lemon skirt and jumper and a choker of pearls. He turned back again and winked, but feared it may've looked merely as if he'd something in his eye.

The tour guide softened. 'OK,' she said coyly. 'As you asked so nicely.'

Friedman was sure it'd nothing to do with his manner of asking and much more to do with annoying the other guide. He'd watched them for at least ten minutes and the level of tension between them was palpable.

'I bet you take risks and walk through the tunnel all the time,' he continued, trying desperately to push home his advantage. 'I mean you have to take some risks in life, don't you?'

The guide was smiling now, her metal-heeled shoes clipping against the tiled floor. 'It's here,' she said, motioning towards an unassuming green doorway, 'but don't tell the old bag I'd anything to do with it. She's on my case as it is.'

'Understood,' Friedman answered. 'Your secret's safe with me.'

She smiled and it was just possible to see her tongue stud glinting in the opening of her mouth.

'By the way,' he added as his hand pushed against the door. 'Where exactly does the tunnel lead to?'

'Pavilion Music Room.' She smiled. 'It comes out in the Band Room and there's a secret door that leads through to the Music Room.'

'Splendid,' he said, pressing his weight against the door. 'And thank you.' And with that he winked again and opened the door.

Vernan's laugh cut through the air as she lowered her hand into the open box and lifted the ashen fragments of manuscript. She let them fall like confetti. 'So, who's the loser now?'

Brodie looked down as the dust and stench from the burned papers lifted in the air like a cloud. It was ruined. Van der Essen's code-book destroyed by the fires of Louvain all along. What sort of joke was this? Why'd a man go to all the trouble of hiding *this* under a cloak of code and cipher?

The palms of the woman's hands were blackened by the soot. 'Not a phoenix after all. Just a fraud.' She stood up, suddenly tall again, her violet eyes dulled.

'Whatever Van der Essen left you is useless, Brodie. And so whether you like it or not, you and Smithies and the whole irresponsible team have to accept that.'

Her eyes narrowed.

'Now, Brodie, lover of puzzles and riddles and codes. Here's a puzzle for you. A puzzle of dragons.' She waved her hands around again as if conducting the dragons in flight. 'Of all these beasts there's only one king. Only one Pendragon, the ruler of them all.'

Brodie scanned the room.

'Can you guess? Which of those you see is the true ruler?' The woman stamped her feet dramatically. 'This one,' she said, pointing down at the ground and the huge dragon woven into the pile of the carpet. 'See how the other dragons fly on outstretched wings? Except this one. This wingless dragon is the true ruler. The lowest,' she stamped her foot again, 'and yet the highest. The Pendragon. He has no need to fly, for his power is greater than flight. He's invincible. Indestructible. All power is his. You do well to remember where true power lies, Brodie. Not in flights of fancy, ideas and dreams. In reality. And facts.'

She kicked out her foot and the toe of her boot clanged against the sooty metal box. 'Take this back to your code-cracking friends and show them there aren't any secrets to find, no great truths to uncover.

Show them you failed. Go home, Brodie. Back to the real world.'

Brodie's grandfather stood at the desk of the branch of Gimlet and Suffolk International Bank and waited. The assistant who'd gone to get the safety deposit clearance card looked, in Mr Bray's opinion, hardly old enough to be out on his own, let alone old enough to be in full-time employment. On another occasion he'd have said something. Asked to see the manager even. But the young boy was pleasant enough, and he seemed, when he returned with the card, fairly competent, so he decided not to mention it. There were after all more urgent issues on his mind.

The footsteps of the junior clerk rang out against the tiled floor as he led the way down into the vault. He gestured with his hand and led Mr Bray through to a wall of deposit boxes clearly numbered. Using a swipe card, the clerk opened one deposit box and slid out the small metal tray it contained.

The contents of the box appeared modest. Simply a shaft of papers and a half-opened envelope with the name 'Robbie' printed neatly on it with purple ink. Mr Bray felt a surge of emotion as he saw his daughter's handwriting. The last thing she'd written on the visit to Belgium that cost her life. In the light, it was also possible to see the indentation made by a tiny key and loops from a chain pressed into the paper of the envelope. This sight made him feel no better. Mr Bray's hand shook a little as he placed all he'd collected into his briefcase.

'Will that be all?' asked the bank clerk.

'For now,' answered Mr Bray. 'Thank you for your time.'

'It's been a pleasure, Mr Bray,' replied the clerk, obviously making use of his fresh 'in store' training.

Mr Bray tightened the grip on the handle of the briefcase and walked back towards the lobby. If he hurried he might just be in time for the appointment with his solicitor.

It was suddenly cold. The light was beginning to fail and Brodie had begun to shiver.

She wasn't sure how long ago the woman in red had left her. She heard her leave and then Brodie dropped to her knees, the blue carpet soft against her legs. It hurt to look at the metal box. Soot-covered silver, a dirty reminder of what she'd hoped for and lost. There'd be no rising of the phoenix. The code-book kept safe for so long by the Professor, hidden to be found by someone worthy, was lost. Turned to ash. There'd be no reading of MS 408 now. No understanding of the strange unheard language, or the pictures that seemed to show another place and time. The only thing left to do was to tell the others. So why she waited as the darkness crept ever closer she wasn't sure. Something told her it was too soon to leave.

When a door opened in the panelling in the wall she wasn't even afraid. The man who stepped out was thin and wiry, blond hair curling round his head like a halo. Something about him looked familiar but she couldn't place where she'd seen him before. Something about his eyes. She supposed at first he must be another government official, come to check she understood it was all over. Or perhaps a guard from the museum wanting to know why she'd spilt ash on to the carpet. And it was perhaps the state of the carpet, the blackened smears across the mighty dragons, that made her begin to cry.

'Hey,' the man said in a voice as soft as velvet. 'Why the tears?'

She sniffed and wiped her nose with the back of her hand. 'I'm sorry,' she said.

He angled his head in question.

'About the carpet. I've made a mess,' she said.

He smiled reassuringly. 'It'll all brush away,' he said gently. 'Do you know this whole room was burnt to the ground in the 1970s? Arsonists threw a fire-bomb through the window in November 1975 and the entire room was destroyed. The splendour you see around you now took eleven years to restore. Remarkable, don't you think, what can rise again from the ashes?' He waited a moment. 'No one will be cross about the mess and besides,' he said, 'it looks to me as if you've been very brave.'

Brodie had forgotten about the cut on her arm. She sat still as he took out a clean handkerchief and pressed it against the wound. As he moved, a tiny golden key glinted on a chain around his neck.

'Who are you?' she said at last.

'Robbie Friedman,' he said.

Something inside her stomach fell. 'Friedman who was thrown out of the Black Chamber?'

He looked uncomfortable.

'Smithies said trying to solve MS 408 cost you your job.'

'It cost me far more than that.' His cheeks coloured a little and he returned his attention to the makeshift bandage. 'I'm very pleased to meet you properly at last. Smithies tells me you've a real eye for codes.'

Brodie just pointed down at the soot-filled box. 'Van der Essen's code-book,' she said. 'It's ruined. I guess we'll never read MS 408 now. Besides, that woman told me the manuscript's a fake.'

Friedman's eyes gave nothing away.

'Are you angry?' Brodie asked.

'Sad,' he said, easing himself into a sitting position. 'It would've been wonderful for Alex's memory if we'd found the truth.'

Her heart leapt at her mother's name. 'You believe it? You don't think it's a fake?'

He breathed in as if he were about to plunge underwater and needed all the air he could take into his lungs. 'It's not fake, Brodie. It's just – the government don't want us to know the truth.'

'What *is* the truth?'

'Something big,' he said at last. 'Knowledge about worlds hidden inside our own, perhaps.' He paused. 'Why'd they go to all this trouble if it wasn't worth hiding?'

'Trouble?'

'Well, chasing you for a start,' he said with a laugh. 'And making the rules. But other things as well.'

Brodie thought for a moment. 'But the code-book was ruined anyway.'

'Maybe.'

Brodie couldn't help but frown. 'Can I ask you something?' she said.

'Anything.'

'You knew my mum?'

Friedman nodded wistfully. 'For many years.'

'I was told she died in a car crash in Belgium.'

Friedman's eyes flickered.

'Do you think there was any way,' Brodie could barely finish her words, 'any way at all . . . ?'

Friedman leant forward and pressed his hand on hers. 'Brodie, your mother's accident was a tragedy. But if you're trying to ask me if I believe others were involved then I have to tell you, yes.' He paused and tightened his grasp on her hand. 'They'll stop at nothing to divert people from the truth behind the manuscript. I have to question whether your mother found out too much.'

A silence stretched between them like a fragile spider's web, yet it didn't matter neither of them spoke.

'You really think MS 408 spoke of a different world and Van der Essen knew how to read it?'

'I really do.'

'Don't you mind if people think you're mad?'

'Sometimes.'

Brodie frowned. 'I think Smithies believes in you,' she said quietly.

Friedman didn't answer.

Brodie reached forward and closed the lid of the box. 'We've got to find the others. Let them know what happened.'

'What will you say?'

'That it's over.'

'You really believe that?'

Brodie lifted the box in her hand. 'It's empty. What else can I think?'

Friedman stood up. 'Your mother would've loved these dragons,' he said, looking again around the room.

Brodie wasn't sure if it made her sadder to know something about her mother she didn't know or if it made her a little happier. 'What would she like about them?'

'The stories,' he said. 'She was always writing up stories about dragons. And of course she loved the stories of Arthur. The real Pendragon. A story of a child. A child very much like you. Alone. Separated from his parents and raised by another.'

Brodie's heart beat against the casing of the box held tight against her chest.

'A child who, despite all the odds, would become a mighty ruler.' He hesitated. 'You know, I don't think we should give up on MS 408, Brodie.'

'But it's all a dead end.'

His eyes twinkled. 'Things aren't always what they seem,' he said.

Brodie looked down at the ground and the noble dragon at her feet.

'It seems this room has doors on only one side. We know otherwise. We'll find an answer, Brodie, if we can just be determined enough to keep looking.' He moved across the room to where, disguised by the painted pattern on the wall, there was an opening. A doorway to a tunnel.

Brodie followed. The door hung open for a moment as she stumbled over the threshold. The light from the Music Room pooled inside.

There was a flight of spiral stairs. The air was cold. Slowly, and without a sound, the secret door swung closed behind them, driving out the light.

The darkness was complete; all-consuming. It took the breath from Brodie's lungs.

There was a scratching sound; a match struck against the stone of the walls and then a spark of light stretching like a cloud. Friedman took one of the candles set in the wall and lit it. He held it in his hand so his face was ringed in a warm golden glow. Then he led her out of the secret tunnel and on into the fading light of evening.

12

Reborn in the Flames

The Director sat with his back to the door. He held a pencil in his hand, twisting it between his fingers like a miniature baton. 'You're telling me there was nothing.'

Kerrith eased the line of her red jumper across her hips. 'Nothing, sir.'

'Just ash?'

'Ash, sir.'

The Director stilled the pencil between his fingers. 'Seems we were successful then, back in the seventies. We had a lead that documents relating to MS 408 were hidden at the Pavilion. It's a shame. The Music Room took thousands of pounds to restore after we destroyed it. I seem to remember they spent years hand-knotting the replacement carpet. No matter. If our job was done.'

Kerrith looked appreciative.

The Director tapped the arm of his chair with the pencil. 'So. Van der Essen's gift is useless, and for that we must be grateful. You've done well, Vernan. Very well.'

Kerrith shuffled her feet.

'However,' the Director added, spinning round his chair so he could face her. 'This ridiculous set-up at Station X is a worry to me. Smithies has always been a loose cannon, and his past association with Friedman always a source of annoyance to me. You've got to admire Smithies' style really, setting up under our very noses.' He tapped his teeth with the pencil. 'But no one takes me or this department for a fool, Vernan. No one.'

Kerrith shook her head in a way she hoped showed full agreement.

'The lead they had about MS 408 may've come to nothing but their interest in the document shouldn't be overlooked. We have a duty to uphold here. Rules to keep. Any work on MS 408 is prohibited.'

'You think they'll keep looking for answers, sir?' Kerrith offered quietly.

'Oh, they'll try, Vernan. That's how it gets, isn't it? Compulsive. Addictive. The search for the missing piece of the jigsaw puzzle, the final letters needed for the crossword. Now they've started they'll be driven to find out more. They'll look for other leads, seek out other sources. Our job here is to prevent them.'

'Sir?'

The Director laughed. 'My dear Kerrith. There's so much you need to learn. So much you've yet to see, about Level Five and its ultimate aim.'

'Yes, sir. I was wondering. If you could tell me about the stamp across the copies of MS 408. The mark of "the Suppressors". Who are they? What do they do?'

'All in good time, Miss Vernan. All you need to know for now is that we'll stop Smithies and his team of code-crackers. They must be prevented from looking deeper. Must give up their quest and leave MS 408 well alone.'

'And how will we do that, sir?'

The Director took the pencil between his fingers and snapped it in half.

Back at Bletchley railway station, Ingham was waiting for them. It was rather unfortunate that because there were five of them, they couldn't fit into an ordinary car. The journey back to Station X in the back of the World War Two land assault vehicle was not the most comfortable of rides. Brodie gave up checking the time of the journey on either of her watches. The bumping around made her feel travel-sick. She closed her eyes and longed to be back at the mansion.

Smithies called a meeting in the ballroom.

Tusia left her books and files on the end of her bed. 'I don't suppose we'll be making notes,' she said gloomily.

Hunter met them by the water fountain. He didn't even attempt to avoid the spurting jet. 'I'll sort of miss it,' he said as they turned and walked towards the mansion. 'I was more than seventy-six per cent used to *that* discomfort,' he added, hobbling awkwardly on his heavily strapped ankle.

The room was organised as it'd been on that very first night. The chairs in an oval and at one side a table where Smithies, Ingham and Miss Tandari sat. This time their faces were grave instead of welcoming. Disappointed maybe. Brodie swallowed. The guilt of failure bubbled in her throat. She thought for a moment Ingham was trying to catch her eye but she was too embarrassed to look up. He'd trusted them to come back with the code-book and they'd returned empty-handed.

After a moment Brodie felt enough courage to lift her head. She realised Smithies was talking and she tried hard to focus on his words despite the confusion.

'We must admit defeat when we see it.' He adjusted his glasses on the bridge of his nose as if the vision through them was at the moment a little hazy. 'We fought an excellent fight! We solved a puzzle that would've stretched the best minds in the land and we should feel no shame about that. We just have to accept our phoenix wasn't intended to fly. Our Firebird Code led us simply to her ashes.' He paused. 'Like an English football team in a World Cup qualifier, I'm afraid we snatched defeat from the jaws of victory. And yet,' he tried to pull himself up taller but Brodie noticed his shoulders were stooped as if he carried a heavy weight on his back, 'we did all we could. I really thought we'd find the answers. That after all these years we'd finally be able to read the secrets of Voynich's mysterious book. Now,' he sighed. 'Now we must accept we'll never know the story its pages hold. The pictures of the plants and animals, the islands and the people, will never really get to share their truth with us. I'm so very sorry.'

His voice cracked a little. He whispered something into Miss Tandari's ear.

'We should acknowledge too,' he continued, 'that the authorities are on to our quest. So the procedure will be as follows. Miss Tandari will spend the week bringing you up to speed on general curriculum work but as of today your work on code-cracking is at an end.' He pulled himself up taller and straightened his rather crumpled tie with the flat of his hand. 'Arrangements will be made with your previous schools to readmit you.

'Plans will be made for you to leave this Black Chamber on Friday. Your families will be notified and as of Saturday your life will return to normality.' He glanced down at notes he had on the table, and once more adjusted his glasses. 'It's been a privilege to spend time with such an excellent crop of young brains,' he said, 'and we must remember, despite the sad demise of our operation, Van der Essen's Firebird Code *was* broken and the message read. Take comfort in that. We just didn't arrive in time to see the phoenix fly.'

Brodie looked down at the ground. She wondered if the final words were really for them or him. When she looked up again, everyone at the long table was standing. Smithies leant his weight against the table. Brodie thought suddenly of her granddad and a tear slipped down her cheek.

'I'm duty-bound to say this is the most unusual of requests, Mr Bray.'

Brodie's grandfather sat nervously in his chair, his scooter helmet resting precariously in his lap. 'And I must say that as my solicitor, your job is merely to tell me if what I suggest is workable and not to offer opinion on the wisdom behind the act.'

Mr Baxter of Pout, Hackett and Gurr LLP winced visibly and lowered his gaze to the desk. 'It's just it's an awfully large amount of money, Mr Bray.'

'And you think at my age in life I should stick to usual?'

'No, sir. Not at all. Not at all.'

'Good.' Mr Bray grasped his bicycle clips which balanced on the arm of the chair. 'So. Is what I've suggested possible?'

'Oh, absolutely possible, sir.'

'And there's no loopholes you can see regarding the education of the children or the purchase of the properties?'

'No, sir. I've checked the land registry and the huts of the building can be sold separately so what you're suggesting is perfectly legitimate. And as regards the education constraints, this Mr Smithies you mentioned seems to have covered every base. We have no worries there.' He hesitated for a moment. 'And my dealing with the US branch suggests Mr Fabyan III of Riverbanks Labs is more than happy to cover the shortfall in costs and act as guarantor.'

'So there's nothing left to discuss, then?'

'Well, no, sir. If you're entirely sure this is the way you wish to proceed.'

Mr Bray took the pen Mr Baxter offered. 'Where do I sign?' he said.

'Come on,' said Tusia. 'Let's go and start packing.'

The three of them made their way to Hut 8. With only days to go they made no attempt to hide Hunter. What could possibly happen if they broke the rules now? They could hardly be chucked out.

Hunter sat on the end of the bed unwrapping a rather squashed Curly Wurly left over from their night-time solving session. It seemed to Brodie to be a lifetime ago. Another world altogether.

'Suppose I should put this room back the way it was,' said Tusia, shaking her head vigorously at the offer of a bite of the crumbled chocolate.

Brodie nodded.

'Great. You can move that ruddy chest of drawers back where it was, Toots. I hurt my toe every time I come in here and surely I'm injured enough without being attacked by your furniture,' muttered Hunter. 'I'm not invincible, you know.'

Tusia paused. 'Well, I'll have to wait until one of you can help me lift the thing. I can't do it on my own.'

Brodie swallowed a mouthful of chocolate. She eased herself down gently into the chair beside the door, wincing with the pain in her arm.

Tusia had just begun to repeat the statement in a high singsongy voice when Brodie stood up.

'You all right, BB?' Hunter said, ceasing his chewing with a look of concern. 'You don't look too good.'

Brodie pushed her hands against her lips and began to breathe quickly in and out.

'You're not having a panic attack, are you? Because they really are my speciality.'

Brodie was pacing backwards and forwards by the window.

'OK, BB. Any time you want to explain what's going on would be great because your rather odd behaviour reflects the actions of the two per cent of the population who are registered as clinically insane.'

'I think we're missing something.'

Hunter soothed his injured leg gently with his hand. 'True, BB. We're missing lots of things. Like a home now, and a purpose and something to work on.'

'No! I mean about the phoenix. It doesn't make sense, does it? To hide a box of ash and go to all the bother of writing a code to protect it.'

'But he didn't hide a box of ash, did he? Van der Essen put the code-book in the box and the fire in the

Pavilion in 1975 just burnt what was inside. Smithies went over that.'

'But the box wasn't in the Music Room, was it? That's where the fire was.'

'Maybe someone just hid the box in that attic after the fire.'

'But why? What's the point? Hiding the box if you know what's inside is ruined.'

'But your version sees Van der Essen hiding the box of ash himself and that's even more nutty.' Tusia was obviously struggling to keep up with Brodie's train of thought.

'Not nutty. Puzzling. But not nutty.'

Hunter frowned.

'If Van der Essen hid the box of ash then that's what he wanted us to find. Ash,' said Brodie.

Tusia was beginning to look a little worried.

'What I mean is, I don't think the ash was all there was.' She rubbed her temples with her fingers. 'When I was in the Music Room with Friedman he said something about there being only one way out.'

'And?'

'And there wasn't. One was hidden. Disguised. Like lots of places in that Pavilion, things are out of sight. The servants' corridor, the secret tunnel, even the room in the sky.'

280

'Look, Brodie,' Tusia interrupted. 'You're tired. We're all tired. We're upset. Disappointed.'

Hunter was pulling a face. Brodie was obviously unnerving him.

'Think about it,' blurted Brodie, resuming her pacing with a vengeance. 'There's got to be a hidden answer. There's just *got* to be.' She stood still. She tightened her hands into fists with determination.

Hunter's eyebrows creased in sudden understanding.

'*Finally*,' groaned Brodie.

'But hold on,' said Tusia, jumping up to stand. 'You think we have to go all the way back to the Pavilion.'

'No,' said Brodie, full of confidence. 'I think the answer's right in front of us. A secret inside a secret.' She laughed. 'The very best type.'

Hunter swept his fingers through his hair decisively. 'Let's not panic about this. We just need to see the box and make sure.'

Brodie agreed. 'We need to go and see Smithies.'

They staggered their way back across to the mansion, and hurried into the entrance hall. Miss Tandari was making her way across to the library. She waved when she saw them. 'Recovered?' she said softly.

'No,' blurted Brodie in a voice that was a little too loud and caused Miss Tandari to step back a pace.

281

'That's the point really. We haven't.'

Miss Tandari looked confused. 'It's hardly been long, has it?' she said defensively. 'I think if you give it more time . . .'

'We need Smithies.'

'Well. It's to be expected you'll feel that way. After all, you've worked very closely with him and it's understandable you'll be attached to him. In times of crisis people often form links with people that stretch across times and generations . . .'

'Miss Tandari,' pleaded Brodie. 'Listen! It's about the phoenix. Not what we feel. We've got to see Mr Smithies. Urgently.'

Miss Tandari hesitated. 'OK. OK. My mistake. He's in the billiard room. I think he wanted to be alone. But if you come with me . . .'

Brodie called over her shoulder. 'We know where it is, but come with us if you want to. We've got something exciting to say.'

The door to the billiard room swung open. Mr Smithies was standing at the window, his hands resting on the sill, his shoulders hunched. Brodie was suddenly nervous about troubling him, but he turned then and tried to organise his features into something he obviously hoped resembled a smile.

'Ah. My merry band of secret breakers. Come to say

goodbye? Really no need until Friday. I suggest until then you make good use of all Station X has to offer. I must say I'm saddened no one yet has ventured for a swim in our beautiful lake. I believe in the war years that was a particularly popular activity but perhaps people were more hardy then. Not spoilt by the luxury of central heating or electric blankets.' He was talking far too quickly. Trying too hard to be jolly.

'Mr Smithies,' interrupted Brodie, beginning to fear no one would actually listen without first giving a lecture. 'We've got to see the box from the Pavilion. It's important.'

Smithies' smile fluttered. 'Of course it's important, child,' he said defensively. 'It's a beautiful relic. One that caused us a fair degree of work to find.'

'But we've got to *see* it.'

Smithies held his hand out to calm them. 'Can't bear to admit it's all over? Want one last look to reaffirm it all really happened?'

'Something like that,' Brodie pleaded.

Smithies led the way over to the high mantelpiece stretched across the fireplace. 'I'm thinking,' he said slowly, 'perhaps we ought to pass it over to the British Museum. Probably best in the long run. Quite exquisite workmanship really.'

He offered the book-shaped box and Brodie took it.

It was as she remembered. Ornate silver with golden firebirds on every side.

She lifted the lid and her fingers were dusted with ash.

She turned the box in her hand.

'What are you looking for?' Miss Tandari asked gently.

'Don't really know,' Brodie answered. 'Just something that's not obvious.'

She slid her hand around the edge of the box, running her finger across a small opening for a key. But as the box was unlocked anyway she dismissed this, and cupped her palm across the lid. 'It's nothing,' she said. 'Just – I was so sure. I thought we'd missed something.'

Smithies watched her. 'Sometimes,' he said, 'we imagine we have an answer when we don't, Brodie.' And the way his brow was furrowed reminded her how long he'd tried to solve this puzzle. Years he'd given to the quest of the unread code.

He took the box from her and stretched his fingers around the base. That was when she saw it. Yellowed and creased, the pointed edge of something sticking out from the join of the lid to the box.

'Look,' she breathed. 'There! In the hinge!'

Smithies put the box carefully on to the baize of the billiard-table. Then he leant forward and jabbed the point of his finger at the protruding fragment.

'Find something small. Something pointed,' he instructed as the others crowded round.

Tusia rummaged in her blazer pockets and after discarding two leaflets on recycling, an aromatherapy lip balm and a stress pig that was looking decidedly battered, she produced a tiny screwdriver.

'What?' she said as Hunter grimaced at her. 'I like to be prepared.'

With the screwdriver, Smithies carefully unfastened the lid hinge of the box. Then he set the lid aside. He pulled the fragment from the hinge. A yellowed piece of parchment curled like a tiny scroll.

'Well?' hissed Brodie, leaning so far forward her nose was nearly against the table. 'What is it?'

Smithies stood back and smoothed the paper with the flat of his hand. Then his shoulders sank even lower, his eyes paled with obvious disappointment. 'It just says "*EXCALIBUR*"!'

Hunter sat with his back against the wall. Brodie presumed he had bad memories of his last recuperation session on the couch and so had rejected the offer and taken to the floor. Brodie squeezed next to Tusia on the window seat.

'Not really what I was expecting,' Hunter said flatly.

Smithies shrugged. 'I must agree. It does seem a little unnecessary for Van der Essen to have written the name of Arthur's sword.'

'Maybe he was just making sure we knew,' offered Tusia.

Brodie fingered the locket hanging round her neck. 'I still think we're missing something.'

'I think, BB,' Hunter said matter-of-factly, 'we may just have to admit that Van der Essen, really did just leave us a box full of ash. No more clues. No secrets. Just the remains of a fire and a phoenix that was never going to be reborn.'

Brodie rubbed her neck again.

There was a long tired silence. Not the sort of awkward quiet where you are waiting for someone to speak. A muted, painful acknowledgment there was nothing left to say.

Brodie gasped, pushed her hands against the seat and jumped to the ground.

'Please,' begged Tusia from the end of the window seat. 'You nearly gave me a heart attack. Will you stop with all the gasps and the jumping.'

'Fire!' Brodie yelled at the top of her voice.

Hunter scrabbled to his feet and Smithies' glasses wobbled precariously on his nose.

'Fire!'

'Where? Where?' Miss Tandari grabbed a billiard-cue from the table and lurched towards the glass-fronted alarm on the far wall. She swung the cue through the air towards the glass.

'No. Wait!' screamed Brodie.

Miss Tandari froze the swing and tottered. 'You said "fire"!'

'I did! I did!' squealed Brodie.

'So I should sound the alarm. Evacuate the premises. Lead people to their assembly points.'

'I mean, we *need* fire. Not we're *on* fire,' Brodie yelped, wrestling the snooker cue from Miss Tandari's hand and dropping it to the floor. 'The paper,' she yelped again. 'It's so obvious.'

'Excuse me?' begged Tusia.

'OK,' said Brodie, trying desperately to calm herself. 'We find a box and we think the secret to reading MS 408 is hidden inside.'

Hunter was nodding frantically. 'And?'

'And then we look more carefully in the box we know was hidden in the Pavilion by a professor of codes . . . a very clever man . . . who spent *ages* trying to leave us perfect clues about where this code-book is.'

'And?' Mr Smithies was getting frantic now.

'And, we're supposed to believe this professor would very carefully hide a piece of paper in the box and just write the name of the sword that went with the scabbard.'

'Excuse me. Does anyone else think she's covering the blindingly obvious?' Miss Tandari said rather meekly.

'That's the point,' snapped Brodie. 'Obvious! The message *Excalibur* is just too obvious. And you keep telling us this whole search is about looking beyond the obvious, don't you? You remember Merlin said it to Arthur. In Malory's poem. Everything's been about *more* than the weapon.'

'And?'

'Van der Essen meant us to look beyond the *sword*.'

'I just don't follow, BB.'

'The writing of the word "Excalibur" is what code-crackers call a piece of disinformation, isn't it, Miss Tandari?'

Miss Tandari's dark eyes were widening now. 'Of course. Of course,' she blurted. 'Something written to throw us off track from the real message.'

Smithies' grin at last was huge, sparkling in his eyes.

'So where,' begged Hunter, his exasperation stretching across his face, 'is the *real* information?'

'On the paper,' Brodie said hotly.

She didn't think it was possible for Hunter to look more confused.

'That's,' said Brodie slowly, 'why we need fire.' She made her words clear and deliberate. 'I think he must've used invisible ink. We'll be able to read it if we heat the paper.'

Mr Bray stood patiently at the barrier in the arrivals hall, waiting for Aer Lingus flight 236 from Illinois. The line of passengers filing through in front of him looked particularly grumpy. The weather was not good and he supposed there'd been a fair amount of turbulence.

When George Fabyan III rounded the corner with his luggage trolley he was smiling broadly. Mr Bray was rather worried he'd be crushed in the generous bear hug offered.

'So,' boomed the visitor, as he followed Mr Bray towards the waiting taxi. 'This really is the start of quite a neat adventure, my old friend.'

'Not so much of the old.' Mr Bray smiled back, tapping the American playfully on the arm. 'I'm not much older than your grandfather was when I first met him.'

'That's practically ancient,' the younger man replied, taking a pair of heavy black glasses from the inside pocket of his leather jacket and slipping them on. 'Surely time to slow things down a bit.'

Mr Bray strode on purposefully. 'Slow things down?' he laughed back before sliding into the front seat of the waiting cab. 'When life's just getting interesting again? I don't think so.'

Fabyan took a stick of gum from his pocket and slipped it into his mouth. 'I like interesting.'

Miss Tandari and Smithies led the way. Hunter stumbled along supported by Brodie, and Tusia followed, mumbling and muttering as she walked.

They crashed into the morning room and Miss Tandari ran straight to the ironing-board in the centre of the room still set up for Steganography class.

They peered at the iron, waiting for it to heat up. A tiny wisp of steam rose from the triangular metal plate.

'You should do it, Brodie,' said Miss Tandari as the thermostat switch flicked to red to show the iron was ready. 'Nice and easy. Smooth strokes, as even as you can.'

Smithies put the piece of paper flat on the board.

'Ready?' Brodie lifted the iron.

No one answered.

She eased the iron face smoothly across the paper. It curled with the heat. Curled and fell again like a phoenix rising in the flames. And as she moved the iron she thought of the old man who'd written the message and trusted them to find it. She thought of her grandfather and her mother . . .

Then she put down the iron on the edge of the board, lifted the paper and held it up to the light.

'Well?' demanded Hunter, stepping in so close she could feel his breath against her cheek. 'What does it say?'

The Golden Key

Smithies got Ingham to close the museum and then called the team together again in Hut 11. They sat, this time, around the long wooden table which had been carved with initials. Brodie traced her finger across the letters AB. The shape of them made her feel safe somehow.

Smithies laid out the tiny sheet of yellowed paper on the table.

'Professor Van der Essen's final message to us, which we've found thanks to Brodie,' Smithies said slowly. 'Contained as it was, in the cloak of invisible ink given life like the phoenix by the heat of the fire.'

He cleared his throat and began to read. There were only five words:

The key to your
protection . . .

'Not exactly over-clear in its meaning, is it?' whispered Hunter. 'I mean, you'd think after going to all the trouble of hiding it and writing the codes, he'd give just a little more. It's sort of like the KitKat of codes rather than a three-course meal.'

'Do you ever think of anything other than your stomach?' hissed Tusia.

'What? I'm starving.'

'Yes. Well,' interrupted Smithies. 'I can see it'll be a testing puzzle. But not one we'll fail. We just need to allow ourselves a little time to make sense of it. And that's what we can work together to do,' he said, his face breaking into the widest of smiles. 'Not much of a lead, but it's a start. We'll take it methodically and word by word we'll make sense of this final message.' He giggled like a child just realising the presents left below the tree on Christmas morning were all for him. 'You see what this means? We thought it was over, but it isn't. We carry on. We do not give up on MS 408. We're back in business, Veritas.'

Excitement bubbled in Brodie's stomach. Only hours before it had been over. Everything. The team, the challenge. Now . . .

The door of Hut 11 clicked open.

Friedman stood in the doorway, his face flushed, eyes wild.

'Friedman, my dear, dear friend,' said Smithies. 'Join us. Wonderful news.'

'I can't,' muttered Friedman.

'But we'll keep you hidden. The authorities think the search is over. You'll be safe here now. Come on.'

Friedman shook his head. 'No, Smithies. My time has passed. We waited too long.'

'What d'you mean?'

Friedman shook his head again. 'For Veritas it doesn't matter.'

'Of course it matters,' Smithies retorted. 'Nothing matters more. You gave up your career for this code. Some gave up their lives. What could stop it from mattering?'

Friedman pointed his hand towards the mansion building. 'Them,' he said quietly. 'Always them.'

Smithies' eyes narrowed.

'I was waiting at the station as we agreed. They're on their way here. I came to warn you,' Friedman said.

'They?'

'Vernan and the Director of Level Five.' Friedman's mouth twitched. 'I saw them make their way over to the mansion,' he said. 'If the Director himself is here, it can't be good.'

The Director walked to the front of Hut 11, gesturing with his hands that all should take a seat.

Brodie slumped down beside Hunter. She'd never felt so tired.

The Director clapped his hands together. Slowly. Rhythmically. 'Well,' he said, 'this has been quite a ride, has it not? Fun while it lasted, you could say. Well, *you* could. We'd just say it was wrong.' He pulled the lobe of his ear, shaking a thought of revulsion from his head. 'Let me, if I may, make things quite, quite plain. The work of the reformed Veritas must stop. It's a point worth noting that by calling your little band of workers the Third Study Group you at least acknowledge the failings of the other two.' He sniffed as if laughing at his own private joke. 'What a shame though you didn't give more thought to the history of the groups. Great men and women, learned men and women have tried and failed to break the secrets of MS 408. And why you'd ever, for a moment, think a band of has-beens and children could come closer to an answer is beyond me.' He allowed a thin spectre of a smile to sweep across his lips. 'MS 408 is prohibited. No exceptions. No breaking of the rules. There's no future for your Black Chamber. You found only ash in the hidden places of the palace. There'll be no more hunting for clues. Smithies and Miss Tandari, your employment is terminated. Ingham, you'll find returning to your retirement most conducive to your health. For you all, Bletchley Park is *out of bounds*. A Ministry of Information ban on your presence here takes force from noon tomorrow.'

Smithies rushed forward. 'You can't prove we were looking at MS 408. A school trip to the Royal Pavilion. There's no rules against that. And if we're all together you can't prevent us searching for the truth!'

Brodie scanned the room to see who'd speak next. The air was charged with electricity.

The Director rebuttoned his jacket and pushed his hand into his pocket. 'No *truth* to find, old man,' he said. 'Your searching is an irritant to me. If we've learnt nothing else from this fiasco then it's the need to be thorough. To leave nothing to chance. All the time the lure of the code remains, there'll be people like you looking for answers. Well, no more,' he sniffed. 'Your operation here, schooling these children, breaks government legislation. You're right. I'll find it hard to prove you're meddling with Voynich's Manuscript. But your trespass on Ministry of Information property is obvious. It's time for you all to go home.' He walked down the aisle between the chairs to where Kerrith waited for him, her form wrapped tightly in a long fur coat.

From outside, Mr Bray had heard every word.

'You all set?' Fabyan released his hold on the older man's arm. 'You gonna break it to them or shall I?'

'Oh, I'd be very happy to tell them the news myself,' said Mr Bray. 'Although of course you should come with me. I've a feeling they'll be keen to meet you.'

Brodie had closed her eyes, trying to squeeze back tears. When she opened them she didn't expect to see her granddad and it was as much as she could do to stop herself from bounding over to him and hugging him tight. From the way he winked at her though, he hadn't just come to speak to her. He made his way slowly to the front of the room, accompanied by a tall, lean-looking man dressed in a rather long black leather jacket and remarkably bright red cowboy boots.

Her granddad turned to face the rest of the room. 'Very interesting speech,' he said with a note of sarcasm.

The Director lifted his lip into what could only be described as a snarl.

'If you'd be so kind as to let me take the issues you raised one at a time, I think there's a few things I can shed light upon,' Mr Bray continued before winking at Brodie once again.

'Who's the old man?' whispered Hunter.

'My granddad,' Brodie said proudly.

'And the other man?' chipped in Tusia.

'No idea.'

Mr Bray teased his rather unruly hair flat against his head. 'Firstly, the issue of the legality of the children being here,' he began, glancing down surreptitiously at the notes the solicitor had prepared for him. 'Smithies was very careful and the issue is clearly covered by section 7 of the UK Home Education Law of 1996. If the guardians and parents of the children involved have no issue with the education being received, then they're at liberty to allow them to stay being taught here at Station X.'

'He's good,' whispered Hunter, covering his mouth with the back of his hand. 'I can see where you get your persuasive skills from.'

'Now of course there's the issue of site ownership, especially if you're making suggestions about banning people from the premises.' He narrowed his eyes to show his annoyance. A look Brodie knew only too well. 'My solicitor has been most helpful in this matter. It seems the mansion house itself was only temporarily in the care of the Black Chamber. A careful testing of the lease documents suggests ownership of the mansion was sold by the Leon family to the government in 1937. But there was a seventy-five-year clause to the purchase.' He coughed then, as if allowing a pause in his words would let the information register. 'It seems now, seventy-five years on, the lease has run its course and the building of Bletchley, and indeed the huts around it, are once more eligible for private purchase.'

The Director gulped. 'Don't be preposterous.'

Mr Bray smiled. 'I am particular about the details, maybe,' he said, 'but certainly not preposterous. I've completed the necessary paperwork to purchase the mansion and several of the surrounding huts so our presence in the grounds of Bletchley cannot be prohibited. I have of course had to sell my own house to do so, but I must say I didn't hesitate.'

'Hey, your granddad knows his stuff,' whispered Tusia.

Brodie swelled with pride.

'Thirdly, there's the issue of employment and funding. Now of course it may very well be you no longer wish to keep in employment those you deem to be investigating a prohibited document.' Brodie shot a look towards Smithies. 'However, it just so happens my involvement with the Second Study Group reminded me the government's not alone in their interest in MS 408. The very first Study Group was funded by the very generous sponsorship of George Fabyan. I've taken it upon myself to contact the great-grandson of that very generous and forward-thinking man and would like to introduce to you George Fabyan III.'

The man to his side lumbered forward, raising his hand in a rakish wave. 'Howdy,' he said, glancing along the lines of those that listened. 'Swell to be here. My own great-grandfather loved the mystery of code more than anything else. It was he who set up Riverbank Labs, the Black Chamber who first looked at MS 408. When Mr Bray called me I was more than happy to lend my enthusiasm for research and, perhaps more importantly, the rather colossal weight of my family fortune behind the project. With funding secured and premises title deeds similarly acquired, I think you'll acknowledge that whether the government wants it or not, the reformed Veritas will continue with their quest to read MS 408. Of course, we'll be making no use of government money or funding, and once Bletchley is under our ownership, proving we're spending any time at all looking at MS 408 will be extremely difficult. I think you'll find access to a now privately owned site and recently closed museum just a little tricky.'

It took a while for the news to sink in. The Director, with Kerrith beside him, seemed totally at a loss, like a passenger arriving at a station to see his train pulling quietly but purposefully away from the platform. His eyes narrowed and small purple patches raised beneath his eyes across the bones of his cheeks. 'It's not over, Smithies,' he hissed.

Smithies smiled his answer. 'I think, sir, that's the very point we've been trying to make.'

'So where does that leave us?' said Brodie.

'It leaves you right here,' smiled Smithies, tucking into a slice of treacle tart which Miss Tandari had heated through by way of celebration. 'All I said this morning remains true. We've solved the code you were brought here to solve. And yet it seems the puzzle that awaits us now is more far-reaching and much vaster than we ever dared to imagine.' He rubbed his hands together.

'More far-reaching?' Hunter spluttered through a mouthful of pudding.

'Look, there must be some important reason why the Director wanted our operation closed down. I accept MS 408 has cost people their careers but that doesn't explain why he's so keen for the manuscript to be so totally off-limits. And I just don't accept his premise that the manuscript's a fake. If it were, then the code-crackers in the past would've proved that.' He dug his spoon into his pudding bowl and lifted it to his lips. 'We've rattled him. And I'd like to know what's got him so angry.' He swallowed the last spoon of custard and wiped a rather large streak of treacle from his tie before continuing. 'Of course we may get no further in our search. We have to remember those who've gone before us, who've been lost to the code, and even those who've been a little damaged on the journey.'

Brodie saw him glance across the room at Ingham, who was sipping from a mug chained securely to the radiator. She felt a strange tightening in her stomach.

'But, you remain the brightest brains in the country, and so your continued service at Bletchley will be greatly appreciated. And of course with Mr Bray and Fabyan on board now, our chances of finding out just what Van der Essen meant in his final code comes many steps closer. And as Bletchley is now out of bounds for those we don't invite there's also no good reason why, if we're careful, we can't bring Friedman up to the mansion now.'

He gestured across the table to Miss Tandari, who

took up his lead and continued. 'Our suggestion is we all take a three-week break in proceedings here,' she said, her silver bracelets sparkling on her arms as she waved her hands. 'A holiday. Time for you to regroup at home and catch up with the family. It'll give us time too, to sort the quarters for Mr Bray and Mr Fabyan.' She smiled rather coyly down the table at the American. 'I'm thinking our accommodation, isn't quite up to the standards of a modern-day billionaire.'

'Billionaire,' spluttered Hunter, spilling a dollop of ice cream from his spoon on to his lap.

Fabyan ran his fingers through his hair. 'Billions, trillions. Let's not get caught up in details. And anyhow, you don't need to give my needs no mind. I'm a gigantean fan of camping. I can cope with the accommodation arrangements inside an English countryside mansion.'

Miss Tandari smiled encouragingly although she was clearly not altogether sure. 'Anyway – three weeks to get our affairs in order. The path we've embarked on is going to be long and challenging.'

'Hey. We're all about the challenge.' Hunter wiped the spilt ice cream with the back of his hand and then licked it. 'What?' he said in response to the dismissive frown from Tusia. 'It's Rocky Road. My favourite flavour. Shame to waste it.'

The feast over, Brodie stood with Tusia and Hunter in the doorway. 'Amazing man, your granddad,' offered Hunter.

'We Brays like to find ways out of a puzzle.'

'You did great earlier, by the way,' Hunter added. 'Your mum would be proud of her daughter as well as her dad.'

'Don't get me crying again,' Brodie mumbled, pushing him so he hobbled on his heavily bandaged foot. 'I only just stopped from earlier.' For the third time that day she took hold of the locket round her neck.

'You'll definitely come back after the break, won't you?' asked Tusia in a way which suggested she'd beat either of them with her stress pig if they dared say no.

'Well, my granddad has sold his house to buy the huts in this place so I'd be out of a home if I didn't want to come back,' Brodie laughed.

'You try and stop me,' added Hunter, 'after all, my crumpled unicycle's still waiting in the garage. It's about time I got around to fixing it properly. Smithies was helpful but admits he's better when a thing has two tyres. Anyway, with a billionaire on site I may be able to afford a new wheel.'

Brodie hit out playfully again and this time Hunter

hobbled clear. Above them the moon shone brightly.

'Seriously, though,' said Hunter, lowering his voice. 'This is all pretty scary. I mean working on something the government wants left alone. What sort of secrets are we going to uncover?'

Brodie frowned. 'Ones people gave up their lives for?'

Hunter smiled and linked his arm through Tusia's. 'Hey, stop with the disgusted face,' he snapped. 'I'm injured and in need of support.'

'Brodie can help you,' Tusia replied.

'I think it's about time Brodie caught up with her granddad,' Hunter said. 'Poor old man's been waiting to get a word in edgeways for hours.'

'Well, you're the one going on about the billionaire and the unicycle.'

'You make it sound like the name of a song,' said Hunter as Tusia led him away back towards the huts. 'Or perhaps the name of a circus act which could appear alongside you and your whacky thai chi or whatever you call it.'

Brodie watched them move off, away from the mansion, the sound of their voices still lifting on the breeze as they walked.

Brodie's granddad was sitting on a bench in front of the

mansion, the broken-headed griffin lit by the moonlight behind him. 'There's so much to catch up on,' he said.

'I wish you'd told me about Mum and the accident,' she said at last, without looking at him.

'I'm sorry,' he sighed, without looking up. 'We were never sure. Perhaps a part of me was frightened of the truth.' He rubbed his hands together. 'Look, Brodie. I shouldn't have kept the truth from you. I shouldn't have hidden what I know. But at the time it seemed best. You'd lost so much. I couldn't face you losing more.'

She put her hand in his. 'I'm so glad you're here,' she said. 'Really glad. It'll make everything nicer.'

'Oh, I don't know. Looks to me as if you've formed a great little team.' He glanced over into the distance where the figures of Hunter and Tusia could just be seen hobbling in the torchlight, towards his hut. They looked very much like a pair of delivery-men carrying an invisible, heavy load.

Brodie and her granddad sat for a moment staring in the direction of the lake. The moon showed only the water as it left the fountain. Darkness obscured where it fell.

'I hope I've done the right thing, Brodie,' Mr Bray said at last.

'I think you have,' she answered.

Mr Bray sighed. 'Anyway, I think I've had enough excitement for one day. As Miss Tandari said, we'll need a few weeks to get things in order. I suggest you go and get some sleep.'

Brodie's brain was racing too quickly for sleep. 'I'll stay here for a while,' she said. 'I like the quiet.'

Mr Bray pushed himself up to stand. 'Don't expect you get much of that sharing a room with Tusia,' he laughed.

'Not much.'

'Still, don't stay up too long. You'll need all the energy you can get. I'll need help packing my rumba records for the move here and I have to admit I've added a little to my collection since you went away.'

Brodie was unsure how long she'd sat there alone before Friedman arrived. 'May I?' he said gesturing to the place beside her.

She moved up to let him sit down.

'Quite a night, wasn't it?' he said. 'After quite a day.'

Brodie waited. 'I'm glad you're part of the Group now,' she said at last. 'I think my mum would like that.'

Friedman sniffed. 'You, your mum and Smithies. Probably the only people who'd be pleased about it.'

'Why?'

'Oh, I saw the way your granddad looked at me. Smithies warned me some people have long memories. It's hard to shake off the "mantle of madness", Brodie. People have a way of holding it against you.'

'He'll change his mind,' she said, in a way she hoped sounded reassuring.

'Hope you're right.' He turned to face her as if studying a portrait. 'Your wonderful mother, Brodie . . . you look so much like her, you know.'

Brodie felt her cheeks colour.

Friedman's eyes sparkled. It was then Brodie remembered where she'd seen his face before. In the yellowed photograph her granddad had shown her, months ago now, when all this first began. Friedman, and Smithies and her mother. When they were children here. Together. Working on the code. She looked up. It was as if Friedman was remembering too.

'Was that locket hers?' he asked slowly.

'Granddad gave it to me just before I came here.'

'He gave me something once too,' Friedman said, reaching down the neck of his shirt and pulling out a thin chain with a tiny golden key.

'Granddad gave that to you?' Brodie said, trying to hide the surprise in her voice. 'Really?'

Friedman laughed and lowered the chain so the key rested in the hollow at the base of his neck. 'It was your mother's too. Apparently she sent it to your grandfather along with a letter to pass on to me just before she died. Sent it from Belgium, before the accident. She sent something for Smithies, too. Some long strip of paper with holes punched in it. But to me, she sent a letter and this key.'

Brodie narrowed her eyes to concentrate.

'I never got the letter. Your grandfather said there was some problem. But he gave me the key. Said your mother thought it was important for me to have it.'

Brodie felt the exhausted cogs in her mind begin to whirl. 'Why was my mother in Belgium?'

'Van der Essen,' he said matter-of-factly. 'We were sure the Professor had known more about MS 408 and your mother went to check out his things. Spoke to his family.'

'And the accident happened before she could tell you what she learnt?'

'Yes.'

'And the key came from Belgium?'

'Yes.'

'And you don't know what the key's for?'

'Yes. No. I thought perhaps it was just a sign, you know.' His face was colouring in the moonlight.

'A sign of what?' Brodie's voice was rising.

'Brodie. Things were complicated between — well,

your mother and me. We had feelings for each other. But I had my difficulties. It wasn't a good time for me. Being accused of madness isn't an easy thing to bear.'

'And you think the key was just a sort of symbol,' she said, her heart racing now so her words fell over themselves. 'That's all?'

'All?' The man looked angry. Hurt even. 'I don't think you can talk so flippantly about things that don't concern you. You're too young to understand.'

'That's not fair! I'm part of this team aren't I? I'm not asking about you and my mum! I'm asking about the key.'

'What d'you mean?'

Brodie had jumped up, pacing about. 'OK. OK. I'm thinking about the hidden clue in the box from the Pavilion.'

'What clue? Come on, Brodie. What are you talking about?'

'You were there. You heard Smithies read it.'

Friedman shook his head. 'I came into Hut 11 and I told you the Director was coming. I heard nothing about another clue.'

'But we talked about it as we ate?'

'Still not there, Brodie. I needed air. Crowds unnerve me.'

Brodie could feel her frustration rising. 'But you

knew we were going on to try and read MS 408. Why do you think we weren't stopping?'

Friedman laughed. 'I don't need to see another clue to decide to go on. I've never given up. Never. My whole life's been about making sense of MS 408. I go on because that's what I do. I don't keep trying because it seems likely or because we're getting closer. I keep going because I don't know how to stop.' He paused. 'They don't claim a man is mad for no reason,' he said.

Brodie tucked her hair behind her ears.

Connections were firing in her mind. The Veritas logo and the symbol of an elephant holding a key. The importance of never forgetting. The value of the scabbard.

'OK. I get it,' she blurted. 'You keep going whatever the odds. But what if I tell you there's another clue? What if I tell you, we found more? I think the key round your neck, the one my mum gave you, is the answer!'

The Director closed the door to his office and flicked the latch. He removed his jacket and placed it carefully over the back of the chair, smoothing the creases in the sleeves. Next he loosened his tie, slipping the opened knot over his head and laying the silk strand across the arm of the suit. Then he removed his cuff links and put them in the silver tray to the left of his desk. They rattled as they rocked across the silver, the engraving on their surface flashing in the light of the neon strip above them.

Finally, the Director rolled up his sleeves.

Seated on the leather chair, just beside the window, the Director picked up the phone and paged through to his secretary. 'I'd like to use the private line,' he said in a voice warmed a little by the cheap wine he'd drunk on the train back from Bletchley.

'Certainly, sir. Is there anyone I can connect you to?'

'No. Just ensure the line's secure.'

He waited for a moment until he dialled. Then he spoke very clearly so his words could not be in any way misheard. 'They are more inventive than we feared. And their commitment seems absolute.'

'So. Are you telling me it's time for direct action?'

The Director waited before he answered.

'Yes. The time has come.'

'This'd better be good, Brodie,' Hunter yawned from behind the sleeve of his rather large dressing-gown. 'I was having a wonderful dream where the water in the fountain in the middle of the lake had turned to chocolate.'

Tusia mumbled something which Brodie couldn't

quite hear but she thought she included the words 'typical' and 'drowning'.

They met in the music room. Hut 11 still had memories of the Director's rant about legalities and legal injunctions and was too far to go in the dark.

'So,' said Smithies, stifling a yawn himself. 'Are you two going to explain what all this is about?' He held the metal phoenix box in his hands as Brodie had insisted he went to get it. The rest of Veritas stood round the edges of the room, although Mr Bray had made use of a chair in the corner and was rubbing his feet in an attempt to bring feeling back to them. Ingham was offering him some painkillers, but Mr Bray refused. The only member of the group who didn't appear to be suffering from extreme exhaustion was Fabyan, who announced happily he was still running on Illinois time and was ready for anything.

'OK,' said Brodie, taking the box from Smithies. 'Stick with this. It's going to be good.'

'Better be worth giving up a dream about a lake of chocolate,' mumbled Hunter.

Brodie ploughed on. 'OK. Listen. I think Van der Essen hid us a new clue in the phoenix box. It's that phrase hidden in the hinge. Those words "*The Key to your protection*".'

'Anyone else having a burst of déjà vu?' asked Hunter,

who was soundly struck by Tusia on the arm.

'Now,' persisted Brodie, 'all the codes Van der Essen left us are about King Arthur. Yes?'

The Study Group mumbled in agreement and Mr Bray tried his best to look as if he knew what his granddaughter was talking about. Miss Tandari began to whisper in his ear, but Brodie only allowed her a little time to help him catch up.

'And all the time we've been looking at the scabbard and not the sword. Arthur's scabbard. Remember?'

Tusia said something about how they could hardly forget as they'd spent the whole day running away from the authorities because of that clue and Ingham agreed, looking strangely usual in his pyjamas amongst a crowd of others, most of whom were also dressed for bed.

'So,' went on Brodie, gaining confidence as everyone began to look more awake. 'I don't think Van der Essen was hiding a code-book in the Pavilion. I don't think it was about what was inside the box. The ash was put there from the beginning. But that's not the point. It was not the *sword* we were after. It was the *means of protection*. Ultimate protection. The scabbard.'

'So?' said Ingham.

'So I think the *box* is the important thing.'

'But we've been all through this,' Hunter said,

sounding exasperated. 'Going back to the box led us to the extra clue.'

'Yes,' Brodie blurted. 'And it should take us back to the box again.'

'I'm not following,' said Miss Tandari, her forehead furrowed in an obvious attempt to pay attention. Mr Bray began shaking his head beside her.

'The box is it. It's the final clue. Not a message *hidden* in the box. But the box *itself*.'

'I see.' It was perfectly obvious from Tusia's comment that she didn't see but had felt the need to say something that'd be considered as supportive.

'It's the box we need to look at,' Brodie said again. 'That'll give us what we need. The box is *the protection*.'

'So what we need then is *the key*?' said Smithies slowly, as if awakening from a dream.

'Exactly,' said Brodie, turning the box in her hand. 'And here, look, in the side of the box, is a hole for a key.'

'Well, that's all pretty wonderful,' muttered Hunter. 'And I am impressed, honestly I am. But not to be too mean about the whole clue-solving thing but I think there's something you've missed.' He waited, then opened his hands out as if showing them empty. 'We haven't got a key.'

'Oh yes we do.'

Hunter lowered his hands to see who'd spoken. 'We do?'

'Yes. We do.' It was Friedman and his voice trembled as he spoke, lifting his hands to his neck to release the small golden chain that hung around it.

All eyes in the room were on him as he passed the key to Brodie.

'But where? How? When?' It was difficult to be sure who was asking what.

'My mother sent Friedman the key,' Brodie said quietly. 'My granddad said she was on to something and that something took her to Belgium. She must've got the key from Van der Essen's things.'

'And she sent the key to you?' Tusia said, her eyes fixed firmly on the man in the centre of the room.

He said nothing.

Brodie held the key in one hand and the box in the other. She moved the key gently towards the lock. 'Are you ready?'

No one in the room answered.

Epilogue

Somehow it seemed fitting the discovery was made in the Music Room. Brodie, as she thought about that moment, was particularly pleased about that.

The key turned slowly in the lock under the pressure of her hand. There was the gentle sound of clicking. A release of air as if the box was exhaling after having held its breath for a very long time. The base of the box lifted. The remains of ash fluttered away like morning mist. There was a secret compartment. A place hidden inside. And in the compartment was a small metal structure with a tiny handle. There was an opening at one end – a slit like a letterbox – and at the other end it was possible to see lines of metal almost like the keys of a miniature piano.

'It's a music box,' said Fabyan.

'But there's no sound,' said Tusia.

'Because it needs music.'

Brodie didn't understand.

'It works if you feed paper into the opening,' Fabyan continued. 'I've seen these things before. Paid a fortune for a few in my time. Paper is fed inside and the workings play the tune.'

'But how do they know what to play?' asked Hunter.

'There's holes,' said Fabyan. 'Punched into the paper like a code. And the metal keys in the workings play a note every time there's a hole. The holes make the music.'

Brodie could hardly breathe. 'Like the holes on our invitations to Veritas,' she said. 'The holes let the light in and told us what to do.'

She turned to look at Friedman.

They both turned to look at Smithies.

Smithies' face was flushed with colour. 'Alex,' he said quietly. 'She knew. She'd found the pieces of the secret and she knew one day we'd reunite them.'

'Erm, any chance you'll tell us what's going on?' Hunter said. 'You lost me with the paper and the holes and the music.'

'Not lost,' Smithies said softly. 'Found.' He took his wallet from his pocket and pulled out the long thin strip of paper he'd carried since the death of his best friend. 'Brodie,' he said, passing the paper to her. 'Make the phoenix sing.'

Brodie fed the paper through the slot in the workings. She turned the handle and she waited. Then, in the silence of the night, a gentle tune began to play. Soft and stirring, the sound of notes rising and falling.

'It's Elgar,' Mr Bray said gently.

Tusia looked confused.

'The tune. It was written by Elgar.'

'You're sure?'

'I'm totally sure.'

'And so that's the solution to the Firebird Code?' asked Brodie. 'Notes of a melody?'

Smithies smiled. 'It's perfect.'

'It is?' said Hunter, turning the statement into a

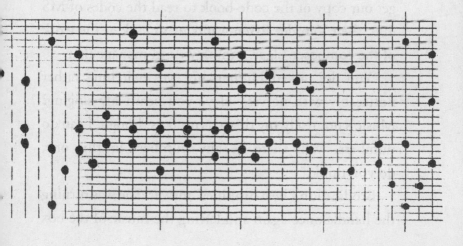

question. 'Because I don't get it.'

Ingham grinned. 'Elgar, my young man, was a master composer.'

'OK. Still not getting it.'

'And more than that. He was *a lover of codes*.'

'He was?'

'He was. Have you never heard of the *Enigma Variations*, a whole series of compositions Elgar wrote to include codes?'

'Wasn't really part of the Key Stage Two curriculum,' offered Hunter. 'We were too busy doing songs about recycling and looking after your teeth.'

Smithies frowned. 'Well, then I think we've some learning to do.' He ran his fingers along his chin. 'I think we finally have our answer,' he said with more than a hint of excitement in his voice. 'If we're going to get our copy of the code-book to read the codes of MS 408, then Van der Essen wants us to look at the work of the composer Elgar. I think we can manage that.'

'You do?' asked Hunter, his eyes twitching rather noticeably with nerves. 'Have you heard my singing? Music's not really my thing. Numbers though. I can do numbers. Will there be any numbers in this one, do you think?'

Brodie didn't hear Smithies' answer. She was turning the handle once again and letting the music of the box fill the room. A sense of expectation rose in her. A tune flew free as if the phoenix was rising at last from the flames and sharing with the world her song. The firebird was singing.

She had her granddad here, Smithies, Miss Tandari and Ingham and all their knowledge about codes. She'd got Friedman, who'd known her mother, and Fabyan, who'd helped see off the Director. And she'd got two of the most annoying but wonderful friends she could ever hope for.

And they'd got a new code to help them decipher MS 408.

Whatever Elgar had hidden in his writings, she knew they'd find it. Because that was what they were here to do.

They'd made a commitment. To each other and to the code.

And one day soon they were going to find out what the greatest unread code in the world was all about.

Acknowledgements

Thank you for reading *The Power of Three* and sharing in its secrets. I'd like to thank here all the people that encouraged me as I wrote it!

So thank you to:

Ann Wright; Barbara Large; all my writing friends from MUSE; all the authors from CWISL and Erica Richardson and the late Rosemary Ingham.

All my friends at Ocklynge School, Eastbourne; colleagues and pupils (especially past and present classes 5BD and 6BD and members of E Plus!); all the team at SLAMS; 'Bumper Book Shop' Eastbourne; 'Stagecoach', 'Rattonians' and the 'Ratty Mums'; David Cane-Hardy, Pete Gurr and Barney Pout; Matt Keogh, Daniel Trott and all the 'early draft readers'!

All the Evason family . . . you're wonderful! Andrew

and Jane Norriss . . . I really appreciate all your help and friendship. John Smithies, John Werner, Tusia Werner, Ron Guildford, Malcolm Barton, Richard Crane and Yvonne Lever – you were amazing teachers! Thank you!

The incredible team at Hodder Children's Books and Beverley Birch, my fantastic editor.

And my wonderful family – David, Andy and Rocky for your enthusiasm; Mum for teaching me to love stories and for being my first *Secret Breakers* reader and Dad for all your support. My fabulous husband Steve, for all your patience and encouragement. And Meggie my wonderful daughter, logbook writer and friend . . . for inspiring me every day. It was you who taught this firebird how to fly!

AUTHOR'S NOTE

VERITAS : The search for Truth

What inspired *Secret Breakers*? The true story of a man discovering a real coded manuscript hidden in a castle. I felt I'd uncovered an incredible secret. I found out all I could about the Voynich manuscript. I looked at every page online in The Beinecke Rare Book and Manuscript Library. I researched attempts to decipher it which had driven code-crackers mad. I immersed myself in the history of codes. The more I read, the more I wondered ... why was the ancient manuscript encrypted? What secret was it protecting? Who was it protecting the secret from? I wanted to write about children who try and decipher the manuscript. Adults had failed for nearly five hundred years! I loved the idea of children using different mental powers to solve the problem. ('Secret Breaking' is the new super power!) The most fascinating attempts to decipher MS 408 were made by real study groups. These involved famous American code-crackers William and Elizebeth Friedman and later John Tiltman a code-cracker from the British Black Chamber based at Bletchley Park Mansion (code named – 'Station X').

STATION X

People in Britain only started to hear the truth about 'Station X' during the 1970s. Bletchley Park Mansion was used during World War Two as a Black Chamber just as I describe in my story. Workers were recruited secretly and not allowed to tell even their families what they did. Many gave the cover story that they worked on